BRANCHES

A Novel

Adam Peter Johnson

Cover design by: Amanda Rose Johnson

For Mom

Contents

From the Author

Under normal circumstances, stories about parallel worlds are an opportunity for fun "what-if" riffs that let readers safely visit fantastical dystopias where familiar events played out differently. The Nazis won World War II and now we all speak German and Darth Vader's the hero in Star Wars, etc. etc.

But, to put it lightly, these are not normal circumstances. How are we supposed to enjoy these stories when reality itself has descended into the kind of dystopia we'd never have believed a few short years ago?

If you were given the opportunity to leave in favor of a different reality—right now, today—would you take it? The question no longer feels so abstract. And if you did leave, what might you find on the other side?

Thank you for reading. If you enjoy this book, please consider leaving a review at bit.ly/reviewbranches

SATURDAY

I'm standing at the water's edge when the phone call comes, sand to my ankles, sinking deeper with each advance of the waves breaking on the beach. Nolan is laughing, suspended in the air, his little arms linked between Meredith and me, his feet strafing the water as it rushes past. I don't want to answer. So I keep tracking the rhythm of the waves, the salty spray against nearby rocks. I search for another distraction, my son straining my arm as he whipsaws beside me, giddy as he's dragged by the water flowing back out to sea.

Along the shore, a black ground beetle scampers toward a driftwood refuge, tiny barbed legs knifing it forward. But it's wiped out by the surf before it has a chance. Seems about right.

Up the beach, Dad's swaying on the old weathered rocking bench where I once spent countless hours, where a few years ago my parents and I had taken one last picture together. And beyond, past the sand berm at the beach's far edge, the quaint old rambler home, same as it ever was. But today it feels like a memory that belongs to someone else. I'm trying to remember what I'd hoped to gain by coming back here. I told Meredith it was to let Nolan have some quality time with his grandpa, to awaken the same love of the trees and the trails that I'd found at his age. Walkie talkie hide-and-seek, plastic bow and arrows with rubber nipple tips, the whole bit. And Dad deserves some time with family again. But if I'm honest, I came for me. To escape. And right now it feels like a mistake.

This is what Nolan needs, not me. I'm closer to forty than four yet I feel so much older.

I told people it was the election that broke me. But that's not the truth. Sure, my feeds were melting down. They always are. Apocalypse now and forever, amen. No, it was the silence after that did it. The sight of everyone going about their days as if the world hadn't ended. All those years, ceaselessly hoping to stop the inevitable. There was no way *He* could win again. Not now. Not after everything that's happened. And of course He didn't win. Not really. We all knew it but it didn't matter. Because apparently nothing matters. And so everyone just kept moving through their daily loops like wind-up toys, in denial, defeated or just oblivious. Nothing short of innocents being gunned down in the street could shake them, and then not even that. I don't know. Some people said I was overreacting, which, let's face it, doesn't help when the problem is that no one seems to be reacting at all. Worse still were those who either decided or revealed they were actually happy about it.

Meredith said she understood. Nolan couldn't possibly, which was for the best. At least he had an excuse.

"Take it." Meredith reminds me of the call still ringing out against the crush of the waves. "It's going to be good news." But I don't think she means it. Then again, any answer is better than no answer.

The voice on the other end of the line doesn't waste time with pleasantries.

"How soon can you get back to the hospital? Your results are here. Why don't you come in and we'll talk about it."

SUNDAY

Ever been invited into someone's home and then they go out of their way to make you feel unwelcome? You make small talk, maybe if you're lucky you score a glass of water, but ice would be pushing it. The front door stays in the host's line of sight at all times. Everyone involved silently agrees to pretend they're having a good time as the whole experience screams *"I was just being nice. How dare you actually take me up on the offer."*

Every moment spent in a hospital is like that. Doctors always insist you come at the first sign of trouble, then they don't know what to do with you. They're embarrassed they can't figure out what's wrong so they keep the meter running until you finally agree to leave them alone.

The walls of the waiting area irritate me. I'm back home, back in the blunt cold of the north, 1,200 miles from the nearest ocean. This is either the eighth or ninth time I've waited here over the past year. I've lost track. Each time I bristle at the sight. Seams in the wallpaper curling at the edges. An old cathode-ray TV sulking on a corner table. An underlit fish tank so barren it looks like a metaphor for the impending fallout from climate change. A grandmother watching rapt as a toddler thumbs her way through board books. Okay, so that one's pretty cute. But the walls irritate me. Mom would have called the color "baby shit green" and then laughed. And her laugh would have gotten everyone else laughing whether they thought it was funny or not. It's probably the first time I've smiled in a week. But only for a moment. The boxy old television interrupts the thought, flogging a wintry view of Washington and the preparations being made for the inauguration. And I wonder again how all this could have happened.

A nurse leads me down a labyrinth of identical hallways, but not to the doctor's exam room I'm expecting. Instead, I find myself in a small conference room with a half dozen professional types in business attire seated around a teardrop-shaped table. None of them look like doctors to me. Maybe they sent me to the wrong room? An unwanted houseguest once again. *I can show myself out, thanks.*

One of the suits looks at me. He stands as I enter, a pale young man — too young, I think, for what we're here to discuss — who greets me with an eager smile and a bristling energy that makes me even more uncomfortable.

"Welcome! How you must be feeling right now!" he says with a posh English accent. He takes my coat, ushers me to the sole open chair at one end of the table. "Thank you thank you for coming on such short notice."

I hover over the chair, reminding myself to ask whether the hospital will reimburse my family for the cost of changing return flights, but my familiar headache is making it hard to concentrate. And that's not what I really need to know.

"How long do I have?" I ask.

The young man squints, glances back at his colleagues. They're looking in the general vicinity of where I'm standing but none look me in the eye except one: a middle-age woman who's wearing an elaborate emerald brooch. The distracting bit of flair is tastefully pinned to a tailored suit jacket that complements her dark skin, but for some reason I think it seems out of place. The woman's eyes are studying me the whole time. By contrast, the mousy bald man seated next to her gives little evidence there's anything going on behind his dim eyes at all. Across the table, a young woman with a blonde pixie cut keeps nervously digging at her cuticles, silently mouthing words as if she's trying to talk herself into something. And the other two make so little impression they're practically human screensavers.

"Beg pardon?" the young man says, puzzled by my question.

"It's not exactly a mystery," I say. "The only time doctors refuse to discuss lab results over the phone and insist you cut your vacation short so you can come to the hospital on a Sunday? It's when you're dying. So there's one question I need answered. How long?"

This gets the man even more excited, all apologies for the misunderstanding. He urges me to sit. I comply. The woman with the brooch is now holding a small clicker of some kind in her raised hand. The man nods and she clicks on cue, firing up an overhead projector.

The word "QUANTGEN" appears on the far wall beneath an abstract symbol:

A quick series of five chimes plays in the background somewhere. Great. Proprietary melody for a nebulous brand. Just the worst. I should know. It's my job to work on these things. At least it was. I half expect to see two horny yet chaste retirees sunsetting in twin bathtubs out in a field somewhere.

"Now then," the woman with the brooch says. "I'm sure your doctor mentioned that one of the tests you took was a new kind of test."

"Where is my doctor?" I ask. "Why isn't Dr. Djawadi here?"

"Don't worry, we're in total communication," she says. "You're free to follow up with her another day. But for now, we are here to help you. You see, your symptoms ... they made you a plausible candidate for something the medical community has until recently never thought to look for. Something special."

She advances the slide and on the wall "QUANTGEN" is replaced by the branching limbs of a massive tree. "It's a big world out there," she says. "In fact, it's much bigger than you know."

"Wait," I interrupt. "Just so I'm clear, because I don't know that I got a straight answer. You're saying I'm not dying. Correct?"

Before she has a chance to respond, the pixie cut abandons her cuticle and jumps in. For some reason she lets out a nervous breath and appears overcome with emotion. "Can't you see in my eyes that I'd rather die than cause you a minute's pain?" she says to me, the eyes in question welling up. "No, wait. Can I start over?" Everyone else glances at one another, not really reacting, and I have no idea what's happening.

The young man in charge cuts her off with an open palm. "Whoa, whoa. Easy. Let's just, um. Sorry about this," he says in my direction. "Let's take it down a notch, okay? Beverly here—"

"Fantine," she corrects.

"Right, Fantine. You see, she's just— *Fantine*? Really?" He turns to the others for validation but gets nothing, so he presses on. "Anyway, she's been in back to backs all day and, well. Let's focus on moving forward with the presentation, shall we?"

"Of course," Fantine says, immediately composed. "Sorry."

The woman with the brooch resumes as though nothing had happened, clearly a pro, her eyes still trained on me. "You know, for centuries, people believed that persistent seizures, like yours, were caused by evil spirits or demons. Some living force. And many believed that epileptics had been granted a supernatural gift that let them see things others could not. Some even called it the 'sacred disease.' Now, advances in modern medicine and the discovery of the neurological basis for epilepsy did away with those theories. But then, not all seizures are made equal. And occasionally, further advances mean we later learn our ancestors were onto something, however imperfect their understanding may have been." She leans forward in her chair. "Tell me, have you ever heard of something called a quantum signature?"

"Hold on," I say, now more angry than confused or fearful. "What is all this? What are you saying? If I'm not dying then what do I have?"

The young man smiles. "An opportunity."

SHARE
scroll
COMMENT
refresh
SHARE

I find myself instinctively scrolling feeds on the bus ride home from the hospital. A flick of a thumb first honed on *Toki* and *Battletoads* delivers the latest news, but the dopamine hits aren't what they used to be. Nights once spent on *Candy Crush* now replaced by doomscrolling. Diminishing returns in everything.

The headlines are bleak as usual. Today it's another long-shot recount effort shot down, overwhelming evidence of voter suppression ignored. And the voices who always claim to know better are out bleating, reminding us of the obvious: it's too late. All is lost. Even though I'm thinking about it constantly, I'm still not ready to accept what all is lost actually means. Some people said I should stop worrying about events happening a thousand miles away. But now, as we pass armored vehicles every six blocks, it doesn't feel so distant. I have to keep on top of it, make sure everyone knows whether they want to or not. *SHARE.* The ground keeps shifting out from under me. It's all I can do to stay on my feet.

To be honest, the distraction is just a way to avoid calling Meredith a few minutes longer. I know that. It's not like I'm in denial. But this isn't helping, so I dial home. We try to talk but Nolan is crashing around in the background so she's catching every third word.

"They were who?" she asks.

I tell her what they told me. "They're a pharmaceutical company that apparently specializes in something called quantum pharmacology," I explain.

Nolan is banging what sounds like pots and pans, upset that Meredith is talking to me and not to him. *Bang. Bang.*

"And it's a what? You have what?"

"I have a *parasite*," I say too loudly. A couple seated across from me gets up and discretely moves to the back of the bus.

Meredith lets out an audible sigh. "So it's not cancer." As she says it I'm feeling relief too. "But how did you get it? A work trip?"

Bang.

I tell her they didn't know. "They asked a million questions, about where I've been, about everything really. But I've traveled so much." *Bang.* "They took lots of notes but didn't offer any feedback."

Bang.

"I bet it was when we all went on your work shoot to the Amazon last year," Meredith says. "You kept saying you were nervous about getting in the water, and I said you were being ridiculous." She's already blaming herself. "I should have stopped you. I thought it was a quick dip. You'd been through so much, and I thought ... God, what if Nolan has it?"

Bang. Bang.

The pots and pans have me rattled now. I keep watching to make sure we're not being stopped at another surprise checkpoint.

"Nolan was never anywhere near the water on that trip," I remind her. "And the truth is we don't know. It could have been any of a dozen trips or not a trip at all. All I know is they didn't seem to know. It's a species they just recently discovered." I'm remembering the look on the woman's face—God, I already forgot all their names, I'm shit with names, the woman with dark skin, thick tousled hair and an emerald brooch, Beverly maybe?—the look when she said the parasite was *special*. The young man in charge was just pushing a product, but she seemed to actually believe in it.

9

I try to explain it the way they explained it to me, how time is like an ever-branching tree. "Every possible event, every possible configuration of every variable in the world, is happening all the time, simultaneously," I say. "It's the set of variables we share that determines exactly which branch of the universe we follow together. But somehow, somewhere, all of those other variables are playing out as well, they're just on different branches of the universe we drift away from. And each new moment brings a million new branches yet again."

Bang. Bang. Bang.

"What are — quiet Nolan — what are you saying? I thought this was about a parasite?"

"It is. The parasite, in a host, makes its way to the brain. But as far as the scientists can tell it doesn't cause any real damage. Instead, it drifts. It's not like any other living thing they've seen before. Sometimes, when branches split, the parasite forks away from everything else and follows a different branch instead. And these people, Quantgen, they can tell because at the tiniest scale possible — the quantum level — apparently everything from our branch has a signature that always reads the same. I didn't totally understand what they were saying, but it's like everything here vibrates the same or something."

Bang. BANG. Bang.

"So you have a fluke or something in you — Nolan, kiddo, *stop* — something that vibrates different because it's from, what? A different timeline? I mean. That's crazy. And you believe them?"

I didn't at first, but I do now. But I don't want to get into it so I don't respond. She's silent for a minute but Nolan's banging continues.

"I don't get it," Meredith says. "Do they think it's valuable or something?"

I watch the other passengers on the half-full bus, everyone looking into the middle distance, swaying together around corners and over ruts in the pavement, past the armored patrols, all somewhere else in their mind, just trying to make it through the winter.

"No," I say. "That's not it. There's a pill, or rather a series of pills, they want me to take. They think they can push it back to its proper branch."

"So the pills will kill it? They'll cure you? You'll be cured?"

"Basically," I say. "Or so they think."

"There's no way insurance will cover this."

Bang.

"They say it's a drug trial," I explain. "Apparently insurance doesn't enter into it. I take seven pills over the course of a week and that's it."

"Oh." I can faintly hear Meredith's reaction, not crying just overwhelmed, and I know the exact expression she's making because I've seen it so many times the past few years. But this time I think it's a sign of relief. Of release. And now I'm feeling it too, like a sense of shock wearing off though I can't remember when exactly the feeling began.

I take a deep breath. *Bang.* I don't want to tell her the last part. *Bang.* I consider waiting, but it'll just be worse if I do.

"The thing about the vibrating," I say. "Quantgen said it's not just the parasite that's vibrating wrong." *Bang.* "It's me." *BANG.* "They're saying I'm from another branch too."

"What? What does that mean? Would the pills hurt you?"

"They told me there was no chance." But then they also had me sign several waivers.

"I don't understand," she says, becoming more alarmed. "So these people, people we've never heard of before, they're saying you have a parasite that's giving you seizures and makes you vibrate wrong, but the pills will make it go back to a different branch of reality or whatever."

"Not exactly. They think the nausea, the seizures, all of it is the result of drifting between branches. Apparently I've been drifting with it ever since I picked it up. In theory, the pills should stop it and send us both back."

Bang. Bang. BANG. BANG.

"Honey, this is crazy," Meredith shouts over Nolan's banging. "This sounds like a scam. We need to call someone. I'm not going to lose you because of —"

"You won't lose me. Of course not. I'd still be here, they said. Same as always. As they described it, you probably wouldn't even know I've changed. And I'd be vibrating right again. I just, I guess, in some way, wouldn't be this version of me."

I know the look she's making now too. "You're scaring me," she says. "And I don't know why you're not scared too, but you need to wait before getting any pills from them. Do not take anything until we can look into this more. Okay? Promise me."

"I promise."

We hang up.

And suddenly I realize I'm the only passenger left on the bus, so focused I hadn't even noticed anyone get off. I listen to the rumble of the engine and think about the pills as I try to decide how I'm going to tell Meredith I already took two.

I t's ten minutes before I left the hospital, just before I raced to catch the bus.

As I stare at the tray in front of me, all I'm thinking about is how I've never seen a black pill before. The next five are standard fare, chalky white horse pills arrayed in a line like ghostly ellipses, but the first is black as tar. At the far end, the final pill is a dark forest green.

Everyone has left the conference room except the young Englishman. He tells me I have a choice.

"The good news is that, unless you walk out that door right now, you will be cured in a matter of minutes," he says. "Your symptoms, gone. No more headaches, no more seizures. No more drifting between branches. You will live out your life here, in this branch. The parasite will live, but the black pill is like an anchor, keeping you here. It trains the parasite to be attracted to the exact pitch at which this branch vibrates on a quantum level."

"You're saying I would live the rest of my life with a brain parasite?"

"A harmless one," he says reassuringly. "Consider yourself lucky. Tens of millions of people live their entire lives with chronic conditions far worse than a benign microscopic slug that wants nothing more than a warm place to live. And all you have to do is take the black pill."

"So what's the bad news?" I ask.

"It will cost you."

"Cost me?"

"Around $50,000, I'm afraid."

"Oh."

He smiles. "Ah, but there's more. In fact, it's the best part. The choice. You could simply take the rather expensive black pill and stay here. Or, once you've taken the black you can take the white pills, one each day. The white pills stun the parasite and weaken it, bit by bit. Think of it like a course of antibiotics. With the parasite rendered inert, you will naturally drift back toward the branch where you belong."

"And how much do the white ones cost?" I ask.

"Nothing. In fact, if you agree to participate in the full trial, the black pill comes free as well. There's even a small stipend for participating."

This sounds too good to be true.

"What about the green pill?" I ask.

"It's just that it's a bit stronger than the rest, so be sure to take that one last," the young man says, handing me a small piece of paper with the same instructions he'd described. "Just a bit of insurance to ensure the parasite is killed and you don't end up back here."

This all sounds crazy. A half hour ago I was a dead man. And now? I don't know what to think. I definitely don't trust these people. This all sounds insane. I tell him I'm not taking anything until I've talked to Dr. Djawadi. I still don't understand why she's not part of this conversation.

"Of course of course," he says, placing a reassuring hand on my shoulder. "All that matters is your health. You have an opportunity to live a happy life. You deserve that."

He says they'll get the pills bottled up for me. I can let them know when I'm ready.

I wander the maze of hallways back to the lobby and wait for the receptionist to wrap up a phone call. It's dark outside now, the late January light already gone. A few people remain seated behind me in the open waiting area and its three ugly walls, everyone patiently flipping magazines. One, an old man held up by an ivory-capped cane, crosses to the TV in the corner and takes it off mute. And now the room is filled with a familiar voice. It's *Him*.

The chyron is banal — "*President holds rally ahead of 2nd inaugural Wednesday*" — but the content is anything but. Terrifying rantings that people once mocked as eye-rolling delusions, now coming true. The old man stands close to the TV and leans on his cane as everyone else pulls their magazines closer.

Finished with her call, the receptionist beckons me forward and I ask to speak to Dr. Djawadi.

"It's Sunday," she says. "Is it an emergency?"

"Absolutely, in a way."

Her eyebrows rise and stay there, but she pulls up the number on her computer, dials and hands me the phone. "Your funeral," she says, washing her hands of it.

I take the receiver, but a moment later the sound of the dial tone is drowned out by the rap of a clipboard on the receptionist's desk. Two police officers stand beside me, steely-eyed men clad from head to toe in bulky body armor like they're fresh off a tour in Raqqa. A glance through the glass double-door entrance confirms the presence of a steroidal armored truck parked in a handicapped stall outside, so massive you can't see the roof from this angle. The officers are consulting the clipboard and one another, looking hopelessly confused, as though they're a lost couple trying to find their way back to the interstate.

The dial tone is replaced by Dr. Djawadi's outgoing voicemail listing her availability every day this week. *Monday's going to be tight between Zumba and racquetball so if you need to reach me it's best to try between 5:35 and 6:05. Now, Tuesday's another story.* I'm patiently waiting for the beep when I notice something dangling from the hand of one of the officers. A black cloth sack with a thick drawstring. The receptionist smiles at them and points toward the open waiting area and its baby-shit-green walls. The officers thank her, set the clipboard on the counter and silently approach the handful of patients still trying to block out His voice blaring on the TV. They stand behind a young black woman seated with her back to us then nod to one another.

Leave a message after the beep.

The woman drops her magazine and begins to yell, her voice muffled by the sack drawn tight over her head. The second officer is fumbling with a ziptie but the woman is struggling so furiously he can barely cinch it to her wrists. She's not wearing a coat, dressed in spandex and sneakers like she's about to go for a run in spite of the January weather, but that's all I can really discern without seeing her face. One officer holds her bound hands while the other struggles to control her flailing legs.

Everyone else in the waiting area flees except the old man with the cane who remains fixated on the TV, unfazed. It's not clear he's even aware of what's happening, but then he leans forward and turns up the volume, ensuring *His* voice rises above the scuffle.

The hooded woman kicks one officer hard in the leg and he careens into the desolate fish tank, the water flowing outward sending glass shards and Styrofoam coral in every direction.

I stand motionless as though everything is taking place somewhere else. Then the phone in my hand reminds me where I am. *If you'd like to make a call, please hang up and dial again.* The officers are working for Him, of course. His long arm, reaching into our lives like never before. I know I should be trying to help the woman. But I don't know how.

When I was ten I watched my best friend Jacob get beaten up by another kid at school for no clear reason other than the kid was mad and decided to take it out on the first person he saw. Mom had arrived to pick me up and, to my shock, she grabbed the kid, pulled him off of Jacob then shoved him on the ground. She was amazing like that. I thought she'd be relieved to know I hadn't been hurt. Instead she grounded me for not helping. "When someone needs you, you're always taking a side whether you like it or not," she said. "So be sure to pick the right side." For months I was furious with her. It was easy for her. She was a social worker. She had no choice but to help. It was her job.

I hear her voice in my head now. Urging me. Chastising me. And of course I take a side every day on my feeds. But it's not the same when the bullies are armed.

The woman in the black hood is still trying to gain her bearings. She staggers left and collides with the boxy old TV, knocking it on its side and finally breaking the old man's attention as the furious rally continues on screen. The old man sneers then swings his ivory cane, striking the woman in the back. She drops to her knees. The officers surround her and drag her toward the entrance, her gasping breaths audible as they pass. They pause in front of the glass double-doors, which open automatically. A blast of icy air rushes in and I drop the phone, my lungs growing heavy. *Take a side.* Mom's voice, always there. I want to step forward, to will myself to intervene, but my body's not listening. Instead, I'm watching it all play out, helpless, the woman destined for one of the new camps they've opened.

And then one of the officers collapses to the ground. A janitor, who'd been standing in the corner unnoticed, had stepped forward and struck the officer with his mop bucket, murky water spraying across the tile floor. He's thin, nondescript, someone most people would overlook, but his piercing eyes suggest he's had enough. Now he shoves the other officer, who trips on the body of his partner. The janitor takes the hooded woman by the arm and they run through the open doors into the night. He helps to remove her hood as they run, the lights of the parking lot casting their shadows in every direction.

The doors close automatically and I let out the breath I didn't know I'd been holding.

Then one officer rises, extends his arm. The doors obey. And he fires a full clip at them. Even though my ears are ringing, I can still hear Him screaming obscenities on the TV now dangling upside down by its power cord. The janitor slumps into the snow at the far end of the parking lot and stops moving. The woman's still running, hands bound behind her back. The officers lumber after her, their armor weighing them down, but she's already crossed the highway.

Without a word, I make my way back to the Quantgen conference room, the sound of His voice growing ever more distant. When I get there, the Englishman is waiting with two pills in his hand. One black, one white.

On the main floor of our house, in the corner just off the living room, there's an old upright piano. A maple-framed Baldwin with deep scratches along its sides. Scars from a former life. It's in tune, but the tone isn't what it used to be, a few sticky keys on the high end. An old mechanical metronome with a broken wind-up key sits atop in silent vigil. Mom left both for Meredith when she passed, though Meredith doesn't really play much anymore. I like to think I'm a pretty lenient dad, probably too lenient if I'm honest, but if I have one rule it's that Nolan is not to touch that piano. Ever.

After the four-block walk from the bus stop, I enter the house to a cacophony of keys. Nolan sways precariously on the piano's uneven bench, playfully mashing away, his dark hair matted back with sweat looking Beethoven-chic. Meredith sits a few feet away in the living room, intently working on her laptop. She goes along with the one rule when I'm around, but it's clear she doesn't agree.

I simply tell Nolan to stop, at least that's how I intend it. But Meredith's reaction tells me I've gone too far. I've scared him again. Now, I want to be clear, I would never hit a child even if one bit me in the face. I know because Nolan has, twice. (Toddlers.) But when it comes to four-year-olds, there's a thin line between not taking you seriously and tears, and, well, the one rule is the one rule. Still, I took it further than I'd intended.

As he cries in the living room I sit on the narrow bench, unsure what to say next.

"Are you going to be all right?" Meredith asks, less a question than an accusation. She's been trying to research Quantgen online, but there's absolutely nothing. Like it doesn't exist. "Please tell me you're not buying into this pitch for a bad sci-fi movie, because this whole thing sounds like some kind of grift."

"I don't see how," I say. "I went to the same hospital where I've been seen for years. There they were with my lab results. What am I supposed to think?"

"But you told me you only met with people you've never seen before."

I look to the living room to make sure Nolan is okay. He's sitting quietly, watching a cartoon, stealing little glances back at me. He's changed his shirt for some reason while Meredith and I were talking.

"Of course I want to believe you can get help. But … this." She folds her arms and looks at the ground as she measures the words. "Has it occurred to you that you might want to believe these people because they're telling you what you want to hear?"

"Oh really? Do you think that I want to hear there might be a way to escape from hell? Well shit, who would want that? I mean, seriously, what am I supposed to believe? Does it sound too good to be true? You bet. It also, honestly, kind of makes sense. There has to be a reason the whole world went insane all at once. Why *wouldn't* this be the answer?"

I still haven't told her I've started the pills. And I don't even want to talk about what happened at the hospital. I shouldn't need to. Meredith knows how bad things are here.

She's quiet for a while. When she speaks, she's much softer. She looks at Nolan the whole time. "You know, in all the years we've been together, I've never once feared you would leave me. It was never even a thought. Even after everything we've been through. Your seizures. Your job. The crash." The election. "But now here you are, saying it to my face."

"But I'm not talking about leaving you," I say. "Not at all. Of course not."

"You're talking about leaving *this* me. *This* Nolan. Your dad? Everyone. Even if it's all some bizarre fantasy, that's what you're saying you want right now."

"It's not like that at all. *Jesus Christ*, Meredith. Of course I don't want to leave my family. Just this horrific situation we've all been forced into."

I want it for them as much as anyone. And I'm pissed at her for the accusation.

We don't say much after that. I join Nolan in the living room and bounce him on my leg, a meager peace offering that cheers him while I discreetly scroll my feeds. And I'm suddenly very aware how big he's getting and know I won't be able to do this much longer. I ask why he'd decided to change his shirt yet again but he's having too much fun to respond.

Am I really leaving them? I was so anxious to be free. I know I should have asked more questions, but I need this to work. And that's when it occurs to me I have no idea what's about to happen.

I met Meredith on a sweltering summer night a few weeks after I graduated college. Though she doesn't agree.

I saw her standing on a street corner outside a local bar that had once been an old nickelodeon theater. She was trying and failing to hail a cab, her long caramel-brown hair obscuring her face. I saw an opportunity to lend a hand and, honestly, to bum a cigarette. It's funny now to think we were once both smokers, or that we used to hail taxis for that matter. She was turning in for the night ahead of an interview for a studio photography gig the next morning. Her dream job, she said. My dream job being one that covered my bills, I didn't quite get it. But we got to talking—about Annie Leibovitz, about Yousuf Karsh—and three cigarettes later a taxi arrived. We decided to walk up the street and have another drink instead. In the end, she missed the interview but said it was worth it.

But that's not Meredith's story.

According to her, she and I first met eight months earlier. It was during a brief moment when I'd harbored delusions of becoming a Serious Actor and landed a supporting role in a university production of *Endgame*, the Samuel Beckett play. I was Nagg if that means anything. Meredith was lead set designer. She crafted an elaborate forced-perspective backdrop made from hundreds of tiny portrait photos in mosaic. Basically her life's work to that point. It was a single, wood-framed piece that filled the stage and wasn't designed to be moved. My memory is that the mosaic, when viewed from a distance, displayed a scene of haunted stone ruins crumbling into a sea that stretched to the horizon.

On the morning of the premiere, the publisher who owned the rights to Beckett's plays threatened legal action against the school for failing to adhere to their strict instructions — that *Endgame* always be staged simply in an "empty room with two small windows" — nothing more or less. It was a whole thing with those pricks. Imagine being that petty? I remember thinking it was bullshit when so much work had gone into the set, though I hadn't the first thought of whose work it was. In my experience, actors and set crew didn't really mix. And I really didn't want to see all our hard work lost at the last minute.

Two hours before opening curtain, Meredith told the director she'd made the decision to tear down her creation. All I remember is being told we needed to strike it and strike it quickly, so I picked up a sledgehammer and went to work. Meredith says she remembers how, at one point, she and I were standing side by side, each eagerly pulverizing her seascape. Canvas shredding, wood snapping like fortune cookies, that primal satisfaction of tearing something down. No words were shared between us, she says, but together we fixed it so that the show could go on. Anyway, that's her story. My position is: when it comes to meet-cute stories, if both parties don't remember it, it doesn't count. And frankly, I wasn't a very good Nagg anyway.

But beginnings are just a story you tell. If every relationship can be reduced to a single sentence, the specifics of how you met barely describe the shape of the first letter. It's the longer arc that matters. At least I hope it does.

MONDAY

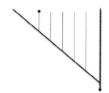

I t's the next day and I don't know what to do. Meredith is at work and Nolan's at preschool, which means I'm supposed to be scoping job opportunities. But I can't focus. So I do what I usually do when faced with uncertainty. Scroll my feeds.

Judge tosses suit to address millions of uncounted ballots

SHARE

refresh

Leaked memo outlines plan to leverage protest violence, expand emergency powers

SHARE

refresh

Local officer Petkoff awarded for heroism in September shooting of Anton Walters

refresh

QUIZ: Which one of The Golden Girls are you?

refresh

Federal government announces it will no longer keep track of hate crimes

SHARE

I read the instructions from Quantgen again but there isn't much to go on. Just a few sentences about when to take the pills. There's nothing written on the bottle at all except a phone number. And as Meredith said, there's nothing to be found online. I could call the number, but it's not like I'm experiencing any side effects. In fact, I haven't had a headache all morning. Maybe it's working the way it's supposed to.

It's not long before I'm back thumbing the feeds and their bleak omens.

In the evening, we all have dinner together. It feels normal, Meredith and I both eating with one hand and checking our phones under the table with the other, Nolan pretending not to notice. No phones at the table, we agreed, but if she doesn't call it out I won't. Mutually Assured Doomscrolling. Or whatever it is she does, I'm honestly not sure anymore.

Like I said, normal. It's as though we've agreed the previous day never happened. Yet I still feel it hanging there.

"Does this taste different to you?" Meredith asks, poking at the freezer-aisle sausage skillet we have every other week like it's betrayed her. "I swear they changed something." We used to joke all the time about her highly attuned palate—in church, age nine, she could tell the week they changed the type of communion wine and spit her sacrament right back into the communal cup—but this time it feels like a taunt.

It's my turn to lay Nolan down for bed and he holds my hand until he falls asleep, faintly whispering to himself in character as his stuffed dinosaurs discuss the mac and cheese they ate for lunch. The whole time I'm remembering the questions they asked at the hospital. All the personal details I shared. As I replay the meeting in my mind I'm thinking it was way more information than they should have needed to diagnose me. And for what? What was I hoping would happen?

I know the answer, of course. That the election would have been fair and legitimate and spared the countless lives now at risk. Which means I wouldn't have melted down at work and been fired. Which means I wouldn't have wrapped my Kia around a utility junction box and spent Christmas day half-conscious in a hospital bed. And now I think it's far too much to ask.

I take the second white pill anyway.

A few hours later I'm still lying awake in bed. I drift in and out of sleep, flashes of the crash between moments of lucidity. Meredith's face is illuminated by the low glow of my alarm clock. Even deep in sleep she looks worried. She's probably right to be. What have I gotten us into? And if I'm not drifting, what do I really have?

It's impossible to know when the headaches started. The stress, constant since the previous election, only grew worse when Mom died. To pick a moment when I started feeling off is pretty much futile. And then one evening, about a year ago, I was standing next to Meredith brushing my teeth before bed.

We'd been talking about the climate. She was the one who brought it up — forecasts in her feeds suggesting we only have a few years to dramatically turn things around or the planet will go full-on four horsemen within Nolan's lifetime — but I was the one who ran with it, the climate catastrophe that looms so enormous you have to accept you can't actually grasp the scale of it. We'd been at it for twenty minutes and I guess I'd really worked myself up.

"We need everyone everywhere to change everything or we're all dead," I'd said.

"I'm going to make some changes," Meredith said, trying to put a cap on it. I could see that she was already making a plan. Always moving forward.

"But it's not nearly enough," I insisted, toothpaste foaming rabid. "The problem is so much bigger than just diligently composting our shits or whatever. That's not going to save Nolan. In fact, it's so far beyond anything you and I could ..."

And that's when everything went blank.

The next thing I knew I was on the ground, Meredith over me, looking terrified — not crying just overwhelmed — and relieved to see I was alive. She thought I'd had a seizure.

I would have three more in the following months. As I began seeing Dr. Djawadi, searching for answers, it became increasingly clear the apparent seizures, the waves of nausea and the frequent headaches were all connected. Eventually Djawadi ran out of tests to run, but I needed to know. After the crash, still laid up in the hospital, Djawadi told me she'd learned of a new experimental test available to patients who matched my symptoms. I wasn't going to argue.

And then to hear that not only was there a cure for my symptoms, but a cure for *everything*. It all fit.

But now I'm thinking again about the young man with the English accent. The man in charge. What he said after I'd taken the black and white pills.

"Just one more thing," he said. Then he withdrew a series of forms from a briefcase, calling special attention to one that required my banking information. "So we know where to send the stipend," he said with a smile.

TUESDAY

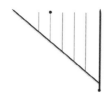

Daybreak. Meredith and Nolan have left again on the bus but I'm still in bed, the shades drawn. I've slept maybe three hours. I keep picturing the moment before the crash, that feeling where everything seems to slow down and you can almost see the individual frames of film on the faulty projector that plays in your head. First a starburst as the headlights shatter. Then the sound of the bumper crumpling as the hood seizes and implodes and the airbag starts to fire and there's a flash and smoke and a ringing in the ears, and ...

Someone is calling my name. But it's not a memory.

It's Meredith's voice, telling me to wake up, that we're late. I get out of bed, confused, quickly dress and stumble into our open garage behind her. A blast of frigid winter air brings me to my senses, but I still don't understand why she and Nolan have returned.

The first thing I see is the dark blue hood that I'd watched implode four weeks ago. Now reflecting sunlight. Pristine. Meredith tosses me the keys to our Kia hatchback, and as we get in I grip the leather steering wheel cover tight. After I'd been discharged from the hospital, I went to the junkyard and tried to retrieve the wheel cover from the wreck, but it had been shredded. This exact wheel cover.

I cry out before I have the chance to compose myself. Nolan, as usual, becomes a tape recorder. "What the fuck!" comes a sing-song cry from the back seat.

"Look what you've started," Meredith says.

I pull out of the garage, not knowing where we're headed. Behind me, Nolan points out how the garbage truck we just almost hit is brown.

"You missed the turn!"

I look over my shoulder to see where Meredith is pointing but don't know what I'm searching for.

"What the fuck!"

"*Nolan.*"

Through short breaths I explain to Nolan how he should never repeat that word outside the car. He beams at me in the rearview.

"School," Meredith reminds me.

An apology, a sharp U-turn, and she gives me an I-told-you-so look as though we've been through this before, but it's not making any sense to me.

Nolan continues narrating. "What the fuck. What the fuck. What. The. Fuck!"

Meredith covers her mouth so Nolan can't see her laughing.

One thing I always loved about my relationship with Meredith was that it was uncomplicated.

Right from the start, there was plenty of overlap in the Venn diagram of things we both liked: hiking in the nearby hills, Sleater-Kinney, Cary Grant's early screwball comedies, those brown oval chips in Gardetto's. But plenty of couples connect over shallow delights only to discover there's not much underneath. As years passed, it felt like every one of our friends found themselves caught in a swirl of toxic melodrama for one reason or another. Yet somehow, a decade on, our relationship remained effortlessly calm, when the money was tight and when it wasn't.

For whatever reason, we had that durable quality successful couples have—we just *got* one another. We spoke our own private language of inside jokes and callbacks. Like when she'd go outside to get the mail she'd return and announce, "Mail call!" and I'd say, "You're lookin' at him," and she says, "Ooh, sorry, first class only today." Just dumb things only we thought were funny, but it was special because it was ours. Never a miscommunication.

Nolan changed all that.

We weren't even sure we wanted kids. "Mutually ambivalent" we would say when nosy people would inevitably ask. Then, suddenly, we were parents with life and death responsibilities and the constant needs of someone who hadn't even been a thought a year earlier. One friend said it would be the greatest thing that ever happened to us. Another said it would be an unrelenting nightmare. What I didn't expect was that they'd both be right, depending on the day. Or the minute. A cry in the night moments after you've fallen asleep. A four-alarm meltdown before the plane has left the tarmac. An embrace of unconditional love. All the tired clichés we'd been bemused to see our friends endure in recent years found us as well, and they no longer seemed tired. They seemed prescient. Even profound.

Nolan was born with an underdeveloped left lung, which meant constantly rushing to his room in the middle of the night to confirm he was still drawing air. He still wheezes when he gets excited. Meredith's dad called him our little accordion. But to us he was perfect. We were, without warning or any real plan, a family. There was less time to spend hiking Buena Vista Ridge, less time to ourselves. It got harder to stay in sync. When you're a young couple in love you crave nothing more than time alone together. When you're a new parent you crave sleep and a few minutes to be completely alone with your thoughts now and again. Sometimes when I went to the bathroom, I'd stay a few extra minutes in a vain attempt to get centered. More often than not I'd just end up scrolling instead.

But even though things were no longer uncomplicated, they were still good. With the benefit of hindsight, things were very good.

A fter we drop Nolan off at preschool, I drive to the Land of Long Yellow Lights and pull up to Meredith's work—a commercial lease management company where she works on administrative contracts all day. An unintentional game of telephone brought her here from her original goal of becoming a professional photographer. (Her *Yelp* review: good pay, nice people, super fucking boring.)

Meredith kisses me goodbye.

"Good luck," she says.

I smile and pretend to know what she means.

After I round the corner I immediately pull over and check my phone. Tuesday, January 19. So it's still today. I drive straight to the hospital and demand to speak with someone from Quantgen. The receptionists exchange a confused look.

"Is there a name I can look up for you?"

I try to think but I can't remember any of their names, so I ask to speak with Dr. Djawadi instead. As I sit amid the baby shit green, my foot tapping furiously, the television—upright once again— confronts me with footage of barricades being put up across Washington for the inauguration, a handful of tanks taking up positions in the streets that strike me as more strategic than ceremonial. Other than my car everything seems unchanged, though now I see the shattered fish tank is still in one piece. I don't recognize the shoes I'm wearing either.

Djawadi greets me and asks how my symptoms have been. I don't know where to start so I ask to discuss my Quantgen medication. It's clear she doesn't know what I'm talking about.

"If you're seeing a specialist it's best if you follow up with them," she says. "I'm your GP and happy to help if I can, but they are going to have answers specific to any medications they've prescribed for you."

In my head I can still hear the little five-note melody that played when QUANTGEN flashed on screen. It reminds me of the tones that drove Richard Dreyfuss insane in *Close Encounters* — *da-dee-dum-dum-da* — but with the pitches inverted. Marketing pro tip: Rip off what works, then season to taste, or just to avoid IP lawyers. But it's nothing to go on. I'm not going to walk around humming nonsense at everyone or I'll be committed.

"I met them in this building two days ago," I tell Djawadi. "Believe me. Here, I can show you."

She follows me through the halls, but the corridors of this hospital are a confusing maze and I'm aware I look plenty crazy as I round corners and backtrack repeatedly. What started as a friendly walk-and-talk soon becomes a grudging indulgence on her part. Eventually, I find the door to the room where I'd been taken. But it's locked. As Djawadi flags an admin to help, she confirms the room is occasionally used for overflow needs. The door is keyed, motion lights click on as we enter. It's definitely the same room but, apart from some dusty chairs stacked in one corner, it's empty. If I was a barely tolerated houseguest before, I'm now the uninvited friend who crashes the party and annihilates the guest bathroom.

So I show myself out.

"I'm sorry, I didn't catch that."

Did you know some of the most horrific torture techniques in history aren't even real?

"I'm sorry, I didn't catch that."

Chinese bamboo torture. Made up.

The pear of anguish. Never happened.

"I'm sorry, I didn't catch that."

And most famous of all, the iron maiden, that grisly human Juicero? Just a prop made by some German museum owner. Just a guy looking to make a quick buck on some pulp fiction. Anyway, I read that somewhere.

"I'm sorry, I didn't catch that."

All of which makes the very real, uniquely excruciating torture of navigating automated phone trees that much more unbearable.

"It sounds like you said, 'hover trucking atoll.' Is that right? Say yes for yes or press pound-six-one for no."

When I got home, I'd located my meds, dialed the number at the bottom and found myself in the most convoluted voice-activated menu imaginable, pacing back and forth between the living room and bedroom as if I might be able to outrun the problem. I've shouted myself hoarse by the time I finally get what I'm looking for, only to be immediately placed on hold to a series of nature sounds straight out of some guided meditation.

With a moment to think, the reality of what's happened is finally catching up to me. I'm in an entirely different timeline. Suddenly, my heart is racing. *Focus. Short breaths. In. Out.* On the line, the recorded sound of a loon's call is almost comically comforting. Finally, a man's voice arrives on the other end.

"By now you are beginning to experience the effects of the medication," he says. "Do not worry. Periodic disorientation is perfectly normal."

He's clearly reading from a script and sounds like someone trying and failing to do an impression of a generic "American" accent. At least I think that's what he's trying.

I want to know why the hospital doesn't remember Quantgen, but I ask the one question I really care about.

"Is this it? Am I back where I'm supposed to be?"

There's a long silence. "How many have you taken?"

"One black and two white."

As I wait, another voice briefly murmurs in the background before the man continues.

"Okay. Sorry, I'm not off book yet. Hold tight, my fellow Christian." He seems to be stalling while he looks up the answer. "Here it is. Day three. So. You likely have begun to notice some changes in your surroundings. These changes are the result of you passing through adjacent branches. The closest branches will be those where divergences—moments where things branched apart—occurred very recently. Everything before that divergence is exactly as you remember your life. As you continue the medication and get closer to your original branch you will pass through branches where the divergences have taken place earlier."

"Earlier?" I ask. "What are we talking about? Time travel?"

"No no. Not time. Multiverse travel. You always remain in the present time. It's earlier events that will have diverged and influenced your present."

"But what do you mean by divergences? Timelines where I made different choices?"

"No," he says. "No no no. Your choices are always your own. No matter which branch you're in, you're still you. It's the world that's different."

"I need some clarification here," I say, trying to make sense of it. "Because last I checked I'm part of the world. What you're saying is that I've already traveled through several branches? Does each white pill represent a branch?"

The man on the line sighs. "No, not at all. The pills attack the parasite and keep it sedated. You've already traveled through many branches, too many to possibly count, with many, many more to go before you arrive at the branch where you belong."

My silence is enough for him to know I'm not getting it.

"Here's the deal," he says, sufficiently annoyed that I think I hear his accent slip. "At the subatomic level, particles are always randomly popping in and out of existence. Total chaos. Okay? The world looks stable and constant to us because if you put trillions and quadrillions of random particles together it all looks like the same grain of sand to us. But if we were able to look close enough we'd see it's all a matter of probabilities."

"I guess I find that concept a bit hard to accept," I say. "A grain of sand will always be a grain of sand."

"Ah, but it's those tiny particles colliding with one another that produce chain reactions that can subtly affect that grain of sand's exact size, weight, orientation. Which in turn affects how it interacts with other grains of sand. Scientists don't have instruments sensitive enough to detect those fluctuations. They're too small. But they're there. And these random particles are what the entire universe is built on. And so the differences between branches — the divergences — originate at that subatomic level. In one branch, an "up" quark pops into existence. In another, it's a different type, a "down" quark. In another, no quark appears at all. And so on. Accumulate enough of those differences, which are happening in every atom everywhere, and you start to get changes that eventually affect things you and I can perceive. And over time those changes begin to snowball. So, for example, given enough time since two branches diverged, a cloud grows slightly more dense in one timeline compared to the other. The larger mass moves just a bit more slowly. And pretty soon, in one branch you look out the window and it's a sunny day. In another, a storm. And that storm might knock down a power line, which might strike and kill a person passing by. Which changes every interaction that person would have otherwise had in that branch. And on and on. Everywhere. Forever. That's what I mean when I say you're always you in every branch. It's the world you're responding to that changes."

"You're talking about the butterfly effect," I say. "Ray Bradbury stuff."

"I guess, sure."

"Okay," I say, still trying to get my bearings. "But if I've passed through to another timeline, where is the other version of me?"

Another disappointed sigh. "Every time," he says under his breath. I just can't win with this guy. "*You* are the only version of you in any given timeline. Remember, the parasite is attached to your brain. It's your consciousness that's traveling from branch to branch, not your body."

"But then, what about the consciousness of the other me from this branch?" I ask.

A pause.

"Huh," he says as though it's never come up. "One second. Umm. Say, while we're waiting, how's your day?" There's a furious clacking of keys while he searches. "It's another great day here in the U.S. of A., no? We're enjoying that Second Amendment, am I right?"

Seriously, what the fuck. While he searches I hear several distinct voices in the background. But I can't make out what they're saying. Who are these people?

"Okay, I'm back," he says. "Sorry, I don't have the answer to that one."

Well that's not encouraging.

"I think I understand the basic idea of all this," I say. "But I still don't get where the transitions between branches happen."

"Right now, as we speak, you are actually passing through thousands of slightly different branches every second," he says. "But in most of those branches, you and I are having this exact same conversation so you do not perceive any difference. You will only notice yourself *passing on*, as it were, when you cross into branches where an earlier divergence resulted in a change to all possible outcomes, including this phone call."

"And when will that happen?" I ask.

"There's really no way to predict."

"This is a lot," I say. "Can I get you to send me some documentation on all this or something? It would help to better understand the science."

Another pause. "Well, there's a section here titled 'Advanced Theory,' but it says answers to questions about simultaneous superposition will only make sense if you have a background in quantum mechanics and that it's not really necessary for you to understand your situation."

"Oh," I say.

"And do you?"

"Do I what?"

"Have a background in quantum mechanics?"

"Well, not formally. I mean, no."

"I see," he says.

"Sorry?"

"Hey, nobody's perfect."

"So," I say. "To recap what you said at the start, I'm constantly shifting into new branches but most are so similar I don't notice."

"That's right."

"And the point of divergence between those branches gets progressively further back in time the closer I get to my original timeline. And anything that happened before those divergences is exactly as I remember it?"

"Exactly."

"And so, does that mean the oldest divergence would have taken place right after I was first infected by the parasite?"

"Yes, that's it, exactly," he says, sounding relieved.

At least I got something right.

"And when will I be in my original timeline? *My* branch?"

"However long ago you were infected," he says, stretching the words as he searches, "you should see changes that originated at that time exactly ... thirty hours after you take the last white pill. That's when you take the green pill."

"I still don't understand why my hospital has never heard of Quantgen before," I say.

"Any questions about your surroundings can be explained by the fact that you are passing through adjacent realities in which recent events occurred differently." Apparently he didn't need to look that one up.

I have more questions but the call drops. I try again, but after letting it ring for several minutes with no answer, I give up.

Justice Department approves order to expand camps in every state

SHARE

scroll

Comedy legend Carl Reiner dead at 94

scroll

In historic 6-5 vote, Supreme Court upholds order extending federal control over local law enforcement

SHARE

refresh

Tom Hanks checks out of hospital after on-set collapse from diabetes complications

SHARE

T he trick is that you have to share something apolitical once in a while or people tune you out. And then, without engagement, the algorithms filter you out of everyone's feeds and you might as well be dead. And when it comes to engagement you can't go wrong with Hanks. But now I'm suspicious. Did Tom Hanks have diabetes in my old branch? Was Carl Reiner still alive yesterday?

I've spent the afternoon on the feeds looking for signs of divergences, but with most updates I can't be sure if today's news is the same or different from my old branch. Without a detailed list it's impossible to know. It's never been today before so these things may or may not be happening everywhere.

And when it comes to news about Him, every day feels like an eternity. News cycles once measured in days are now reduced to seconds, and He dominates every one. He never stops, like a toddler who asks "why" so long you begin to question whether you know anything at all. One day's horrors will leave you sick to your stomach, only to be memory wiped the next day by an even more terrifying development. For almost four years I'd been able to keep track of every detail. Every law broken. Every scandal uncovered. Every new low revealed. I had to. It seemed too important to ignore, especially if that's exactly what most people insisted on doing. But ever since He stole re-election, it's all started to wash over me. Attrition has finally worn me down. I can't keep it straight anymore.

Today there are several navel-gazing features on preparations for inaugural balls and military parades. Sure, that tracks. There's a story about the administration ignoring anti-nepotism laws when setting up its new Radical Elimination Task Force. I don't think I've read it before, but then it's the kind of story I've read fifty times.

Still, I keep scrolling, hoping to spot a change for the better.

Later, when I arrive to pick up Nolan from preschool, it's the same thing all over again. I'm searching for changes everywhere. His teacher looks the same, at least I think so. Did she always have a limp, or did I just fail to notice it before? I scan his classroom, scrutinize his friends on the way to the car, only to discover I'd never really focused on the little details and wouldn't know the difference. What I'd give to have paid better attention. I didn't know there was going to be a test.

I'm a few blocks from Meredith's work when the lights of an armored patrol truck strobe in my rearview. One truck quickly becomes three and I'm boxed in as I pull the Kia to the shoulder. An officer steps out of the truck beside me and approaches my open window. Nolan is buzzing with excitement. To him, flashing red and blue just signals party time. We may as well have been pulled over by *Paw Patrol*.

The patrols appeared the week before the election, setting up random checkpoints throughout major cities that didn't feel random at all. Ostensibly they were here to "ensure the integrity of the vote" but it was clear they intended the opposite. Soon the election was gone and they weren't.

I've cranked up the heat so Nolan doesn't get too cold, but the officer instructs me to cut my engine. A second officer taps the glass of my passenger window with the sidearm he's already drawn and I'm forced to roll them all down. I want to reach into the back seat to protect Nolan but he's loving every second of this. And I don't want to make any sudden moves that could set them off. One officer asks where I'm heading while the other checks my trunk then shines a flashlight in the backseat, gun pointed through the window.

"Awesome," Nolan says.

The lead officer again demands to know where I'm going and I explain I'm just picking up my wife and son. Then he asks if I'm a loyal patriot. I have no choice but to lie. He takes my ID and we're forced to wait ten minutes in the cold with the windows open. The whole time Nolan is singing to himself and I'm hoping to pass through to another branch.

Eventually the officers return and say I'm free to go.

When Meredith gets in the car I apologize for being late. The first thing she says is, "How'd it go?"

"Fine," I bluff.

"So, do you think you want it?"

I don't know what to say so I just shrug. Apparently this version of me had a job interview of some kind. A shrug is definitely not the feedback she's looking for. So I try to change the subject and casually make conversation, but it's very awkward when I have no frame of reference. It's been at least a month since our timelines diverged. Every topic of conversation I can think of is another chance to reveal I'm not supposed to be here. The space between us has suddenly grown.

What I want to know about is the crash. But how do you ask about something that never happened? As I drive home, I start making small talk about past holidays we've all spent together, memories from years ago that should have happened the same here. Soon Meredith's laughing about the time I accidentally dropped her birthday cake on her brother Noah and the candles singed his trucker's cap. And I comment how, after so many years, all those holidays start to blur together. *"We old"* we used to say to one another, tongue-in-cheek. But that was five years ago now. I act as if I'm half-joking when I ask where we went for Christmas four weeks ago.

"That's not ____ing funny," Meredith says, mouthing but not saying her swear words like she always does when Nolan can hear us. I take my eyes off the road and see the pained expression on her face. "Do you have any ____ing idea what it was like to have to cancel on my family at the last ____ing minute?"

"Excuse me," I say, the rhythms of the argument all too familiar even if the details aren't. "I had just been fired and, if you haven't noticed, the entire world is burning down around us."

"As if I don't know?" she says. "And if I hadn't hidden your god____ keys you might have spent Christmas dead."

So that's it. That's the variable. The difference between the hospital and a hangover. In my timeline she's been upset for weeks, but right now I'm seeing more anger than empathy. It's only been a month yet somehow she seems different here.

We stop for a red light. I look into her pained hazel eyes and thank her. "You have no idea what it means that you did that for me. For us." She can't.

But I'm having the opposite effect I'm going for. She's not buying it one bit.

"Oh ____ off."

It's' time to come clean.

"You know those pills from Quantgen?" I say. "The ones you told me not to take? Well ..."

"Quant what? What are you talking about?"

I reach into my coat pocket to confirm I have the bottle. It's still there. *Da-dee-dum-dum-da*. But if this version of me has the pills, why doesn't she know about Quantgen?

"What the ____ is going on with you?" she asks.

"Yeah!" Nolan chimes in from the back seat. He hates it when we carry on extended conversations without him. "What the fuck!"

Two months after Nolan was born there was an election. But I'd been so busy with work and endless business trips, all while straining through the larval stage of becoming a parent. To be honest I was barely paying attention. I'd shut it all out as a distraction. We all knew things would turn out fine.

Then the votes were tallied. And everything changed.

Suddenly, people were in the streets. The floor beneath our feet, the one everyone had assumed was solid, turned out to be rotted beyond repair and buckled at the slightest pressure. *He can't do that*, my feeds would reassure me. *Don't be hysterical. He'd never get away with it*. But then, day after day, He did get away with it. Then He'd take things further. And further again. And those same voices would tell everyone to calm down. *After all, He's just doing what He said He'd do.*

And then, two years later when Mom died, nothing else mattered. The stakes of the next election went stratospheric. You go through life always living in the future, so when the future you expect is taken away, you need to make sure it can't happen again.

Finding a way to repair that broken foundation, restoring the floor beneath our feet. It became everything. It swallowed up the world I thought we'd been living in. Even as every day brought events I'd naively assumed could never happen, everyone I knew continued to go about their days. Sleepwalking survivors. Not me. I needed to ensure it couldn't happen again, even if that meant days and nights were consumed by feeds that continually fed the latest horror. I spent dinners cursing the ways everyone was failing to rise to the challenge while clucking out propeller noises in a vain attempt to get Nolan to open up.

It didn't help that by that point Nolan had entered the terrible twos, growing more stubborn and defiant with every passing day. Raising a toddler is like traversing a minefield with a genie who only grants wishes for more mines. It's hard to feel as though you can save the world when, night after night after night, something as simple as putting on a kid's T-shirt plays out like the end of *Oldboy*. Meredith kept joking that he has too much of me in him. I don't see it.

After years of those second-by-second news cycles, each ratcheting up the tension until something had to give, violence spilled into the streets. Every day everything somehow spiraled even further out of control. It consumed me. *He* consumed me. Always there. Hiding beneath everything. Inescapable.

At some point, with the weight of parenting, with work, with I-don't-know-what bearing down, Meredith drew a line. *He* didn't live in our house and the only way for things to get better was if His presence was banned as well.

"There isn't enough room for all of us" is how she put it.

Unsurprisingly, I disagreed. You can ban His name but He's still there, a God of the gaps filling the space between us.

And in the end, none of the endless hours obsessing, posting, donating — raging — none of it was enough. And it wasn't simply that the outcome was unfair. It was that it was flagrantly, grotesquely unfair without even the pretense of legitimacy. And yet, the minute it was over, everyone around me seemed to pick themselves up and go about their day as if nothing had happened.

I couldn't do that.

For eleven years I'd worked for Macey Windom Irving. I was good at my job too. My MWI title barely fit on a business card, but when asked about my job I could always say I'd been blessed with the opportunity to travel the world. I handled marketing for our corporate clients. Produced content. Solved problems. I was the guy who could fix it. Whatever they needed, I would do. It had its share of ups and downs, but it was a career. But then, as soon as it became clear we would never be rid of Him, everything changed once again.

All eleven years, gone in a day.

Meredith is silent the rest of the drive home.

As soon as I pull the Kia into the garage, Nolan asks me to do some drawing on his Lil Tyke easel in the living room. Sounds good to me. I don't need any more drama right now.

I grab a Crayon and quickly run through my limited repertoire of semi-competent doodles — duck, steamboat, hobo — but it's enough to impress Nolan, who counters with a stick figure dog that seems to have at least four heads. I scan for Meredith, but she's in the other room on her laptop, deep in thought. Nolan asks for more, so I pull up a new sheet of paper and begin freeform drawing.

Within a few minutes I've sketched the gangly, gnarled limbs of an old oak tree, its branches splitting and splitting again. But it doesn't look right. So I try adding more shading. I'm not much of an artist, but I lean into getting the details right, fleshing out the weathered older limbs, the mottled north-facing lichen, the fresh upper growth stretching toward the sun. It occurs to me that what I'm really drawing is a map. The end of each branch is now, but the distance from the previous fork determines what now looks like, with the trunk a baseline that all the branches share. If this morning I entered a branch that diverged before the crash a month ago, then I should already have reached branches that diverged before I lost my job. And soon, any time now, the November election. Him. The key variable. Jackpot. Who knows whether it can be undone, but any change is better than this. Follow the green shoots and let the dying limbs tumble into the dirt.

I'm adding more branches when my Crayon slips, startled by a booming, discordant sound. Nolan isn't next to me. He's wandered off to bang on the old piano again. Bouncing. Wheezing. Breaking the one rule.

What follows plays like a beat-for-beat replay of Sunday night. Whether this Meredith and this Nolan had experienced the same thing, I don't know.

I confront Nolan. But I get too heated and scare him. Meredith confronts me. But this time it's not about Quantgen, and she's not accusing me of trying to leave. This feels different. There's something off in her reaction. There's that same hardness in her that I saw in the car. She's not even bothering to blank her expletives now. I'm trying to work out what could have happened to have changed her from the Meredith I know in such a short time when she tells me she's leaving. She's already taken off work for the rest of the week. She and Nolan are going across town to stay with her parents.

"With the inauguration tomorrow, you're just going to spiral again," she says. "You already are. And I can't always be the one to fix it." She gathers her things without looking at me. "And before you say anything, don't worry. We'll go straight there. No stops. I've got my ID for any checkpoints."

She says it's going to be up to me when she comes back.

I don't know what to say. This isn't my life. This isn't my family. Meredith methodically dresses Nolan for the cold and hands him a packet of applesauce for the ride.

"Come on, kiddo," she says.

I don't know what's happening. This sweet little boy can't possibly understand. But then he gives me a hard, hurt look. And I think maybe he does. Nolan flings his applesauce packet on the ground and stomps it, splattering a cupboard door in a Rorschach blot that reminds me of *Him*. Meredith begins to scold Nolan but I say I'll clean it up. And they leave.

As soon as I hear the garage door shut, I take the third white pill.

WEDNESDAY

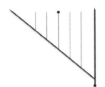

refresh
refresh

I t's mid-morning the next day. My temples strain, eyes sandblasted from staring at feeds all night. I'm sitting in my living room in an old Pixies T-shirt and flannel pajama pants, ritualistically flicking my phone. No matter how many times I refresh, it's still coming.

> *Hours before inauguration, violence breaks out in DC, military parade personnel reposition to engage*
>
> *refresh*
>
> *Surprise indictments unsealed for president's top critics*
>
> *refresh*
>
> *Senators placed under house arrest, DOJ won't reveal charges*
>
> *refresh*
>
> *WATCH: Clip of Timothee Chalamet petting baby duck goes viral*

It's only when I occasionally look away that my thoughts return to Meredith. Could the car crash have changed things between us that much? Is that the key variable? In my old branch, maybe she felt guilt for not preventing it. Could she have been that close to leaving before I ended up in the hospital? Or did something else happen differently here? There's no way to know without asking directly and sounding insane. If I could even get her to answer my call.

I'm once again reminded that I've experienced something more profound than maybe anyone in history has ever experienced. Everyone around me remembers recent events that happened to me but I don't. Like an amnesiac with benefits. I don't even know how to begin to unpack it.

But right now I'm much more concerned with knowing what comes next. If the crash could be undone, what of my job? I text Karl at MWI to test the waters. He responds right away.

How are things here? Calmer since you left LOL

Me: *I bet. It already seems like it was forever ago.*

It was just before Thanksgiving, right? Two months already? Time flies. I was sorry to see you go man. Howve you been? How was youre Christmas?

No change.

I wish there were some way of knowing which things are changing and which aren't. If more recent events change first, perhaps those are locked in and it's only earlier and earlier events that will change. Unless, of course, those earlier changes then changed how later events played out. Butterfly effect. Change begets change. Turn and face the strange. This parasite could have taken me through radical changes or barely perceptible tweaks. I'm not going to be able to game this out until I reach the end of the line. And there's no guarantee any changes will be for the better. For all I know, in my original timeline I'm already dead. Hell, maybe everyone I know is dead, killed in some black swan event, a nuclear war or a pandemic. And I wonder once again how I let myself go along with this.

It's at this moment, as I'm considering my mortality, everything completely beyond my control, there's a thump and the staccato sound of objects skittering across the ground.

Someone's in the house.

I look around the living room for the source, but everything is still, that deathly still that you only sense in the winter, when the pulse of life you took for granted all year ceases to beat and there's nothing for months but an oppressively loud silence.

Another thud, more distinct. It's coming from downstairs.

There isn't much down there. Just an unfinished half basement and some wine and cheese we keep in a makeshift cellar, light sommelier cosplay. It's too damp for much else. There's no exterior door, but there are several hopper windows someone could theoretically break and crawl inside. I check around the corner, in the awkward transition where the living room meets the kitchen. But the door that leads downstairs is shut.

Of course my mind immediately goes to Him, to the armored patrols positioned everywhere. And now, with the inauguration minutes away, with everything I've seen in my feeds, with everything that's happened, expecting the worst is almost never bad enough. And even worse: what if He controls everything in every timeline? What if, no matter what happens in every infinite branch, He only gets worse?

I creep forward while searching for a makeshift weapon, but I don't see anything useful. A plush dog toy. A spongy kids soccer ball. I'm suddenly very aware that childproofing is not an asset when it comes to home invasions. Everything within reach is supremely soft and squeezable. With light steps I enter the kitchen, wincing at a creak in the floor joist as my weight shifts, and draw the smallest knife from the butcher block. No need to overdo it, I figure. Sharp is sharp. Get cocky, get stabbed.

Then, quick footfalls on the steps. Someone is coming upstairs. And fast. I rush to the door, grip the handle and fling it open, hoping the element of surprise actually gives me an advantage and isn't just something they say in war movies.

A shadowy figure approaches, and as it sees me burst into view it cries out in alarm at a high pitch, a surprise I'm not ready for at all. So it does work. In that brief fog of war, there's a loud *bang* and something strikes me in the chest.

I'm laid out on the floor, remembering those scenes where the hero's been shot ten times but the shock is so great he registers no pain. Picks up his blown-off arm and inspects it, unimpressed. Am I the hero now? Sure don't feel like one.

"*Shit*! Shitshitshitshitshit." Meredith rushes past me into the kitchen as though she's trying to dispose of a bomb.

There's no sign of an entry wound on my chest, but I've fallen on top of something. Still prostrate on the ground, I reach behind my back until fingertips brush the shrapnel. A champagne cork.

"Sorry," Meredith calls out from the kitchen, wiping champagne from her shirt with a dishtowel. "I was trying to loosen it and you startled me." I stagger to my feet and try not to draw attention to the knife in my hand.

"But why?" I ask.

She shrugs. "We didn't have any Extra Dry up here."

"No. Why are you here?"

"I made a promise and I'm sticking to it," she says. "I know how much it means to you."

She carries two glasses into the living room. It's a relief to see her smile again, but there's something else in her look I'm not sure how to read. I replace the knife in the block and follow her, uncertain what else to do. Has she come back? Or have I passed to a branch that diverged earlier, where this Meredith never left?

We sit on the couch. She snuggles up next to me and turns on the television. As the screen brightens I'm greeted by an enormous sea of people bathed in sunlight. And in the far distance, the U.S. Capitol building cradles a large platform brimming with patriotic fervor.

Breathing stops. Vision narrows. Time seems to contract. In movies they call it the Vertigo Effect, that trick where the camera dollies back while zooming in and the field of view warps around the hero like a dilating pupil. I don't understand. Why would she agree to this? Why would she put herself through this now after everything we've been through?

And I'm reminded that this is it. The moment I've been dreading for the past four years. Everyone gathered. Far more than last time. The camera cuts to a succession of shots of people cheering. Who are they? How can there be such overwhelming joy and enthusiasm on one of the darkest days in history? But this is it. It's really happening. Cut to a close-up of the stage as the Mormon Tabernacle Choir finishes "America the Beautiful" and I feel as though I'm about to break all over again.

Meredith squeezes my hand and I sense she's watching my reaction.

"Almost there," she whispers.

The Chief Justice has already begun administering the oath by the time I realize it's not Him.

I watch the rest of the inauguration as though I'm trapped behind a pane of glass, observing everything play out as I hadn't dared to imagine it. Meredith wells up a few times. But I feel nothing. I'm seeing it all happen but somehow it's not registering. I should be as elated and relieved as the people on screen but for the moment I'm a total blank.

As the presidential motorcade embarks up Constitution Avenue and onto Pennsylvania, I instinctively pull out my phone to determine what the hell happened differently to change things here. But Meredith places her hand over the screen.

"You promised." Her eyes remind me of the way they looked last night, right before she walked out. "This is it," she tells me. "I promised to be with you today and you promised it would all be behind us from now on."

This should be the greatest day of our lives. We're finally free of Him. Everything broken, mended. Yet it's clear that the pain of what came before is still there, the worry merely pushed beneath the surface. I'm dying to know what happened, but if I look now I'll cross a line I don't want crossed. So I put the phone away.

Feelings are starting to come back to me, the shock wearing off, that feeling when you come to after a nightmare and waking life is a cypher, totally alien, but soon the immediacy fades and you're left with just the sense memory of the terror. It's still there, but gradually it gets harder to connect it to the real world.

This is it. We're free. All of us.

So. Now what?

As crazy as it sounds, it's a question that I never really spent a lot of time on. Details to be sketched in at a later date. *TBD*. It's been more than two million minutes since I started thinking about this moment—believe me, I figured it out—most of them, even in sleep, consumed by Him. The horrifying truths He revealed. About the people we pass on the street. About people we love. And yet. All the buildup to get to this peak, and now to finally peer over the edge. Feeling as though you should be doing something with your hands. You need to move, to do something. Anything. But you don't know what.

I should call Dad, if nothing else to bask in the good news. Meredith squeezes my hand. She thinks it's a great idea, but I can barely hear her. I'm adrift, gripping my phone like a life preserver. I know it's just that it's too fresh. Fear has a gravity to it that's hard to break. But still.

Now I'm listening to the rumbling purr on the line, waiting for Dad to pick up, and an unwelcome thought briefly arises before I push it away.

It was supposed to feel better than this.

There's a story Mom always used to tell about her piano.

Supposedly, long before it was a fixture of my childhood home, the piano once sat in the corner of a bar where she'd worked back in college. Some dive bar in Upper Manhattan, I'm honestly not sure where. The metronome was there too. Just sat on top gathering dust. Mom could never figure out why it was there or who'd left it. She had been a pianist since she was six, so she used to sit and play during her breaks. The owner was a crank, she said, but the tips were good and she got to meet interesting people, so in retrospect she thought it was one of the best jobs she ever had.

The way she told the story, she'd been working one summer weeknight, shortly before closing time, when it was slow and she was noodling on the keys with little to do. When, suddenly, in walked Paul McCartney. All by himself, looking a little lost but unhurried, seemingly with nowhere else to go. This was the mid-seventies, his post-Beatles early-Wings heyday, but by his demeanor you'd never know it. Mom immediately jumped up to fix him a drink. His favorite drink, he claimed, but every time Mom told the story the drink seemed to change. A pint of Guinness, whiskey sour, hard lemonade (which wasn't even a thing at the time), an old fashioned. He asked what she'd been playing on the piano but she insisted it wasn't even a song. With the owner in the back balancing the till and only a few people left finishing up, Sir Paul walked his drink over to the piano and started fiddling with the metronome. It struck Mom as odd that one of the most famous musicians alive, who could fill stadiums to overflowing with his superlative talents, would need help to keep the beat. But he set it to ticking, sat and watched its andante beat like it was imparting some special wisdom. *Tick. Tick. Tick. Tick.* And then, without a word, he started to play. Again, the name of the song changed depending on when Mom was telling it, but I chose to believe her when she said it was "Maybe I'm Amazed." She stood next to the piano as he played and, at his invitation, they sang it together. After that first song, he messed around with a brief ditty, finished his drink and then began to play "Golden Slumbers." Her favorite song. And the metronome kept the beat. *Tick. Tick. Tick. Tick.* Then, at that heady moment, just as Paul was starting in on the second verse — "*Once there was a way*" — the bar owner emerged from the back room to weigh in: "Shut the fuck up! Get up and let someone who knows what they're doing have a chance! We're closing!" Apparently he was more of a Davy Jones fan. Mom always really sold this part and left her audience howling. So with that, Sir Paul got up, handed her his empty glass and a twenty-dollar bill, politely apologized in the direction of the back room and left without another word, Mom left staring in disbelief, the metronome continuing to conduct even though the proceedings had ended. *Tick. Tick. Tick. Tick.*

Incredible. One of the greatest moments of her life, she claimed. I was always baffled how anything else was even in contention. Though I swear the first time I heard the story she didn't mention the duet. When she eventually quit, the owner said he wanted to get rid of the piano anyway and let her have it for twenty bucks. Insisted she take the metronome as well.

It's midafternoon, two hours after the inauguration's end. I'm thinking about Mom's story for the first time in ages. When I called Dad, the first thing he'd asked about was the metronome. I have no idea why. When I called last week, in my old branch, it had been a while since we'd spoken. But the way he sounded today, I got the feeling it had been longer here. I wanted to talk politics but all he wanted to know was whether I ever got Mom's old metronome fixed. It's been busted ever since we brought it home from my parents' house two years ago. Since the funeral.

Still, I'm not sure why the piano story came to me now. Maybe it's because today I'm finally free, my thoughts able to drift, the story something I could always burrow into for warmth. I don't know.

I look up to find Meredith staring at me. Mouth agape. It's because I'm sitting at Mom's piano. My fingers are resting on the keys but not actually playing. I'd wandered over to the bench, lost in thought.

"What are you doing?"

I apologize.

"No, it's just ... I can't remember the last time I saw you go near it."

"I know," I say. "Still. Mom left it for you, not me."

"Your mom didn't *leave* it for anyone," she says. "But if she had, it would have been for you."

"But you're the pianist. You're the one who likes to play. I haven't so much as touched a piano in twenty years."

"When was the last time you saw me play?" she asks. "I don't dare anymore. Look, I get it. I'm not blaming you. But this is *your* piano whether you admit it or not. So if you want to play, play."

I don't want to discuss this again. There's no point. I clap the keylid shut as if to seal it off, though the key to its lock was lost in that New York bar a long time ago. Still, I can't get rid of that feeling I've had all afternoon. That I should be doing something right now. I just don't know what it is.

How are things here? Calmer since you left LOL

Me: *I bet. It seems like it was forever ago.*

It was 2 weeks after Thanksgiving, right? 5 weeks already? Time flies. I was sorry to see you go man. Howve you been? How was youre Christmas?

I check again as I wait in the car, the windows quickly fogging in the cold. Everyone else lets their cars run, a line of little carbon chimneys puffing away. Eventually the windshield is so frosted up I can't see anything.

So here I sit. The nightmare of the election is gone yet somehow I still lost my job. I don't understand. But I'm not going to dwell on it now. How can I be upset when I haven't seen a patrol truck pass by our house once all afternoon?

It's time. I head into Nolan's preschool. He doesn't want to go home, but when I explain we need to stop at a music shop on the way he's immediately on board. As we exit we pass a series of animated zoo animals on the wall demonstrating how to piss and shit with rapturous expressions, friendly reminders for those preschoolers — like Nolan — who haven't yet mastered potty training. They might be setting the kids up for disappointment by making it seem as though shitting is akin to nirvana, but hey, whatever works. I'm trying not to laugh at the thought as I wave to his teacher on the way out. She's not limping anymore.

Google guides me and Nolan to the only instrument repair shop within five miles. It's only a block and a half from Meredith's work, but the name — Down-Tune Beats — doesn't ring a bell. No wonder. It's a narrow storefront around the corner, one you'd never notice passing through on Main. I park across the street. The storefront is two large windows framing a glass door, but all I see inside are dark clusters of musical instruments.

For whatever reason I'm still thinking about the expressions of ecstasy on all those animals' faces as they dump at Nolan's school and I suppress the urge to laugh. *Piss and shit! Piss and shit!* the animals rejoice.

Nolan holds my left hand, mitten on fingered glove, and I cradle Mom's metronome with my right as we cross the street. There's a soft electronic chime as we enter. Inside, there's a half-eaten sandwich sitting atop one of two short counters that flank the entrance, but there's no one in sight. An old Wyclef song I've heard but don't really know plays on a '90s-era Magnavox set on the floor.

The shop is much bigger than it looks from the outside, narrow yet quite deep, but there's very little room to maneuver. Musical instruments are stacked everywhere with no obvious organizing principle, though a few clusters of similar items stand out. A tower of drums here, a ziggurat of guitar pedals there. A mass of vivisected tubas and sousaphones takes up an entire corner. A precarious wire-framed tower that looks as though it could topple over any minute stands adorned with electric guitars like a Coachella Christmas tree. It's not clear whether any given item is for sale, awaiting repair or just busted and the owner couldn't bear to throw it out. But it's fascinating. A bit like touring the warehouse at the end of *Raiders of the Lost Ark*, thinking about all the history gathered, all the stories stacked and unsorted. Nolan's eyes are wide as he plans his method of attack. I have the urge to explain it all to him, to make sense of the madness, but there's so much I don't know where to begin.

The metronome's pendulum lolls to one side as I place it on the counter beside the forlorn-looking sandwich. Nolan is drifting past a spiky mass of woodwinds when a man emerges through a door at the back of the shop.

"Hold up and I'll catch you in one sec," the man calls out.

At first glance I think he might be elderly, but there's a bounce in his step as he threads the stacks.

"It's just me, sole owner and proprietor as they say, so bear with me."

"No rush," I reassure him.

He crosses past us to a tiny microwave set into the back wall behind the counter and extracts a steaming mug. Up close, he's maybe a few years older than me. A slight build, black skin with graying close-cropped hair, a purple Prince T-shirt that seems like it wouldn't be nearly enough to keep him warm in a drafty shop like this. He carries himself like a band kid, if that makes any sense.

He dials Wyclef down and, as he squirts a little plastic bear of honey into the mug.

"Looks good on a cold day like this," I say.

"Ah, it's just for my voice. Everyone in my family runs hot, you know, so I'd just as soon skip it. But never mind me. How can I help you and your little man over there?"

"I'm not actually sure if you can," I tell him. "We have this old metronome that used to work, but while transporting it to our house a couple years ago it stopped."

"Ah, so you a big music guy?" he asks, interested.

"Used to be, I suppose."

"But not anymore?"

"I don't know," I say. "Guess I've been distracted."

"Hey, I get it," he says, pointing in the direction of muffled sounds coming from where Nolan has wandered off. "Kids are full-time. Been there, man." That's not exactly what I meant. "Oh wow, nice." He looks over the metronome with an air of reverence. "An old Seth Thomas model."

"I guess," I say. "I don't know. Does that mean it's valuable or something?"

"Eh. Not really." He sips from his mug, thinking. "I suppose a restored one might go for a hundred or so. Nothing crazy. Only important thing is that it goes *tick tick*, you know? This one just brings back memories. My daughter learned to play piano with something similar."

"Yeah, I guess that's it for me too. More of a sentimental thing. I don't know. The winder seems to work, but the pendulum doesn't feel like it's connected or something. Thought it would be nice to get it working again."

"Right on," he says. "I'll take a look tomorrow and let you know what I can do." He reaches into a drawer below the counter, retrieves an invoice pad and scribbles a note. "This is your receipt for your metronome," he says, pointing to the slip, then gestures playfully at his pad. "And this is *my* receipt for *your* receipt."

At first I think nothing of it. But as I'm poking my head around the stacks of instruments, looking for Nolan, there's something familiar about what the man just said. It's a quote from something.

"I'm sorry if this doesn't make any sense," I say. "But ... the way you just said that? Isn't that a line from *Brazil*? The '80s movie, I mean."

The owner takes on that look kids get in viral videos where a relative shows up after serving overseas. "Right *on*," he says. "Nice get. I am impressed. You know what? That's my favorite movie."

"It's a good one for sure," I say, still unsure where Nolan is hiding. "Python meets 1984. What more could you want?"

"You a big movie guy?" he asks.

"I used to be."

"Hm. Used to be a lot of things. So what was your thing?"

"Excuse me? My thing?"

"Well, given the choice, would you have called yourself a music guy or a movie guy?" The owner coyly folds his arms and leans on the shelf behind him.

"I don't know," I say as I wander deeper into the shop in search of Nolan. "I guess music was like ... let's say a seven out of ten? And movies, maybe more like nine out of ten? So, movie guy?"

Nolan is around the back of one stack, down on all fours with his face in the bell of a trombone. So I return the counter.

"Ah, right on," the owner says. "Say, you ever see the 'love conquers all' cut of *Brazil* the studio made?" He makes a sour face. "The one with the forced happy ending that misses the whole point?"

"Okay, maybe I'm more like an eight out of ten."

"It's all right, not keeping score," he says. He's got that ineffable quality some people have, energy bursting off him in ribbons, yet talking to him is strangely relaxing. "Just making conversation, man. Find it interesting when we're forced to choose between the different parts, which way we go."

"I take it you're more movies than music then?" I ask.

"Me? You know, I'm just a guy," he says with a laugh, now distracted by the metronome. "A dad like you. Gonna be a grandpa, actually."

There's a small tray of business cards for Down-Tune Beats next to the till. I take a card, inspect it, read the name at the bottom. Then read it again.

Oh God.

"Wait," I say. "You're Anton Walters? *The* Anton Walters?"

"Only one I know of," he says, still poring over the metronome. "Not famous or anything. Like I said, just a guy."

But he is famous. At least, he is where I come from.

I'm talking to a ghost.

Anton continues to play with the metronome's pendulum and sweat begins to bead on my back as I recall the news in my feeds. Last fall. Local cop. Courage under fire. This guy, Anton Walters, owned some local store. And one day in September he'd apparently pulled an officer's gun without warning and fired point blank at some woman standing in his store. Somehow, thankfully, he missed. The officer— Petkoff I think—he was on the news a dozen times as the story went national. Shot Walters in self-defense, got a medal for saving the woman's life. To be honest, I'm not big on reading crime stories.

I don't really see the value in constant grief porn. And there's plenty of it. But a month later, when the administration argued it needed to take control of police departments to "safeguard the election" they cited the officer by name. Petkoff became the face of change. All because Anton Walters the attempted killer had given them an excuse. I knew the incident happened somewhere close, but never realized it was here.

Bang.

I jump at the sound, and my reaction makes Anton jump. And now I'm startled all over again.

Bang. Bang.

It's Nolan. He's found a mallet of some kind and has taken to wailing on a suspended snare drum. As soon as I see him I know we need to get out of here as soon as possible.

"Tell you what," Anton says optimistically. "This might actually be a quick fix. We're closing, but if you've got a few minutes I can stick around and get you set and on your way. Why don't you guys follow me into the back."

"No. No, that's not necessary," I say. "You know what? We'll come back tomorrow."

I try to think of some excuse but my mind is locking up. The only thing that comes to mind are those flashcards on the wall at Nolan's school. *Piss and shit!*

"Come again?" Anton asks.

Wait, did I say that out loud?

"I mean. What I mean is, my kid's potty training, and, you know I don't wanna mess up your store. He could … you know. At any time, so. So we should really go."

"Suit yourself, man," he says. I grab the metronome off the counter. "Oh hey, you can leave that here. I'll have it done in the morning."

"No, really," I insist. "I'm sorry but we have to. Right now."

I'm backing away, trying to act casual while also trying not to take my eyes off him. But I only succeed at the second part. He has a look on his face like he's used to this for some reason. I'm sure I don't want to know why. He's not exactly menacing, to say the least, but his store suddenly feels less like an eccentric workshop than a honeypot designed to lure prey like me. And Nolan. I continue slowly backing away and Anton holds up his hands as if to say *"it's all good."*

The front door is five feet away, but I can't see Nolan. He's stopped his pounding.

I need to get out of this shop. I need to get out of this branch.

"Hey Dad?" I hear Nolan somewhere behind me and know that I have to move fast. As I turn, I immediately collide with the wire-frame scaffold adorned with guitars, the heavy-duty kind you might use to hang lights or speakers at a concert. I look up to see a single three-string bass shift like a Jenga block, swinging by its strap on the top-heavy structure. The weight shift is just enough. The whole thing seems to play out in slow motion, a chain reaction pulling the precarious mass down, down, down. And I briefly see Nolan smiling beside an assortment of piano keys arrayed on the floor before he disappears beneath it all.

He's gone. The echo of the crash is still ringing.

I cry out. But he's gone.

"Oh my god," Anton says, rushing forward.

I instinctively step forward to stop Anton and hear the metronome bust apart on the floor beside me. But I don't know what good it would do to stop him so I join him instead, trying to find a way through the shattered mess on the ground, a gnarled mass of poles and wires, severed necks and humbuckers strewn everywhere. I start to grab random pieces and throw them aside. I tense up as Anton puts a hand on my shoulder.

"Hold on man, we need to find him first," he says. "Don't want things to shift further under there."

We listen but it's silent now, the rubble at rest. I wait to hear Nolan's familiar wheezing. But there's nothing.

Anton apologizes. It's not nearly enough.

So this is fate.

We were free. We'd finally broken free. Of Him, of all of it. And now. What now?

Someone will say at least Mom will finally get to meet Nolan but I don't think I even believe that and I'm trapped behind glass once again.

A faint sound.

I look back at the Magnavox but it's not playing.

There it is again.

It's a note. From a bass guitar. It's coming from somewhere inside the destroyed scaffold. Maybe even the one that tipped the scales, I don't know.

"It's him!" Anton says. "Hey, little man," he calls to the pile. "Don't move, okay? We're gonna get you."

"Nolan," I sputter. "His name is Nolan."

"Hey, Nolan, if you can hear me, keep playing, man. Keep it up."

I can't tell where he is, but Nolan keeps plucking the same low string. Again. Again.

We're working together now, sifting through the wreckage. Anton is methodically moving each piece, surprisingly strong for his size, lifting away broken instruments and scaffold fragments until the sound gets louder and finally I see Nolan's sparking eyes looking back at me.

"Damn," Anton says to him. "You've got a good sense of rhythm, little man."

Nolan crawls out. I ask where he's hurt, frantically inspecting his small frame, but he says he's totally fine. It all fell around him without hitting him.

"Like that one movie we saw," Nolan says. "With the guy. Bubster Keaton." Close enough.

"What do you know," Anton says. "Little man's a movie guy, too."

Then Nolan makes an expression as though he regrets saying anything.

"Can I still get a treat anyway?" he asks.

"Yes," I say as I hug him tight. "You can definitely get a treat."

"Can I get a toy?"

"Sure. Of course."

"Okay," he says, thinking. "Can I get a gun?"

"What? No," I say. "Why would you even want one?"

He shrugs. "Jaxton at school has one."

"I highly doubt that. But you should really stop talking to Jaxton just to be safe."

"Why?"

"Look, let's start with a treat and go from there."

"Oh *okay*," he says, as if getting a treat has now become a punishment.

We help Anton make a path through the broken instruments though I'm not sure what more to say. He apologizes again about the scaffold, but I know it's not really his fault. He picks up the metronome, now in several pieces. Says he'll see what he can do.

It's the least I can do to say yes.

Now I'm feeling ashamed for having been afraid of him earlier. Maybe, I don't know, this branch might be a fresh start for him too. A chance to make better choices.

I write down my number and he says he'll let me know either way.

"Thanks," I say, "and say hi to your daughter."

"Jill."

"Jill. Like the character in *Brazil*, Jill?"

He seems wistful, playing with his mug. The liquid's probably cold now.

"You know," he says. "In twenty-four years no one's ever made that connection but her."

"Well, tell her she's got a good movie-guy dad. And thanks."

"Yeah," he says. "If I hear from her again, I sure will."

Nolan's asking about the specifics of his treat as we exit into the cold dark. A squad car is parked behind my Kia, its interior dome light on, and for a moment I freeze up. But the officer inside is just sitting, idly talking into a walkie.

We're not in those branches anymore.

As I drive away, I check my rearview and catch a glimpse of the officer stepping out of his car before I turn onto the next street.

Later, at home, Meredith puts Nolan to bed and I check once again.

How are things here? Calmer since you left LOL

Me: *I bet. It seems like it was forever ago*

It was just before Labor Day weekend right? 5 months already? Time flies. I was sorry to see you go man. Howve you been? Hows youre family?

Still no job. Yet other things have begun to shift more frequently. All this evening I've been noticing changes. Nothing major. Objects around the house seeming to move from one place to another when I'm not looking. First a pen, then a lamp, then the pictures on the living room wall. After dinner, I opened the cupboards and saw they were completely bare until I reached the very last door. Then when I backtracked they were full again. And apparently we have a cat now. As the divergences from the timeline I know originate earlier, changes in the present are growing harder to understand or predict.

It's more than a little unsettling. Like someone keeps hitting reset on the universe whenever I look away.

But in spite of the brief terror at the music shop, today was a good day. In fact, the first truly good day in years. It's like I've been buried in a dark pit for so long I'd forgotten what it was like to feel sunlight. *He* lost here.

We're safe, I keep reminding myself. Nolan is safe.

The pill bottle is resting on the master bathroom vanity and it's time to take another. But I don't want to leave this place. I've finally gotten what I want, what my family wants. What everyone needs. Hell, even Anton. Who knows what the remaining branches will bring? The man on the phone said I would stop drifting thirty hours after I stop taking the pills. Sometime tomorrow morning I should be locked in.

I head down to the garage and toss the remaining pills into the garbage bin so they won't be found. When I enter the house again, the metronome is back on top of the piano. Still in one piece.

THURSDAY

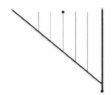

7 months already? Time flies. I was sorry to see you go man. Howve you been? Hows youre family?

V ariations on a theme, but always the same answer.

Any time now I might be locked into this reality — I think — so it would be nice to land in a place where I have a job again. I'm passing through branches that diverged from the timeline I know at least seven months ago, but no luck yet. If anything, the length of my unemployment keeps growing somehow.

It's early morning and I'm riding the bus with the metronome in my lap. Maybe it's because I feel bad about what happened yesterday. Like I need to make it up to Anton or something. Or maybe I just want to do something nice to remember all this, to celebrate how far we've come.

I would have taken the car, but when Meredith awoke this morning she seemed extremely anxious. She left unusually early in the Kia with Nolan without saying a word. It's not how I imagined the afterglow of victory would be but it'll do. The most important change has been made. We're safe. And I'm looking forward to some predictability again.

I'm checking the feeds as the bus slowly lurches toward Down-Tune Beats.

First Act: Incoming president signs order to close detention camps within one year

scroll

Militia members occupying D.C. building say siege will continue indefinitely

refresh

THREAD: Here's why Garfield always sending Nermal to Abu Dhabi is so problematic (1/42)

This morning isn't like it was last night, with items constantly shifting around. It's as though the changes have slowed all of a sudden. In fact, it's been more than an hour since I've been able to spot any changes at all. Either they're too small to notice or the last pill I took is wearing off.

I step off the bus into an unseasonably warm day. It's three blocks to Down-Tune Beats. I know the neighborhood well. People refer to it as the Land of Long Yellow Lights since no one wants to stop here. Given the things she'd heard, Meredith had been concerned about coming here when she first started her job. But to her surprise she found the small shops and soul food restaurants really charming. The problem seems to be one of petty vandalism. Broken store windows drive away foot traffic, which is necessary for businesses to remain open. There's an unfortunate number of boarded-up storefronts here because owners can't afford to replace windows when they break, which only adds to the mythos that it's a place where you should hit the gas rather than slow down.

As I approach the music shop, a woman inside is making elaborate gestures with her hands to someone I can't see behind the counter. She's young, white with a blonde ponytail, a walking ad for

Lululemon. She's gesturing toward the bedazzled smartphone in her hand and she is not happy.

There's a familiar chime as I open the glass door, but the woman doesn't acknowledge me. She's talking to someone on speakerphone instead. Behind the counter, it's not Anton but a young woman who's visibly pregnant. She could be the daughter he mentioned, but I'm not sure. Anton had said he worked alone. She even looks a bit like him, but with longer hair and braided dreads on one side. She's doing her best to ignore Lululemon's drama, instead focusing on the invoice ledger on the counter. Janelle Monáe is quietly grooving on the Magnavox in the corner.

"I'm sorry, how tall did you say she is?" comes a question from the bedazzled phone.

"I told you, she's about yay high," Lululemon snaps back. "Are you even listening?"

"Ma'am, this isn't a video call. I don't know how tall you mean."

"Oh Jesus Christ. I said, she's yay high. Can you get your manager on the line? Preferably someone who speaka Inglés? Domo fucking arigato?"

The woman behind the counter acknowledges me and asks how she can help with a *what now* look. I tell her I'll just wait my turn and she goes back to staring at her ledger. I have the overwhelming urge to hide behind one of Anton's stacks of instruments until the situation is over. But now, as I look around, I realize they're not even there. In fact, the entire store has been rearranged. All the dismembered brass. The toppled tower of guitars. It's all gone. Instead, everything is meticulously organized on mounted display shelves along the walls, *Rentals, Repairs* and *Sale Items* all clearly demarcated with well-designed signs in a sleek stylized font.

Marketing pro tip: spend as much time on designing your signage as you do your product and your business will survive at least a year even if the product sucks.

It's incredible how much more spacious and welcoming the shop appears. Maybe after the tower fell on Nolan yesterday Anton decided to finally clean up in here? But then I remember the metronome in my hands and know none of that happened in this branch.

"Ma'am, I've got my supervisor here," Lulu's phone chirps. *"We're sending someone to you now. If you're in a safe place we can continue to take down details."*

"Look, I don't have the time and I definitely don't feel safe ..."

I exit the shop to get some air until whatever's happening blows over. It's significantly colder outside all of a sudden. I check my phone, try texting Karl again but he doesn't answer. There isn't much left for me to do but wait. It's 9:15. If the timing is right, this could be my last attempt. For all I know I've already ceased to drift.

Inside, Lulu continues to gesticulate wildly every time I steal a glance.

I'm blowing tufts of steam, watching my breaths slowly dissipate. Even as I'm crossing through branches, every moment in time must mean everything's still splitting then splitting again, the future an infinite maze of even more branches we all leave behind in our wake. In one, the steam of my breath drifts left. In another, it drifts right. Right now, it doesn't seem to be drifting at all, just hovers in place until the warmth has been drained, the little cloud slowly becomes invisible again and I can see through to the other side.

What I see on the other side is Meredith. But she's facing the other way and doesn't see me. She's inside Nat's Soul Food Kitchen next door, seated at a two-person table next to the window. A man in a three-piece suit sits across from her, slicked hair, maybe fifty. And I picture the look on her face when she left this morning. She was so nervous. And now she's laughing, the man laughing with her. Is it a business meeting? An interview? Or something else.

No, I can't imagine it. I've never seen anything to suggest … And then I think of her walking out the door and now I'm replaying the last fifteen years on fast-forward, scanning for clues.

Lulu storms out of the store behind me. "Motherfucker wants to charge *me* full price and make me late for brunch, bitch, I will eat you alive." She slams the door of her double-parked Range Rover and drives off.

There's a chime as the door to Down-Tune Beats opens again. The pregnant woman sticks her head out. "Ready now if you are," she calls out to me. She sounds tired.

I tell her I'll be there in a minute.

I look back at the restaurant but Meredith and the man aren't there. In their place sit empty plates and a receipt as though someone had just left, so I don't think I've passed onto a different branch. I head into the restaurant but there's no sign of them. Looking out the back entrance I see the taillights of a Tesla heading down the alley. Meredith and the man are seated inside, along with a third person I can't make out.

I check the table where they'd been sitting. There's a crease in the linen tablecloth that looks like the mark of two arms reaching across the table, but then maybe it's just my imagination. A credit card receipt has been left behind, signed by someone named Chaz Bennett.

I text Meredith: *Everything okay?*

She responds right away: *sorry, in a meeting, talk later*

That's not good. But then, maybe it really is just a meeting.

A minute later I'm back in the music shop. I ask the pregnant woman if everything is all right.

"It's fine," she says as though it happens all the time. "What can I do for you?"

I set Mom's metronome on the counter.

"Are you Jill?" I ask. She looks uneasy.

"Why?"

"I'm a friend of your dad, Anton," I say. A half-truth at best. "Brought this broken metronome in for him to repair and was hoping I could just say hi."

Her whole demeanor changes. She's angry at me in a way she hadn't been at Lulu.

"Dad's dead," she says. "Don't you read the news?"

Dead, here? Again? The branches should be splitting farther apart, not converging. Why would it have happened here, where everyone's been spared? Where things are good again.

"And no," she adds. "You weren't his friend."

"No, I really am," I say, not sure why I'm trying to convince her. "We just, we like to talk movies is all."

"No. You're not."

"How would you know?" I'm feeling indignant at the idea he wouldn't have befriended me.

"Because if you were really his friend, you'd know his name isn't pronounced like *wonton*," she says. "It's Anton, like *Scranton*. So you'll excuse me if I don't have time for another supposed friend of An-*ton* the Attempted Killer nosing around for a scoop." She shifts her attention back to her ledger and starts writing, ignoring me as she had ignored Lulu.

And now I'm remembering all the times I heard reporters say his name. All the times Officer Petkoff said it in interviews. How Anton didn't even stop to correct me when I said it to his face. And this is the person who tried to murder someone? More than once? Maybe he and Petkoff had a past. Maybe he'd been planning it in every branch, and only in some did he get the chance. Or maybe none of us knew him at all.

"I'm sorry," I say. "You're right. I didn't know him well. But from the time I spent with him, he seemed like a good man. And he did talk a bit about you. About Jill from *Brazil*."

Jill stops writing but doesn't look up. "What do you want?"

"I don't know. Just to say I'm sorry for your loss, I guess. I don't even know if you work on things like this now, but. My metronome stopped working and I thought Anton would know — "

"I'll see what I can do," she cuts me off and looks at it. "I can't guarantee how fast I can fix it though. This isn't my only job. But there wasn't anyone else who could take over. And what little money he had is gone."

"I'm sorry," I say. "I know that must be hard, especially if this is where it happened."

She nods, looks at the ground like she's trying to stay composed. "Hey. A paycheck is a paycheck," she says. "Honestly, I'm just trying to keep the lights on for now so I can sell the place. You close down, pretty soon there's boards on the windows and then you got bigger problems."

"No, I totally get it. As for the metronome, Anton told me it reminded him of one you used to — "

"Did he really call me Jill from *Brazil*?" she asks, now looking at me with a faint smirk.

"Well," I say. "It was more like he implied it."

Now I realize I've seen Anton alive more recently than she has. There's regret in her eyes, I think. Or maybe I'm just projecting.

"He was a stubborn man in many ways," she says. "We disagreed about lots of things. How to fix things. But ..."

She tries to complete the thought but it's too much.

I'm not sure what to say. I try to think of something comforting, open my mouth but nothing comes out.

Bang. There's a rap on the glass door. We both jump, startled, and turn to see a silhouette outside the door, backlit by the morning sun. As my eyes adjust, the silhouette resolves into a police officer.

I've seen him before. He's too far away to read the name on his uniform but I know it's Petkoff. The face of change. Last time I saw an image of Petkoff he'd been standing in the White House Rose Garden. Beside Him. Sealing our fates.

"It's him," I mutter. "The one who shot Anton."

"I thought you said you didn't know he'd been killed," Jill says, confused. "And no, this guy wasn't involved."

"He wasn't? That can't be right. I *know* it was him."

"I was right *here* when it happened," she says. "I'd think I would know."

Petkoff says something into the walkie talkie clipped to his shoulder and Jill and I remain still. He somehow looks both physically intimidating and pathetic. Clearly out of shape. Like someone who probably once had leading-man looks, everything square and symmetrical, but with the added mileage and baggage he looks to me now like some kind of alcoholic bullfrog.

The door chimes as he enters.

"Got a report of a female suspect," he says to me, as though I'm the one in charge here, then gestures toward Jill. "Fits this woman's description."

"It was just a misunderstanding," Jill explains, sounding light, trying to wave it off. "Some lady trying to use an expired coupon. It's nothing."

I assume this is either the end of the conversation or the beginning of a negotiation, but before I can say anything Petkoff has her head pressed down on the counter and her hands held behind her back. *Take a side.* Mom's voice in my head.

"Whoa," I say, trying to help. "She didn't do anything. I was here. If you're looking for a suspect, it's not her."

"Thank you for your input, but stay out of this," Petkoff says. Now I see his name clearly emblazoned above his pocket. "Please leave, citizen. I have the situation under control." The script is formal, polite. But he says it with total contempt.

I step closer. "No, really. This isn't the person you're looking for. She's expecting, for Christ's sake."

"It's definitely her. The description was clear. About yay high," he says, but Jill's laid out so it's not even clear how tall she is.

He cuffs her wrists so tight they go white.

"No, I'm serious," I say. "*Stop*. It was just someone trying to get her in trouble. *She didn't do anything*."

"Step back," he barks, "or I'll arrest you for interfering."

I step back.

Jill doesn't say anything. He walks her through the front door, she complies. Why is she going along with this? Especially after her dad was killed. I can't imagine. Maybe it's because of what she saw that day. Maybe she just knows how this kind of thing goes. Or maybe she really did something wrong and I'm the one who's confused. Maybe I've been naive to give either Anton or Jill the benefit of the doubt.

Petkoff shoves Jill into his squad car out front. Her eyes remain fixed straight ahead as the car drives out of sight. I'm left standing in the doorway of the empty shop, filling up with shame for just standing here and letting it happen. But then what was I supposed to do? It all happened in less than five minutes.

There's vibration in my pocket. It's probably Meredith. I exhale and check my phone.

How are things here? Calmer since you left LOL

It's Karl. He did get my message.

Me: *I bet. It seems like it was forever ago*

???

Me: *When did we last see one another? You know how it is, you get old and it all starts to blur together*

Shit. You take 1 day off and you start getting wistful for old Karl LMAO. You coming in today or what?

Jackpot.

"**L**et's talk about your pain points so we can right-size a solution *for you and your stakeholders.*"

Oh God. What am I doing here? Why did I ever think this was a good idea?

It's surreal being back in the office. No one giving me looks, whispering, jeering. It's been less than two hours since I got the text from Karl and I'm sitting at my old desk, as though I'd never left, in Macey Windom Irving's free-range Open Office Collaboration Zone™. We lost the cubicle walls a few years ago, and now we're grouped into desk arrangements the office managers call "pods" and "clusters" like we're fresh produce. Not much seems to have changed in the two months since I was fired back in my old branch. Though I do see that Reggie—an admin who left MWI for a new job last summer—is still here in this branch, and still hoofing it to the bathroom every twenty minutes.

The office is perched on the 25th floor of a prestigious building downtown, one that costs three times as much to rent as the equivalent space a mile away, the workspace an overwrought diorama of consultant-crafted mindfulness buzzword fuckery. Every scarce inch of wall surface is drenched in a different branded color intended to foster productivity and inclusiveness. Paradigm Purple. Synergy Sunset. Transformation Teal.

Marketing pro tip: Who needs affordable health care when you get your rods and cones stimulated every day for free?

"Let's talk more about our value prop. When we're done today we're gonna want to aggressively move the needle for you as fast as possible."

As soon as I got the text from Karl, I'd felt my work phone buzzing on the inner pocket of my coat. The same phone I'd last seen busted into a dozen pieces on the street outside the office. Marketing pro tip: never let your employer talk you into juggling two phones just because it's easier on accounts payable. It sucks, and you feel like a meth dealer. Plus, when they're the same model but only one lets you bypass the numeric lock with your fingerprint, you spend even more of your days frustrated and confused.

"Yes, absolutely. It's on our capabilities roadmap for Q2."

The phone was vibrating with a 60-minute reminder for a 10 a.m. consult call led by Trent Gadsden. Trent's my manager, the man who gave me my big break here, whose politics are abhorrent but until recently had been off-limits at work, who let my family spend the weekend at his beach house twice, who fired me. So if I was really going to come back, I figured I should take the call in person. Even if he's the one doing all the talking. Even if things never went bad here. Only after I arrived did I learn he's dialed in from the beach.

"One of the biggest challenges innovators like you have is that your teammates get siloed. Soon no one has the bandwidth to be able to pull everything together. That's where our work family comes in," Trent says.

The faces are what stay with me the most. I'd worked with the people on this floor for years, some for more than a decade. But when it came time to push back, to take a stand and defend me, their faces showed either apathy or outright contempt.

It was only a few weeks after election day. Five minutes into our weekly team meeting Trent said, "I have reason to believe we have a radical in our midst." He let the comment just hang there.

Now that the election had revealed the hammerlock *He* had on us, any pretense toward tolerance dissolved. Of course our "work family" had always been little more than a benevolent dictatorship.

Aren't they all? But until that moment Trent had felt the need to at least pretend otherwise.

As soon as he'd said it I knew he was talking about me. Even though I'd always been the first to step up or fall in line. Whatever they needed, I did it. I don't know. I guess I'm competitive like that. I'd kept politics out of the office, even as it became increasingly difficult. Work had become the one place where I could go five minutes without thinking about Him.

But then, at that moment, it was as though He was there in the office with us. Trent was the one speaking but the words were channeled straight from Him. Trent even used the same language. "*Radical.*" I half expected my boss to start screeching like something out of *Invasion of the Body Snatchers.*

So there I was, first against the wall. And I made a choice. I took a side, pushed back. And everything spiraled from there. I was certain I'd never see the inside of this office again. Eleven years, gone, with no plan for what came next. But when I think back on that day, it's mainly the faces I remember.

Now here I am, sitting in on an intake call with Trent as he tries to woo a new client. Like nothing happened. We used to exclusively work with hip, interesting brands. Silicon Valley startups claiming they're going to change the world. The cool kids. These days we get all kinds.

"*The optics on oil spills aren't great, I agree. But we'll help you focus on the positive, remind everyone of all the jobs you've created. Employees, first responders, claims adjusters. You're keeping that economy rolling, my man.*"

It's not a job I ever expected to fall into. Just happened. But it pays well. Decent benefits. And I get to travel the world for free, though since Nolan was born travel doesn't feel like the perk it once was. Not to mention the carbon plumes belched by every flight, overdraft fees that will eventually come due.

My hope in coming back is that now, with Him gone, maybe things can go back to the way they used to be. And if not, it'll have to do until I can find something else. Like Jill said, a paycheck is a paycheck.

"My team and I will huddle later and ideate on that for you. When we're aligned I'll loop you back in and we'll make this happen for your stakeholders."

The call ends. Now I wait for Trent to send the email telling me to deliver the plan he just promised.

I sense someone approach from behind, hovering only inches away. I know without looking that it's Karl, the one person who reports to me. He's an assistant project manager, and my only real friend here. Tall, stocky, a relentless bullshitter, not particularly bright or good at his job. But all in all a good guy. At least we're able to talk politics some.

"You found your way back, good for you," he says, and I turn to see him habitually strangling the small foam football he likes to tote around the office in one hand while, to my surprise, the other rests in a sling. "You get my message?"

I haven't seen him in almost two months, so I ask which one and act like I'm joking. Hopefully that's enough to cover it.

"Ah, it's okay, I was kidding anyway," he says. "Just givin' you shit."

"Your arm," I ask, probing. "How's it feeling today?"

"Still pins and needles in the elbow, but you know, I've come a long way." It's not at all clear to me what happened to him or whether it's something that had happened in other branches as well. "Listen," he says, "Speaking of which, I've been meaning to say. Just wanted to thank you for covering everything while I was out all those weeks. Obviously I'm in better shape than the motorcycle, but it's been tough as you know and I appreciate you letting me ease back in." He really is a good guy. Ambitious, sort of funny at times, definitely not smart. But good. I tell him I've got his back, whatever he needs.

"But seriously though," Karl says as he pulses his football and wanders away, "good luck today. You'll need it."

Great. No clue what that means.

As he continues his rounds, I check my calendar again. There's a three-hour meeting starting in less than twenty minutes. Title: "All-Family Workshop: Day 1 of 2." I saw it earlier, assumed I could dial in from my desk and mostly ignore it. I expand the entry. It's in Auditorium 1 down the hall. Eighty-five people on the invite. The listed host? Me. No other context.

As Nolan would say, What. The. Fuck. Eleven years here and I've never once had to lead an all-staff workshop. I scan emails, recently opened docs, PowerPoint decks. Nothing helps.

I've been back at work for an hour and already I'm in every nightmare where it's opening night and I haven't learned any of my lines. I consider taking the loss, getting up and leaving. After everything I've seen the past few days—the shooting at the hospital, Meredith leaving, Nolan almost crushed, Anton dead, his daughter arrested for no reason—everything here feels completely pointless. Why did I come here?

Then again, this is my new branch now. It isn't some "what if" game. This is reality. I've been given a second chance. The truth is that I came back for the same boring, unglamorous reason most people continue to show up for work. There are bills to pay. Meredith and I just paid off the medical bills from Nolan's birth a few months ago and we're forever monitoring his wheezing lung for another costly attack. Plus, we're still paying down more than thirty grand in student loans. Do I really want to mess things up all over again? I need to figure this out and get through the day. Take one thing at a time.

Scanning the other "pods" on the floor, there isn't much to see. The usual crew is grazing over by a foosball table that's gathering dust, trying to caffeinate enough to propel themselves through another hour. Gillian, who spends most of her day on *FarmersOnly* cruising for dates even though she lives behind an Urban Outfitters and doesn't drive a car. Jake from HR, who thinks calling people "chode" is a personality. Karl appears to be telling them the one about how he used to work in Hollywood and a bunch of directors all owe him favors, everyone from Brett Rattner to Lev Upton. You can tell because they're nodding in that way where you know they're being nice but don't believe a word he's saying.

I head toward the auditorium entrance, searching for clues. Past the Inspiration Indigo walls. The Punctual Pink. The Bonhomie Blueberry. Kathryn from internal comms walks past, says "good luck up there" with a smile, and I'm remembering her flipping me off as I carried a box of my belongings out the door. The sign posted next to the auditorium door just says "Reserved: WORK FAMILY TIME, Thurs & Fri, 12–3." No help at all.

As I'm reading, my vision blurs for a moment. I'm questioning whether it had just been a trick of the eye when I'm struck by a wave of nausea. I have never been nervous about public speaking before. Of course, I've never been in a situation like this either. I grip the door handle to inspect the auditorium setup but I'm starting to feel lightheaded. Rather than enter, I steady myself against the wall. Deep breaths as I focus on the two flatscreens embedded in the Optimize Olive on the far wall.

One TV is in commercials, showing an infomercial for a 3-in-1 Telescoping Reacher Tool I've seen dozens of times. On the other, cable news is holding on a live shot outside a federal building in D.C. In voiceover, the anchors are dispassionately discussing an ongoing standoff with militia members who have taken an unknown number of hostages.

Jake from HR passes with a grin. "What's up, chode?"

This shit isn't helping, so I head to the men's room and splash water on my face. In the mirror, my reflection stares back. It's not great. Public restroom mirrors can be particularly cruel. *Deep breath. I can do this.*

I need to focus on why I'm here.

My family needs this. This job is too good to walk away from.

Twelve more years. Just twelve more years if I play my cards right. Save, invest. Hell, if I'm lucky I might not ever need to work again. Retire early.

Then who knows what I'd do. I could dedicate my life to helping people. Maybe become a social worker like Mom.

I've bluffed my way through client calls before. I can do this. Hell, the people in that auditorium know me. They like me. Or at least I thought they did before I was shown the door.

The looks on all their faces. Karl was the only one who offered to help carry my things to my car. *Stop.* Focus on why I'm here. *He's* gone. We won. It's a new day. Meredith has been through so much. She deserves to have today go well for a change.

I'm considering whether to surprise her with a nice dinner out when everything goes blank.

I can't move.

I'm sitting at a table in a spotless white room, no windows, an empty chair on the opposite side, the outline of a single door cut into the far wall. But I can't move. It feels like the beginning of an interrogation in some poorly written cop show that follows all the standard tropes, completely unmoored from reality. A mechanical clock is loudly ticking somewhere but I can't turn my head to see it.

I wait, but I have no idea what for.

Then, the handle of the white door slowly turns. The ticks grow louder.

The door opens, and it's exactly who I'm expecting. It's Him. He's been here all along, of course. He's been with me every hour of every day for years. But for the first time, He's here for real. He takes the chair across from me, tie pooling on the table as He seats Himself. I want so badly to leap across the table, but I can't.

"You thought you could get away from me that easily?" He calmly asks, expressionless.

Not really, no.

"But you did. You actually thought it was all going to work out, didn't you. But you can't escape Me."

He smiles His Cheshire Cat smile. "The escape, like so many things, it was all a hoax. You are a radical. An enemy of the people. And I'm, like, smart."

The door opens again but I can't make out who's behind it at first. And then I see. He looks older but I can tell it's Nolan. I'd know him anywhere. Older Nolan enters and He rises with warm greetings, arms enveloping, His eyes trained on me the whole time.

It takes me a while to realize I'm in a dream. But by the time Trent enters the room with my third grade teacher and Slender Man, I'm pretty sure.

W hen I open my eyes again, everything is blurry. There's a hulking form standing over me. Slowly, things come into focus. The form has a mouth, eyes, pretty much everything you'd expect in a face. The person's lips are moving but the sound is slow to return, like it's on a lag. It takes a minute for everything to sync up again.

"What are you doing in here?"

It's Reggie. I lift my head and immediately strike my temple on something cold and hard. A toilet bowl. I've collapsed in the far stall.

Another seizure.

The nausea rises, then dissipates, as I get back on my feet, now reminded of the time I walked in on one of our execs doing a line in this same stall. This probably isn't a great look. I offer an embarrassed grin and shrug, and Reggie backs out of the room without another word.

Back in the hallway, people are streaming into the auditorium. On the far wall, both flatscreens show the same live footage. Several overturned cars are in flames on a city street as a military tank advances in the background, wisps of white smoke rising all around. It's not clear where it's taking place, but it looks like some far-flung battlefield, far worse than things had been before the inauguration in my old branch. On the left screen, a chyron at the bottom says *"Report: Arrested senators denied access to lawyers."* On the right, a talking head discusses why he believes "both sides are to blame for this latest crackdown."

My familiar headache is back and I feel another passing wave of nausea. I reach in my pocket for my bottle of pills but it's not there. That's right. I tossed the pills and the contact number with it. I check my personal phone and my work phone but the number isn't listed in the history. Apparently in this branch I'd never called them.

The broad headache slowly fades to a localized throbbing. The parasite symptoms have gone for now but I still have a tender bruise where I hit my head.

It's time for the workshop to begin.

Inside, everything in the auditorium is dark except its dramatically lit stage. Every seat in the audience appears to be full. I quickly make my way to the stage, where a single lectern stands in front of a large white screen with the words "WORKSHOP" projected onto it. On the lectern there's a clicker, presumably to advance slides.

I step forward, palm the clicker and watch dust motes floating in the light. "Thanks to everyone for attending," I say. Time to riff and hope for the best.

"Why are we here?" I ask. "Why do we all work here? What is it about MWI that gets each of us out of bed every day? Who is it that ultimately benefits from what we do?"

Normally, in a meeting like this, the audience would give the session leader an enthusiastic cry: "Our stakeholders!" But today, total silence. Shoes squeak, chairs groan as people shift uncomfortably.

A click to advance the projector, one that I hope provides an answer. I half expect the Quantgen theme to play. *Da-dee-dum-dum-da.* Instead, I've conjured a nightmare. The image is that of a gruesome wreck, a sensible commuter car hugging a tree, innards both mechanical and biological splayed before it. *Click.* In the next image, a young girl screams in front of an oil derrick that's caught fire, a thick black rain falling over her. *Click.* A bulldozer belches smoke as it fells a tree hundreds of feet tall, with what appears to be an indigenous hut lying in the tree's shadow. *Click.* The images only get worse. Death. *Click.* Child slavery. *Click.* Gingivitis. *Click. Click.*

And then it clicks. Crisis communications. That's what I'm here to talk about. I've been handed this responsibility because there's no one better at toeing the corporate line. When a client served up shit, I ate it without complaint. And what did it get me in the end?

"Let's be honest," I begin, without any plan for what I'm going to say next. "Often what we need from our clients isn't time or patience. What we need are different facts on the ground. But we don't have that luxury. We can't untaint that groundwater or unburn that village. No. What's done is done. When we're brought in to manage a crisis, we're brought in to communicate away a very real problem. And if it were easy, they would have handled it themselves. So what do we offer them? Peace of mind. The ability to weather the storm. Warm reassurance."

In my peripheral, Karl steps onto the dais, quietly watching a dozen feet away from stage left. On my opposite side, a burly man I don't recognize takes the stage and slowly approaches me. Maybe he's my guest? My assistant? I'm pretty certain I've never worked with him before. And I'm guessing I haven't won an award.

Not knowing what else to do, I keep going.

"So why do we do what we do? What do we have to offer? On the other side of the crisis, the public will still hate the client's guts. Of course they will. We're just sanding down the spear tips for as long as the check clears. *We're* managing *them* through as much as we're helping them. What do they really need? A hard slap in the face. But they don't come to us for that. They come to us for a tranquilizer. Palliative care. What we offer them is a better story."

The man draws closer but to me he remains a stranger, a craggy jaw resting on the broad shoulders of a linebacker. And then he breaks into a sprint. I haven't had the wind knocked out of me since I was ten, so when he tackles me to the ground I feel like I'm drowning.

A few employees cheer as I'm dragged from the auditorium, struggling like the hooded woman in the hospital as I'm carried past its inspirational walls. Holistic Hazel. Proactive Peach.

I'm taken to a small room in the building's security office on the first floor, sat in a chair, the door locked, alone. I'm in a different branch than I was twenty minutes ago. That much is clear. But the details are anyone's guess. I half expect Him to enter for real this time.

Soon, the door unlocks and Karl enters. The one person I can trust here.

He doesn't look happy to see me.

"You know, old pal, we need to have a talk about your future," he says, impatiently rubbing his temples. "Because it isn't here in this building. I can tell you that. Now, I'm not sure how you could have failed to get the message before? But to be clear: You. Were. *Fired.*" He somehow manages to stretch the word into four syllables. "Are you trying to get arrested too?"

The only way forward is to tell him some version of the truth. That he's my closest friend at MWI. That we've been through a lot together, and even when the culture started to turn these last few years I could always count on him. Now that I'm here, maybe he can help make things right.

"Is that some kind of joke?" he asks. "What exactly is your plan here? You're going to get your old job back?"

"Of course not." I know he was promoted after I left, at least in my old branch he was. And good for him. I'm guessing he was supposed to be the one giving that presentation. And here his old fired boss shows up and tries to take over. I try to think of a good excuse for coming back but there isn't one.

"Look, you don't have to worry about me," I say. "I'm sorry, Karl. I wouldn't want to get you in trouble. It's just that we've been through a lot together over the years. Maybe, I don't know, I thought I could make things right, I guess. Maybe you could put in a good word with Trent?"

"Put in a good word?" Karl crouches so we're on the same level, a look of menace I've not seen in him before. "If you wanted to continue exchanging bullshit texts that's fine. Whatever. But to come back here?"

"I thought you might be able to help smooth things over," I say.

"We're done, you and me. You knew what I wanted." He did talk about advancing his career to a nauseating degree. "I mean, use your head. Who do you think told on you in the first place? Trent isn't very bright under that rug of his. He never would have figured you for a radical on his own."

It's a betrayal so unexpected I have no words. Karl, of all people. So that's why I kept getting fired. Even in branches where He didn't win. Apparently Karl screwed me over every time, in every branch except one where he was on medical leave. I probably only have a job there because he hasn't yet managed it.

"Leave," he says "And don't come back. Lots of radicals out there, you know. It's an easy call to make these days."

For some reason, the thought occurs to me that if Mom were in my place she probably would have found the right words to talk her way out of this. She had this way with people that almost always ended with them on her side, like she'd recited some secret incantation. Maybe forty years as a social worker conveys some kind of superpower as a reward, I don't know. By the end of the day she would have had Karl offering her family to stay at his cabin.

But then I'm not her, so I agree to leave.

T he bus ride home is like touring a war zone. Public transit is still operating for the moment but several bus windows have been broken and snow is blowing in. As we pass through the Land of Long Yellow Lights, several buildings on both sides of the street have been burned to the ground. Meredith's work has been fenced in by an expensive-looking barricade, but where Down-Tune Beats had stood there's only rubble. I call Meredith repeatedly but she doesn't answer. At one point the bus is forced to wait as a tank slowly crosses in front of us, its treads tearing up the asphalt as it crawls.

The four blocks from the bus stop to my house are a dead sprint through whipping wind and heavy snowfall. The streets are deserted, but there's a constant pop-pop of gunfire echoing. It sounds close, but I can't tell which direction it's coming from. Maybe all directions. On my block, a body lies in the middle of the street a few doors down from our house. A woman with long red curls, but that's all I can discern. I have no idea how long she's been there but she's slowly being buried by the snow coming down. A trail of blood has spread in every direction, red ripples on a white canvas flowing out from the center.

As soon as I get home, I overturn the trash bin in the garage and start riffling through bags of filth, foraging for the bottle of tossed pills. But they're not there. Seems about right. I rush inside and slip on a streak of applesauce left on the kitchen floor. For a moment I'm confused, but the Rorschach splatter left on the cupboard door is unmistakable. It's the same one Nolan made two days ago. Right before Meredith took him to her parents.

I'm back in a previous branch, drifting away again. The parasite's awoken. It's taking us back to the branch where I started. Where everything is broken.

I call the hospital. As before, no one has heard of Quantgen. *Da-dee-dum-dum-da.*

Out of options, I head to the master bathroom. And there it is. Resting on the vanity. Exactly where it had been two days ago. There are still three white pills and the green left. By the time I'd taken the latest white pill I must have already passed beyond this branch. For whatever reason the other version of me from this branch must have chosen not to take it. Or wasn't able to.

I dial the number on the bottle and parry and thrust my way through the tortuous phone tree. Finally, I'm put on hold to nature sounds again. But the meditation track doesn't sound soothing this time. Instead, the calls of nature sound ominous, sadistic, the animals mocking, threatening. Outside my bedroom window, an armored truck is quietly rolling down the street. It's flanked by a dozen heavily-armed men in riot gear who step past the dead body as if it weren't there. Two officers lag behind the rest. One is consulting a clipboard and giving instructions to the other, who fires yellow tracer rounds at the front doors of select homes.

In my ear, whales sing, crickets fiddle, birds warble as more homes are singled out. The El-Sayed family at the end of the block. The Nguyens across the street. The elderly Iglesias siblings who live next door. Then one of the pages flies off and the officers are chasing it across our neighbors' yards, always a step behind the next gust of wind. I'm pressing myself against the wall now, hoping I won't be seen by the men standing little more than twenty feet away. The officer with the clipboard retrieves his paper, reclips it, then stands in front of our house as he holds the paper up to his face, trying to decipher the writing. Animals in heat are braying, screeching, calling out for a mate. I'm gonna punch that goddamn loon in the throat.

The patrol moves on. We're safe for now.

Finally, I'm connected.

"By now you are beginning to experience the effects of the medication," a man says. "Do not worry. Periodic disorientation is perfectly normal."

This time, the voice on the other end of the line isn't disguised. Or maybe it's just someone better at faking an American accent.

"I'm drifting backwards," I say.

There's a pause as he seeks the right script.

"Did you miss a pill?"

"Yes."

A long pause. "Intentionally?"

"Yes."

"Sir. You must take *every* white pill, not *some* of the white pills. *One* at a time, *one* per day. Then you *must* take the green pill or the parasite will recover and you will drift back to where you began the trial."

Faint gunshots from farther up the street. I ask why I'm having seizures again.

"Because the parasite likes to, for lack of a better term, 'swim upstream' within the multiverse, whereas the medication renders it inert so that it — and you — can drift 'downstream' to where you belong. Traveling upstream is, as I understand it, a less pleasant experience for the host. But ultimately harmless."

Again I hear other voices in the background of the call, what sounds like people having other conversations though I can't make out what they're saying.

"So," I ask, "if that's true, why can't I just take the green pill once I reach the branch I like best?"

"Because, sir, if the parasite — *ancylostoma everetti* — is not sufficiently weakened before termination, it responds by releasing a toxic compound that kills its host. This is not a 'choose your own adventure' situation. Your only options are to take the full course of medication and end up in your original branch, or stop and you'll end up in the branch where you first met our team. At this time I must call your attention to the terms of the contract you signed, which state that failure to complete the full trial will result in a $100,000 fee that *cannot* be waived."

"What?"

I don't remember anything about a fee. This is absurd. Now I know this is some kind of scam. I mean, technically speaking, I didn't take the time to read the full terms and conditions. It must have been fifty pages long. And let's be honest. Does anyone?

The man asks whether I have enough pills to complete the full course now that I've begun to drift back. I explain that I have one additional pill now due to the slippage and he pauses to check something. As I wait, the voices in the background become more distinct. As do the sounds of the room. It sounds like a call center. Other people having the same conversation with other clients. Some voices speaking in English, some not. Drones toiling in a machine. But what machine? Just how big is this drug trial?

The man returns to confirm the extra pill should be enough medication to proceed and encourages me to take it as soon as possible. "Remember now, you're still only on the third white pill. You've lost a day because you let the parasite set you back, which means you won't be in your original branch until Sunday now. Any more questions?"

"Once again, I don't understand why I've retained my pills in every branch yet no one ever remembers me meeting with Quantgen."

"Any questions about your surroundings can be explained by the fact that you are passing through adjacent realities in which recent events occurred differently." The one thing they never need to look up. "So, if there's nothing else today, would you mind taking a brief survey after the call? Any notes you have for me would really help."

"Notes? For what? To help with what?"

"With my craft," he says eagerly. "Like, did you think it was believable? You know, I felt pretty good about it, but I felt like I could have gone further with the $100,000 part, you know? Like, really sell the gravity of it. Like, 'surprise, you're fucked, man,' you know, really dig deep. Glengarry and all that, you know. I don't know. What do you think?"

This is not the day to mess with me. "What do I think? I think there's a dead body lying in the road in front of my house and if I don't get out of this branch soon I could be next. I think you just said if I don't take all your pills I'm going to get taken for every cent I have and then some. What do I *think*? I think I don't want to take your shitty survey. In fact, no one in the history of mankind including Alexander Graham fucking Bell has ever wanted to take the survey at the end of the call. Ever."

And the line goes dead.

I'm exhausted but can't sleep. I take a pill and spend the afternoon at home watching the feeds, listening for more gunshots, that familiar feeling of being held captive, of watching the world burn and not being able to do anything more than just hope it gets better.

Senator taken off life support after tragic fall from window

refresh

Newly federalized police quell protests in 38 cities as fallout from 2nd inaugural violence continues

rinse

Claim of assassination plot prompts Capitol lockdown, Congress prevented from convening indefinitely

repeat

Kobe Bryant takes first steps, almost one year after his debilitating crash

refresh

Climate bill already stalled as new president tries to press 100 Day agenda

rinse

Militia members say they're 'hunkered down' for indefinite occupation unless election overturned repeat

*Mercury is no longer in retrograde: here's what that means
for your cats*

Three hours later it's clear I'm back in a better timeline, the headaches gone. There's almost no snow on the ground anymore. More importantly, no body. No yellow tracer marks. Tension begins to unwind as well.

I get it now. I need to see this thing through to the end, come what may.

My phone shows I have a missed message. I hit play and am soon relieved to hear a familiar ghost.

"Hey there, movie guy, this is Anton Walters." He says it like *Anton* from *Scranton*, and I'm sad for him all over again. "Sorry about the delay. I intended to work on your metronome last night but got a little detained for a bit. Anyway, the good news is that it was a quick fix. I've gotta head out now and get some rest but feel free to come by tomorrow and pick it up anytime. No charge. Hope you and little man have a good night."

I still haven't slept, but I feel like celebrating. It's time to take stock of all that we've gained. I'm back where things are good again. Headed in the right direction. We're free, we're alive. Another hour later, fortified by a lowball of bourbon—the good stuff I never touch—I look up to find Meredith standing in the doorway. She's watching me with a smirk, as beautiful as I've ever seen her, and I picture her standing on the corner the night we met, the ambient glow of a now-forgotten bar's illuminated marquee cast upon her. She's more beautiful even than that.

"What's the occasion?" she asks.

"It's a good day," I say.

I suggest the two of us have a night out on the town, but she reminds me it's Thursday and she can't take off work tomorrow.

A nice dinner for two instead? Too late to find a sitter, right. So the three of us venture out to our favorite steakhouse as a family, even though my Nolan isn't exactly batting a thousand when it comes to behaving in restaurants.

It's dead at the steak house. Pretty normal for a once-again-snowy weeknight in January. So we take a table in a cozy corner nook. We take our time chatting with a young server with plenty of time on his hands. And pretty soon Meredith is telling him the story about how she and I first met. Her story. How we worked together to tear down her *Endgame* set. It always makes me uncomfortable to hear a story I don't remember in which I'm a main character, but I'm feeling so good tonight I'm not going to let it bother me. I focus instead on helping Nolan navigate the maze on his placemat. I'm not sure helping a cow find its way back to pasture is very inspiring when it's going to be on our plates in a few minutes, but who am I to argue. Nolan's having a blast.

Our drinks arrive, and I'm about to propose a toast when my phone vibrates. A text from Karl. I tell Meredith it's work. She gives a resigned look.

> *Hope your feeling better, man. Dont worry about today,*
> *Trent wasnt there anyway. Weve had our share of benders*
> *but Ive never blacked out an entire morning before LMAO.*
> *Some king shit right there.*

Blacked out? So that must be how it works. As soon as I passed out in the bathroom at MWI, the other me must have woken up. Apparently when I pass through other branches, the version of me who's living there ends up with a memory gap during the time I'm there. Of course, now I'm thinking of all the times I've ever been forgetful or blanked on what I'd been doing. If every second brings more branches, there might be an infinite number of slightly different versions of me, all doing the same thing at different moments. It's a strange thought. Hey, maybe I contain multitudes, I don't know. But then I've never lost a whole morning before.

"Still with us?" Meredith says with a frown. "You have 'work face' again." She has that same I-told-you-so look she had the other day, but I can't connect it to anything. This person I love, whom I know so well, is indecipherable again. I'd felt space growing between us over the past year, a wedge He'd created, a space He'd filled. But now, even with Him finally gone, there are so many missing details. The space between us feels wider than ever.

I remind myself that I'm only passing through. This is still far better than the alternative. Just enjoy the ride while it lasts.

"Time for a toast," I announce. Meredith hesitantly raises her wine glass as Nolan raises his milk. "With the election and inauguration behind us, I promise I'm going to make more time to focus on you, and to recommit myself to my work. I know this has been a hard time for all of us. But things are going to be different from now on. Better. We're here, together. And nothing can stand in our way."

As I'm speaking, Meredith slowly lowers her glass and looks away.

I ask what's wrong.

"Why are you doing this to us again?" she asks. We sit in silence. There's an intense tension I can't explain.

She then recounts how I had taken her and Nolan to this same restaurant nine months ago, to this same table in fact, shortly after *He* had died of a sudden stroke. And I had made this exact same toast. "Almost word for word. Remember? But things haven't changed, have they. Actually, I take that back, they have. They've gotten worse. Christ, we were all so hopeful—*I* was so hopeful—and yes, of course I'm glad he's gone as much as anyone. But we don't have Him to blame anymore." How could things possibly be worse with Him gone? It's so absurd my mind can't even entertain it. She's fighting back tears now. "And your work? You hate your job. You've been practically daring them to fire you. So what is this? Why should I believe things won't just break again? It's not fair to Nolan. And I can't always be the one to fix it."

This was the culmination of something. Clearly. But all the important pieces are missing.

The pain on Meredith's face, in her whole body, looks like something inflicted by one of those torture devices that never existed. Iron maiden incarnate. I don't know what to say, so I don't say anything. She excuses herself, heads to the restroom to recover. Nolan continues to silently draw on his placemat, that look of a child who's seen and heard enough that he's learned to cope by tuning it out. So different from the Nolan I know. What's happened to them here?

Soon the server brings our food and Nolan digs into his mac and cheese, never taking his eyes off his plate while I wait for Meredith to return. Unsure what to say when she does.

The more I try to parse what could have happened to these Merediths I keep meeting, the more I wonder about the parts of these branches I'm not seeing. Everywhere I go there's a me-shaped hole, a ghost I can't see. If it had been *me* in these timelines things could never have happened this way. There's some missing variable I'm not seeing.

Eventually, once Nolan is close to finished, I acknowledge the inevitable. The night is a bust. I try to flag down our server for to-go boxes so we'll be ready to go if Meredith ever comes back. But we're the only ones eating, the limited staff apparently consigned to the kitchen. I instruct Nolan to stay put and rise to find someone, wandering the seemingly vacant steak house.

A host breezes through swinging kitchen doors as I approach, startled to see me. With apologies, I request some boxes. But get a blank expression in return. Apparently they don't have the A-team working nights like this. I begin to describe our server, though not his name because I'm shit with names. And then, as I watch the wide, blank face staring back, no hint of recognition whatsoever, the truth sinks in.

I don't want to look. But there's nothing else for me to do. Vertigo Effect, like a dilating pupil. And somehow the emptiness is worse than the pain it replaced.

The worker returns to the kitchen. I walk past the empty corner table where my family from a different branch had been sitting and leave behind a twenty-note for a confused server to find.

It was the day we learned families were being torn apart at the border. About the camps. Two years before the camps expanded everywhere, before random people who'd been critical of Him were snatched off the street and never seen again. We knew the news was bad, even if we couldn't yet imagine how much worse things would get. If there was one day when things between Meredith and me took a turn, where things weren't the same afterward, it was probably that day.

We'd taken Nolan to Buena Vista Ridge. An opportunity for us all to get some fresh air after the long, cold winter. I remember the sun was very hot. Unusually so. An SPF100 kind of day. A triple-antihistamine kind of day. A record-breaker that's been broken twice since. Nolan was twenty months old at that point, right at the age when he started launching into Olympic trial heats without warning.

refresh

Reluctantly, we stuck to the easy trails. The reason you go to Buena Vista is for the views up top, but with a toddler your mind always goes to the worst-case scenario. The threatening root underfoot, the bare rock face with a death wish along the ascent. Over time you start worrying a bit less about the same things, usually because something new has taken its place. But the first time anywhere with a newly-mobile toddler plays like a horror flick in your head. *The call's coming from inside.*

It was all Noah's fault.

SHARE

Meredith's older brother used to be a fun guy. Maybe not someone I'd have chosen to be friends with, but he was funny enough and mostly apolitical. We weren't interested in the same things, but I never felt the need to tiptoe around certain topics either. All that changed pretty quickly after that first election. To me, it was a disappointment. But it was devastating for Meredith.

refresh

Meredith loved her brother. She still does. But for some reason he was determined to put that love to the test. It wasn't just that Noah disagreed. He couldn't leave it alone. Constant attacks, constant rationalizations. I took to calling him Whatabout, which she thought was funny at first, but quickly less so. Her parents tried to stay Swiss about the whole thing, keep the peace, though that meant pretending Noah's increasingly shocking comments were perfectly normal. *Why, yes, of course all human beings have worth. But then again, maybe not? Who's to say, really.*

We were certain this time would be different. Surely children put in camps, ripped from their parents, sleeping on cement floors, the shocking images, the intentional reckless cruelty of it, surely that would be the breaking point. But of course it wasn't. Instead, Noah doubled down, Meredith's phone pinging constantly as we walked with deflections, taunts, accusations.

Whataboutwhataboutwhatabout.

She knew they couldn't continue like that.

COMMENT

We'd gone to Buena Vista to get away from it. Of course that wasn't possible. He could reach her anywhere. Likewise, I'd promised myself the trails would be a feed-free zone, a place to finally clear my head. But as we walked I lost count after a dozen pickups.

He could reach me anywhere.

scroll

refresh

SHARE

Meredith had announced she was finally going to cut Noah off before we'd even left the house. She spent our walk through those hothouse trails fighting raging allergies while trying to find the right words, there but not really there.

I'd agreed to stay out of it, but there were a thousand different Noahs right there in my feeds every time I looked at my phone. And they were too much to resist. The trolls, the true believers, the bandwagon believers, the cynics, the pedants, the sycophants, the spammers, the both-siders, the no-siders, the mercenaries, the devil's advocates, the anti-anti crowd, the anti-anti-anti crowd, the bots, the grifters, the grifters who accuse trolls of being bots, the Nazis, the quote-unquote ironic Nazis, the incels, the TERFs, the anime chuds, the anti-anti mercenary pedants, the TikTok teens and the K-pop stans. The last two were cool enough, at least.

COMMENT

You can try to ignore them all. But they're still there.

COMMENT

And ignoring the problem is exactly how we ended up here in the first place.

MOCK AND BLOCK

COMMENT

refresh

SHARE

Something that only just occurred to me: they're all still there, aren't they. Right now. Even if *He* isn't. What is the shape of victory again?

Anyway, after the dopamine rush from vanquishing a few Noahs, I looked up to find I was completely alone on the trail. Apparently my family had gone on ahead.

I walked farther up the path, around the next corner, and found Meredith sitting on a tree stump, phone in hand. Her eyes were red, and not from the allergies.

"There," she said, slowly nodding with a sense of finality. "It's done." I asked if she was okay. She said she would be eventually. She had no choice. Then she looked at me, confused. "Where's Nolan?"

The search probably lasted less than five minutes. But it seemed to stretch on for hours. The lower trails avoid any sharp drops or rugged terrain, but they roughly follow a stream that cuts across the park reserve. We split and ran in both directions then met again, panic rising, my mind conjuring horror movies I'd never imagined. Meredith's voice broke as she cried Nolan's name again and again. We darted through the brush. Shouting. Pleading.

When we stopped all we could hear was babbling water.

I approached the edge of the stream in a panic and the soft ground on the edge of the bank gave way. I slid into the frigid spring water, a sudden shock in the blistering heat. The stream wasn't deep, maybe a little more than a foot. But plenty deadly for a toddler. Meredith ran along the bank while I sloshed through the water, searching frantically for any signs under the rippled surface.

When Meredith cried out, I knew it meant he was safe. I rounded the bend in the stream to see an odd sight. A woman was sitting at the water's edge, confidently leaning against a ridged black pan. She was calmly playing patty cake with Nolan as he giggled along.

I don't think we ever even asked the woman's name. She had that look where she could just as easily be twenty-five or fifty, you really couldn't tell, carrot-colored curls draped over a dark linen shirt, cut-off jean shorts and no shoes, seated in the mud like she didn't have a care in the world, her toes resting in the icy stream. She informed us she'd spotted Nolan walking near the water and thought she should keep him company until his guardians came looking.

"I figure a kid this cute, someone would be by before long," she said matter-of-factly. "Best to stay put."

We both rushed to hold Nolan, who was having a great time on his first adventure and let out a squeal.

Meredith asked what the woman had been doing out there, so far from the trail.

"Oh, just panning," she said.

Supposedly she dealt in all kinds of stones and gems—tourmaline, amethyst, topaz, aquamarine, you name it, grew up in North Carolina near one of the only emerald mines in North America, now closed, and never stopped looking to see what was under her feet, not that we asked for her life story—and she'd heard rumors there might be some gold remnants churned up in the old glacial till nearby.

Exhausted and grateful, trying to be polite, I asked if she'd found what she was looking for.

"Not so much," she said with a tired grin. "But you know how it is. You gotta keep at it."

She returned to her work, and we returned home, far more stressed than when we'd left. A stress that never really went away.

Looking back, we were extremely lucky the woman had been in the right place at the right time, but all I could think about that day was how it was the last thing we needed on top of everything else. It was the first time I remember thinking fate had it in for me. By the time Mom died, five months later, I was sure.

The house is dark when I return home from the steak house. I trudge through the front door and shed my coat on the floor, not bothering with the lights, and collapse in the armchair in my darkened living room. Somehow it's still Thursday. The longest day of my life. I still haven't eaten anything, the pulsing pressure in my head like bilge water sloshing back and forth in a sinking ship. At least it's not from the parasite this time.

I just want to get to the end. I don't want to keep meeting these Merediths I don't understand and can't help only to leave them behind. The pained looks from Nolan, the Nolan who now won't even look in my direction for reasons that have nothing to do with me. I can't do anything about it, so I'm better off hiding out somewhere until I'm back where I belong. I have two more white pills to take then another thirty hours until I take the green. I just need to get through the next three days.

I'm considering booking a hotel room, somewhere I can hole up alone, when the phone rings beside me, a flare on my armrest firing in the dark. Meredith. I let it go to voicemail and soon the room is dark again. Rather than leave a message, she calls back. After her third attempt there's a ping to signal she left a long message.

Years ago, when I traveled for work and we couldn't be together we used to leave one another long, unhurried voicemails. Before Nolan was born. Most voicemails automatically cut off after three minutes, but we'd set our phones to let them run as long as we wanted. When our schedules made it impossible to talk, she'd leave a message to tell me everything about her day, ask about mine. I'd do the same. Audio pen pals, distant yet connected.

I check the length of the voicemail she left. Seven minutes. But after the Merediths I've seen this week, I don't want to play it.

Hotels downtown, anything with a bed and a TV will do. I'll just wait and read my feeds. Better yet, I could shut off my phone and rest. I finally have the chance to turn it all off. I'm booking a reservation for a standard king size when the brown tabby cat we apparently own jumps onto the couch beside me and starts to purr with friendly vibrations. It has a small notch in one ear and white gloved paws. I reach out to pet whatever-its-name-is but the cat hisses and scurries under the couch.

It's funny. I always wanted a cat when I was young, but Dad liked to refer to them as "sociopathic parasite farms" so it wasn't happening. Always a dog family. I wonder what moved us to get one here. I watch it watching me, like it knows I don't belong here, its eyes reflecting the light from the entryway. I've known people who think cats have a mystic ability to see things people can't. I highly doubt it. But in this case I suppose it's actually true. This cat knows more about my life here than I do. For all I know, we took in this cat in my original branch and it's what gave me the parasite that started all of this. But no, that can't be right. I've never had a cat. Only things that happened after my infection could have changed. Whenever that was. If we'd gotten a cat before the infection I would remember.

This damn parasite. It's been with me throughout all this, my invisible partner as we hitchhike through hell together. Soon I'll be rid of it and this can end.

I get down on my hands and knees and inch toward the tabby. I'm not even sure why. It's not as though it can whisper secrets in my ear, point out all the missing variables I'm not seeing. As I draw near it hisses and runs again. Seems about right.

The cat flees down the hall. A light is on at the far end. Nolan's room. It's not clear whether it's been on since I arrived or if I've passed through to yet another branch. Inside, Nolan is quietly lying on his alphabet rug, scribbling with crayons on construction paper, his face illuminated by his plastic camping lantern.

"Where were you?" he asks without emotion, without looking up. I tell him I'd just stepped out for a few minutes, then inquire about his mom. "I don't know. You were fighting," he says to his drawing that, from what I can tell, appears to be a chicken with legs ten feet long shitting on a school bus. Guess he's finally showing an interest in potty training, at least.

"Did she leave?" I ask.

"Uh huh."

"Do you know where she is?"

"Uh uh."

"Do you know why she was mad?"

"She wasn't mad. She was sad. You were mad." He looks at me. "Are you going to leave, Dad?" It's the first time I've ever heard him call me dad rather than daddy.

I assure him I'm not leaving.

Nolan and I work together to change him into his pajamas, and it's every bit the power struggle as it is with my Nolan. Once changed, I remove two pebbles and a LEGO block from his pants pocket before tossing the clothes in his hamper. I lie beside him until he nods off then lie awake in his bed watching him sleep. Meredith was right. He has her mouth and eyes, my nose, my stubbornness. There's nothing to distinguish him from my Nolan in any way that I can see. In fact, he's no more or less mine than the Nolan I'm headed toward nor the one I left behind. And I know that even if I'm bound to pass beyond this Nolan at any moment I can't just leave him here alone. Presumably, the other me will take over as soon as I pass beyond this branch, so I need to stay close.

FRIDAY

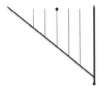

The doorbell rings, and keeps ringing.

It's loud. Far too loud, actually. I rush to open the front door but there's no one there. Yet the doorbell keeps growing louder. I step outside, inspect the doorbell buzzer. It looks normal. Then I realize it's not the sound of our doorbell at all. It's that door chime. From Down-Tune Beats. I step back inside and see there's a police officer standing in my living room. The door chime stops. And now it's too quiet. The officer is facing me, idly buttoning and unbuttoning the holster snap on his sidearm. But I can't make out his face. The features keep shifting, like bubbling water.

So, first off, this is a dream. I get that. Noted. But it still feels so very real.

"An-ton Walters," the officer says with a familiar voice, his finger pointed at me.

No, I'm not.

"Of course you are. You fit the description. About yay high?"

Why does this keep happening? What did he even do?

The officer's facial features finally settle into place. And now it's Him.

Great, here we go again.

I tell Him I'm not afraid of Him anymore. And I'm not. He's gone now. "Fake News" is the reply.

And now He draws His gun, points it at me, tells me I don't understand. And then He proceeds to explain how He could have had Susan Dey at that Emmys after party in 1988, how she came onto Him and He was the one who turned her down, because she wasn't a 10, not even close, an 8 actually, 7 if I'm being honest, just nasty really, and some people, many people in fact are saying "L.A. Law" had a good run, you know eight seasons is a helluva thing and not many people know that, and after it was all over this big guy came up to Me, big beautiful beefy guy, straight out of central casting, medals up to his epaulettes, on top of his epaulettes actually — the epaulettes were themselves medals — so beautiful we fell in love, and he came up and he was a grown man crying and he said, tears streaming down his face, Sir, he said, I saw everything Sir, you could have had Susan, Sir, you turned her down, Sir.

He continues in that vein for a while.

By the time He finally pulls the trigger, more than anything I'm just relieved.

I awaken in Nolan's bed. Apparently I'd been so tired I slept through the night.

Nolan's playing on the floor and immediately notices I'm up. He's excited, which makes me happy, which means his breaths rattle, which makes me worry about him. It's never simple.

The phone confirms it's Friday. Two more days to go until the green pill. To my surprise, the notification bubble in the corner suggests Meredith's voicemail message is still there. All seven minutes of it. I must have passed through an unimaginable number of branches in the hours since she left it. Somehow, all those little changes yet that stayed the same. But I still don't want to get drawn into the drama of someone else's life, problems that have nothing to do with me.

The Kia isn't in the garage, so I get Nolan dressed. We walk four blocks through a blanket of fresh snow to the bus stop and I ride with him to his preschool. On the ride there I watch the other bus passengers, some looking under-caffeinated, others clearly hung over as they face the workday ahead. One thing I'm noticing as I pass through branches that diverged many months ago: the weather is now constantly in flux. Snowing one moment, and then when I turn my head the other way it's sunny, the accumulation on the ground varying between a foot, nothing and everything in between. Beyond that, the most common changes are little things. The old woman sitting across from me was wearing a different shirt a minute ago, but ten minutes before that she was wearing the same paisley shirt she has on now. And yet the young man sitting next to her hasn't changed at all. It's been the better part of a year since the divergences we're passing through, and yet he's a constant. Is it because no variables changed that directly affected him? Is the woman next to him more indecisive about what to wear, so tiny differences were enough to nudge her one way or another? But then maybe some people are just rigid like that, butterfly effects be damned. A change in the weather might throw you off your schedule by the end of the day, but every new day is another reset, a chance to make a fresh start or stay the same.

Who is and isn't riding the bus is changing as well, the composition shifting every so often, and yet I never catch the changes as they happen. One minute they're there and when I look away and back again they're gone. Like watched pots, never boiling. The only explanation that makes sense is that I can't really trust my senses. I read once that people have almost no ability to see color in our peripheral vision. But we think we can, because our brains cope by filling in the gaps with an educated guess. Maybe a similar survival instinct is at play here. Anything totally incongruous and the brain just filters it out.

Just to be safe, I keep intentionally looking away from Nolan and back again, but he's always there, eagerly watching the other vehicles on the road, commenting on every kind of truck he sees. And not a military patrol in sight.

I don't know what I'm going to do to pass the time between school drop-off and pick-up. I still don't want to face Meredith. Whatever she's dealing with, whatever the other me in this branch is dealing with, I don't want any part of it.

But I've got eight hours to kill. I suppose there is one thing I could try. One variable I can control.

"Welcome to day two of our MWI workshop."
Trent's jowls shake as he introduces me, and I wonder why I was ever surprised to learn that Trent supported *Him* and would surround himself with others who did as well, the culture deteriorating little by little and then all at once. The blowhard attitude. The bad hairpiece. The inability to take even the slightest criticism. It's all right there.

I pop the next pill right before I take the stage.

The room is much more enthusiastic than it was yesterday. Though it would have to be.

"Our stakeholders!" And the crowd goes wild.

I announce I want to kick off by gathering a few people on stage for a quick team-building exercise. The lights go up, and I'm struck by how lilywhite they all are. I tell Trent to stick around, then call up Kathryn and, of course, my man Karl, still cradling his arm in a sling.

First, I talk a bit about exactly what it is Macey Windom Irving does, just so there's no confusion.

"Because let's face it, MWI doesn't cure communicable diseases or feed the homeless or even make those little coffee sleeves that keep your hand cool. No, MWI excels at exactly two things: telling our clients the story they want to hear and molding our employees to become more like us. But who are we? Let's find out."

After my remarks, the crowd's applause is more tepid than usual, but they get excited when I announce we're going to play a game about how well our work family knows one another. Trent has that look of feigned enjoyment he gets in client meetings. He hates not being in control, not knowing every answer in advance. Karl and Kathryn clearly think they're about to win an extra vacation day or something.

We start with Karl. I ask him to look at Kathryn and name the biggest impact she has made on our office. He regurgitates a line about her being "detail oriented and not trying to boil the ocean." Cue polite applause.

"Unfortunately that's incorrect," I say. "But close. The correct answer is that our office's medical supply cabinet is now kept under lock and key because Kathryn kept stealing anything that contained pseudoephedrine the moment it was restocked, so when Alice in accounting had a heart attack last year it took ten minutes to retrieve the first aid kit and now she walks with a cane."

This does not go over well.

I move on and pick up the pace. I ask Kathryn, who's no longer listening, "what do you think Karl's first thought was once he discovered the woman he took home from the office ballgame last summer was actually Trent's underage daughter?"

By the time I've finished the question Kathryn has fled the room and its Beatific Beige walls. Karl seems to have gone catatonic. Trent, on the other hand, is very much present. And furious.

So I ask Trent the million dollar question: "Tell me, in fact tell everyone, reenact for all of us if you can. What was the look on your face when you first heard the news that *He*, thankfully, mercifully, had died from that stroke last year?"

Trent's face is now a deep red—Results-Oriented Rouge—and I'm in a state of near bliss as I grab the hairpiece off his head and set it aflame.

I catch the midday bus home.

I want to end things on a high note. Book a hotel room and wait things out until Sunday. Until my new life can begin again. I just need to make sure Nolan is being cared for and I can go. And so, much as I don't want to, I need to call Meredith. I don't want to hear the pain in her voice again, but one quick call and this will be over.

When I check my phone, the little "1" symbol is waiting for me. Her voicemail from last night. Seven minutes. It's still there.

Reluctantly, I tap play.

"Hi," Meredith says. "I was hoping I could reach you in time. I'm sure you're still mad after what happened." I can only imagine. "What was I going to say? ... Yes. Right." She pauses. "I met a man just now. A tall man in white. Actually, he kind of reminds me of a man I used to know when I was a little kid." Is this a confession? I consider stopping the message but now I have to know. "A friend of my dad's who used to come by the house. He stopped by for dinner at least once a month. Was probably younger than I am now, but as a girl I thought he was really old. Very tall. Hair darker than Nolan's. And he had these truly massive hands that never stopped moving when he talked. And he was always talking. He had so many stories. About everything, really. We'd gather on my parents' rickety front porch and he'd talk and talk, the hands narrating it all. How meteorologists use computer models to measure the probability it'll rain tomorrow. How Cleopatra lived closer to today than to when the pyramids were built. How Jupiter is tearing its moons apart bit by bit, causing some to catch fire and others to melt their ice into briny oceans that just might contain hidden life. No one would ever interrupt when he spoke. Not even Noah. It was like ... I don't know ... like the world came spilling out of him and we just wanted to let it in. Because for whatever reason we knew he knew so much more about it."

There's something off in the way Meredith is speaking. She's sort of unfocused, listless. She's not drunk, I know that voice well and this isn't it. I'm not sure what it is. Maybe it's because she's leaving again.

"I know I've told you before," she says. "But when I was a kid I was convinced there were people in the world who knew everything. I wasn't sure where they lived, but I was sure they were out there. I knew Dad didn't know everything because Mom reminded him every day. And you know how my mom always has this way of criticizing herself when she speaks, like she knows an insult is coming and she's determined to beat everyone else to it. So certainly *she* couldn't know everything. But that man who visited us. I was sure he did. I didn't know what he did for a living or if he even had a job. It didn't matter. That's who I always wanted to be. Nothing was more important than knowing everything there is to know."

Where is she going with all this? Why did she even call?

"And then I met you," she says. "I remember the night—not when we first met, but on the night you always say we met—on the corner by Barclay's." The name of the bar I'd forgotten. "I remember you knew right away I was interested in photography. You tried so hard to convince me you loved it too. Tried to talk about Yousuf Karsh even though you clearly had no idea who he was. It was endearing. You were cute. And you kept at it. Not just on our first date, but for years. And you made me think. That maybe knowing isn't enough. And I didn't think about that tall man for a very long time. Then, I'll never forget. The night before our wedding. After the rehearsal your mom came up to me. She was so sweet. I never told you this before, but I asked if she had any advice and she just told me to 'keep pushing.' I asked what she meant, and she said something to the effect that her son was a very smart young man but sometimes she was worried he didn't try enough. I actually laughed. It wasn't at all what I was asking, and besides, that wasn't what I saw in you. But then your mom was always very perceptive. I miss her." Meredith is quiet for a few moments. "I'm sorry. I can't remember why I called. I'm having trouble … That's right. The man I met just now. Tall. The one who reminded me … he was a doctor. *Oh God.* I remember now."

She lets out a long breath.

"After our fight, I needed some air. I hiked up Buena Vista Ridge to clear my head. Beautiful, but I could tell a storm was coming. On the way back down it began to snow and then the wind picked up." There's a sort of forced cheeriness in her voice now, which always worries me more than when she's mad. "I started to hurry and I think I slipped on a patch of ice, in that spot where the trail takes a sharp turn by the first overlook. I must have hit my head on the rock face but I don't remember … Thought I was okay, made it to the bottom fine." I hear the shakiness in her voice. "But then, as I was driving home my head started to hurt and vision went fuzzy. I was right by the hospital so I turned in. The doctor … he says they think it's something called an epidural hematoma. I'm actually feeling fine again, so he said I could call. I just seem to be getting … distracted. Look, I don't want you and Nolan to worry. But the doctor also said it's not uncommon to have … have lucid periods even when the situation is severe. Or fatal. Anyway, I'm waiting to go in for a scan and depending on what they find they think … there's a good chance I may need emergency surgery." She's got that sound again, not crying but overwhelmed, and now I'm feeling it too. "So that's what's happening. I just wanted to call. I … I don't know. I don't want Nolan to be scared. Tell him—"

I wait for her to finish the thought until it's clear the call cut out. I pull the voicemail log again. But the message is no longer there.

I've passed on. But I need to reach her. Not any Meredith but the one whose voice I just heard, trying in that terrifying moment to be brave. I call her cell but there's no answer. I call the hospital. And wait. After several minutes on hold, they confirm she never checked in. It's a new branch. Things happened differently here.

It's early afternoon now. If she's safe, she's probably at work. I get off the bus and board one headed the other way. Toward the Land of Long Yellow Lights. I call again. The moment I step off the bus, Meredith answers. But it's clear it's not the same person from the voicemail. She's not happy to hear from me.

"What do you want?" There's this carbon-fiber edge to her voice that's like nothing I've heard in fifteen years together.

I stammer, standing on the street corner as the bus lumbers away, trying to remember why I'd even called. Eventually I ask if she could pick up Nolan today.

"It's your week," she says, exasperated. "I will pick him up Monday, as per the schedule. You don't get to change this on me right before the weekend because you can't handle it. We talked about this. I have my own life now." And she hangs up.

I grip my phone until I think the screen might crack. How is this happening? I'm passing from one nightmare to another with no apparent reason. No, it's worse than that. Because these aren't nightmares. They're real. All the pain goes on whether I'm there or not. I'm playing Russian roulette with a fully loaded gun and forced to feel every bullet.

Actually, no. That's not it. There's clarity in a bullet. If every relationship can be described in a sentence, what's a bullet but the period at the end? At least the finality of it offers some sense of perspective, the ability to step back and see the shape of things. And if every relationship is a sentence, then life is just the paragraph where they all fit into place. Each of them half-written until they suddenly end.

I start walking but I don't know where I'm going anymore.

Every day, we're just living with all these sentence fragments we like to pretend are complete. It was the best of times. Give me liberty. Tis better to have loved. You can't see the full message until you reach the end. And by then it's too late to change it. But there's no clarity to be found here. Sentences that were all identical until a year ago have, somehow, spiraled apart to make the whole unrecognizable. Ballistic mayhem. Worse, there's no period at all, no ability to step back and read it for what it is, for what maybe it always was. What changed? I can't make sense of all these fragments with missing pieces and no discernible endings.

I'm in front of the soul food place where Meredith had been eating a day and several lifetimes ago, remembering how she looked. How it made me question everything. The same man is eating there. Chaz Bennett. Guess some names stick better than others. He's in the same seat right now, at the same table. But with a different woman.

Chaz with his pin-striped three-piece and greased thinning hair, trying to pretend he isn't growing old, growing pathetic. He looks as though he's trying to channel Gordon Gekko but instead comes across like some grotesque heavy straight out of *Dick Tracy*. What could Meredith possibly see in him? And here he is with another woman and now I'm furious on her behalf too.

Take a side. Mom's voice again. I'm remembering the priceless look on Trent's face while his coif burned to ash before his eyes. I have to do something. I enter the restaurant and knock Chaz's glass of beer into his lap.

"Jeez, man," he cries out. "The heck are you doing?" He stands and I realize just how big he is.

"The fuck are *you* doing," I shout. "And who is this? How many women are there? You think Meredith won't find you out you piece of shit?"

"Who?" he asks, carefully dabbing at his crotch with his napkin. "What are you … what?"

"Who do you think you are? I saw you with her yesterday. Maybe you think the rest of these women are all whores, but Meredith's not like that."

The woman seated at his table calmly looks at me, unamused.

"I'm his wife," she says.

"Excuse me?"

"I'm his wife." She does appear to be around his age, I see now. "We've been happily married thirty-two years. I think you've mistaken Chazzy for someone else."

"No, I'm quite sure," I say. "Believe me. I mean, how can you be sure this asshole isn't cheating on you?"

"Well for one thing," she says, folding her hands on the table, "he's been in the hospital for sepsis the past five months. Chazzy was finally strong enough he returned to work this week. But he still can't be on his feet for more than an hour. I drive him everywhere he goes."

Now I'm remembering the third person in the Tesla. The one I couldn't see.

Chaz slowly seats himself as his wife steadies him.

"Kid, I don't know who the heck you are," he starts, then pauses to regain his breath. "But if I were healthier right now, I tell you what, I'd clock you right in the noggin."

Noggin? Did I just assault Guido Mr. Rogers?

"Easy dear, please don't get worked up," his wife says, patting his hand. "We need to get back to the studio and I need you at your best. Remember, keep doing such a good job and you can get that McFlurry later."

He brightens at the mention.

She turns to me with disgust. "Now if you'll excuse us."

They get up to leave and I stagger outside, into brutal cold. I slump against the side of the building until I feel the sidewalk under me.

Yes, things with Meredith had been tense in my old branch. But the reason was obvious. It was Him. Of course it was. He swallowed everything, shadowed us everywhere we went. But now He's gone, His fucked-up sentence complete.

Yet here we are.

What changed? Is it possible we were always this close to the end and I failed to see? And somewhere, right now, in another branch, she's lying in a hospital bed because of me. If she's lucky.

My only hope is that the remaining branches can offer some kind of answer, a way to make sense of it. Then again. Not knowing when and how the sentence ends is torture.

But sometimes the period is worse.

S ay it.

     Even just to yourself, it'll feel good to say it. I think.

     So say it.

I told everyone it was the election that broke me. But that's not the truth. The truth is, I was broken the day Mom died.

The last time I saw her she looked tired. I knew it was because she was as worried about Him as I was. At least I thought I knew. Her defining trait was what Dad always kindly called the gift of gab, and yet that day she didn't say much.

It was mid-summer, maybe a month after we briefly lost Nolan at Buena Vista Ridge. I was on a work trip close to my old hometown and decided to stop by for a few hours. Mom and Dad seemed glad to have the company. We talked and talked about Him and what He was doing to the country. The lives being destroyed. Technically I was the one doing most of the talking, but they were right there with me. They asked about Nolan—they were so excited to finally get to meet him in person—and I apologized for not making it home sooner. Though privately I thought they were just as guilty for not flying to see us in the almost two years since he'd been born. After all, we were the ones busy with work, with the stress of parenting. It wouldn't be until months later, until after the funeral, that I'd learn how tight the money had been.

I wish I could remember more about our last conversation. I know we went to the beach behind their house. Some neighbors passed by on a walk, took a picture of the three of us together on the old rocking bench. The weather was unseasonably cold and windy and Mom's hair was whipping in her face in the photo. That much I recall. But mostly I remember talking about Him. One thing I do recall Mom saying: "You know my friend Jackie at work? The way she sees it, she says He's just doing what He said He'd do." She said it in such a way it was like she neither accepted nor rejected it. Just a view that's out there, and isn't that interesting. I said something to the effect that it sounds like Jackie is a sick person. And Mom reminded me Jackie had always been there for us. That was how she saw things. Kindness plus time equals someone worth listening to, no matter what they believed. And that bothered me. Because it meant there was a chance I could lose her to Him too. Like Noah. Like so many others.

And that was it. It was a casual goodbye because we'd agreed to get together soon. As though I were leaving for school for the day. I believe I told Dad to take care of her, thinking but not saying that Mom seemed stretched thin somehow. But in truth I'm not sure I said anything at all.

Months passed. I talked to Dad by phone once or twice. The funny thing about Mom, she was extremely warm and gregarious in person but never a big phone talker. We'd put Nolan on the line a few times when he first started talking but he was usually too shy to say much. One time he announced he'd pooped in his diaper, and to hear my parents tell it you'd think he'd invented differential calculus.

Then, a few days before she died, Mom called my cell. I didn't answer. And she didn't leave a message. She never did. I'd like to say I was busy with something important, but I just didn't feel much like talking at the moment, lost in my feeds. And then I forgot all about it until I got the message from Dad.

She'd had pancreatic cancer but never knew it. We can only guess how bad her pain must have been, but she was never one to complain. And I'm left forever wondering why she called.

The funeral passed in a blur and soon we were back home. I felt restless, like I needed to do something — fix something — but there wasn't anything I could fix. I know it was hard on Meredith too. She was so supportive. I should have done more to make sure she was okay. Nolan didn't really understand, which we said was for the best, but the lack of understanding was hard too.

Dad said we should take the piano and metronome, that Mom would have wanted it that way. But I don't think she had any intention of ever parting with it. Somehow it had never really occurred to me that she would ever die. I thought of her as invincible somehow, never considered a world without her in it. So, reluctantly, I agreed to have the piano shipped home and told anyone who asked that it was meant for Meredith.

That was a little more than two years ago, yet it feels like another lifetime now. I suppose it technically was. I shut most of it away, kept the grief hermetically sealed. And I funneled all the pain, the guilt, all of it, into the election. Stopping Him was how I could undo it, could make things right. But of course He was never something I could stop, any more than I could stop death itself.

Maybe Mom's death was the missing variable, the reason things keep going wrong regardless of whether He lives or dies. If only I had known what Mom had been going through, things would have been different. I could have been there for her, could have been by her side every step of the way. Meredith and I could have quit the jobs we hate, moved closer to be with her. Sure, we had bills, but we also had some savings. We would have made it work. She could have met Nolan. Loved Nolan. And he could have loved her. Even if I couldn't save her, at least we could have said a proper goodbye.

Meredith and I could have been happy. The grief wouldn't have driven us apart.

But I didn't get that chance.

And now, hearing the voicemail from Meredith, it's happening all over again. Another call left unanswered, another sentence fragment I can't decipher. I have to do something. I can't let these things keep happening. These branches were supposed to be a chance to start over. But I still don't know how.

Cold. Warm. Cold.

I can't see the changes, but if I close my eyes and concentrate, seated on the sidewalk, I can almost feel when the weather shifts. It's changing more frequently now, every few minutes. Sun. Clouds. Snow. Sun. Then there's the people on the sidewalk, walking carefree with no armored patrols in sight, blissfully ignorant of how good they have it. The people change less frequently than the weather. They're stickier somehow. Now I'm thinking about that viral video a few months back where you listen to an audio clip with two words listed, and whichever word you look at is the one you hear. The brain is a very good filter. If I'm really traveling through thousands of branches a second, branches that now would have diverged nearly a year ago, I'm probably missing lots of tiny changes and only really seeing those things that are most consistent, like not seeing the breaks between movie frames.

And yet, despite all of it, some things have stopped changing. In my phone, Meredith's name no longer appears. The number is still listed, under "Ex." I keep checking, waiting for a change.

I still feel like I need to do something. But now I fear I'm only making things worse.

I slowly get back on my feet and peer into the restaurant behind me. Chaz and his wife have left but their credit card receipt is still there. Then I hear that familiar chime next door, and I find myself stepping toward Down-Tune Beats in the hope that someone might have a happier story here.

Jill's inside, talking to Anton. He's alive again, standing behind the counter with his arms folded, slowly shaking his head. Dressed exactly the same as I saw him two days ago. Jill's standing by the deadly tower of guitars, dressed like she's about to go for a run. In fact, she's dressed exactly like the woman I saw the police try to abduct at the hospital on Sunday.

Anton and Jill are clearly arguing about something, talking loud enough I can just make out what they're saying. I wait outside and hang back out of sight.

"No. No, it's not *safe*," Anton says.

"It's never going to *be* safe if I don't," Jill says. "You think we're safe here? Now?"

"No, we're not. And that's the whole point," Anton says. "I don't need you to be a hero."

"I'm not. Believe me. Heroes usually just end up getting people killed. Dad, we know what we're doing. This isn't like how it used to be. There's more of us now."

"I'm not doing this again," he says, turning to his little microwave. "I won't have this same argument. Choir tonight. Not gonna waste my voice. You know exactly how I feel about it."

"Goddammit, Dad," Jill says. "I just ... please stop worrying. I'll be fine."

Anton squeezes his plastic honey bear into his steaming mug. "You can't know that."

Possible clues to what happened in those other branches? Or maybe not.

They've stopped talking, so it seems like as good a time as any to interrupt and I press open the door. *Chime.* Jill says hi but there's no sign of recognition. Not that there would be.

"Well look who it is!" Anton says to me. "It's music guy! I figured you were never coming back at this point."

Wait. This isn't the same version of Anton I met two days ago. It can't be.

I apologize for interrupting.

"No worries at all," he says like we're old friends. "How've you been?"

I don't even know where to begin.

"Let's just say life's been interesting."

"I bet, man. I bet," he says. "Say, I've got your Mom's metronome in the back room. All fixed up. You know, after ninety days I tend to put abandoned items up for sale. But I could tell how much it meant to you so I thought I should hold onto it in case."

He threads his haphazard stacks of instruments with a spring in his step and disappears in the back. It seems I actually came here before in a different branch? So many things happened differently here, yet apparently I still made that same choice. I guess it shouldn't be too surprising, but it's strange to think there's another me out there who made the same decision I wouldn't make until months later. But why didn't I pick it up?

"So, music guy," Jill asks, making small talk as we wait for Anton. "You just been busy or what?" She crosses behind the counter, hoists a blue backpack on top and begins sifting through it.

"Me? Yeah, you know," I say. "One thing after another lately."

"Mmm hmm," she says, setting a seemingly random series of items on the counter: hair scrunchies, Sharpies, bottle of ibuprofen, swim mask and snorkel with some sort of filter taped over the spout, a few maxi pads, granola bars, a full gallon jug of milk. Then she starts to methodically repack them.

"Me? I'd say you're lucky my dad's so sentimental," Jill says. "If I were running this place I probably wouldn't be so quick to bend the rules." She laughs at the thought as though it's thoroughly ridiculous, and I'm sad again for the Jill I met before.

She has no idea what's happened to him in those other branches. Somehow, it keeps happening. Even though the world is so much better here, I have this terrible feeling she won't be able to see him much longer. Then again, maybe he died twice by coincidence. An unlucky twist of fate. But I doubt it.

"Hey, Jill," I ask. "This might sound random, but have you noticed police coming around a lot here lately?"

She looks at me like I'm crazy. "Uh, yeah."

"Any particular reason?"

She raises her eyebrows. "Is what it is."

"No, I mean, I guess I was just worried about Anton. Is he in trouble or something?"

"What kind of trouble?"

"Maybe legal? I don't know. Is there somebody who has a, like, a beef with him or something?"

"A beef? With my dad?"

"I don't know why anyone would. It's hard to imagine, actually. I mean, he seems so ... so ..."

"Gentle," she says.

"Right."

"He is."

Now I'm thinking of the words she tried to say yesterday but couldn't.

"I'm sorry, where are you going with this?" she asks, and I have to find a way to say it without saying it.

"You know," I say, "I'm sorry if this seems too personal, but my Mom passed away a few years back. And, well, I've been thinking lately about what I'd want to say if I saw her again. Do you ever think about stuff like that?"

"About stuff like what?"

"Like what you might say to your dad. If you knew you wouldn't get another chance, I mean."

She stops rearranging her backpack and looks at me.

"Is he telling his customers he thinks I'm gonna die now?"

Dammit. She's so focused on her own thing it doesn't even occur to her she could lose him at any moment.

"Okay, first off," she says. "That is *not* acceptable, and second, don't you worry yourself, mister music guy. I can take care of me."

I want to shake her out of it, to tear off the blinders that keep her from seeing him, from appreciating the time they have.

"That's not what I meant, Jill. It's just—"

"Here it is," Anton calls out from the far end of the shop, emerging from the back with the metronome. "You know, it was actually a very quick fix."

"You know what? Forget it," I say to Jill. "It was just a thought. Oh, and by the way, I meant to tell you congratulations. About the baby, I mean. When are you due again?"

Jill zips her pack shut, slings it on her back. "*Seriously?*"

She steps out from behind the counter and it's clear she's not pregnant.

"Dad, you've got an interesting choice in friends," Jill says as she walks out the door, then looks back at me. "Rule number one, dude: never *ever* assume a woman is pregnant unless she's in the middle of giving birth." She lets the door shut, then opens it again for a moment. "And even then, just no."

So. That was bad.

Anton arches his eyebrows as he sets Mom's metronome on the counter.

"Do I even want to know?" he asks.

"Probably not," I say.

He has this expectant look like he's waiting for me to say something.

"So?" he asks.

"So."

"So where were you? After our talk, I was so sure you were going to show for choir rehearsal. You were so damn eager. And then you straight-up ghost for months, and now here you're back. So?"

136

Wait, I said I was going to join his choir?

"I don't know," I say. "I guess life got in the way."

"Right on, but isn't that exactly what you said though?"

"What did I say? Remind me."

"You said you didn't really value simple things like singing and dancing with other people until you couldn't do it anymore. At least I think that's how you put it. Remember, I was giving you shit, like what are you living in the *Footloose* town or something?" He cracks himself up and slaps the counter. "What you said stuck with me though: that, in the end, music is as much life as anything. Right?"

"Right," I say. "Right." Dispatches from another me. I have no idea what I meant. But I can understand that desire for connection, for something comforting to cling to.

"Anton," I say, taking care to pronounce it the way only people who know him would. "You tell me what you would do. Let's say you were given a Get Out of Jail Free card, the chance to leave all your problems behind and start over. Would you take it?"

"Like how do you mean?" he asks, as though the question itself is nonsensical. "If this is your way of saying you want to be Kevin Bacon ..."

"No, I mean as a thought experiment. Wouldn't you want to get out of here? Away from all your problems, everything weighing you down. Start over. Like in that Lev Upton movie where they flee Berlin to find a better life."

"Upton? Total trash director," Anton says, shaking his head. "Take a drink every time a shot lasts for more than three seconds and you'll be stone sober at the end."

I point out I actually have a friend, or at least I used to, who claims he knows Upton and says he's a good guy. Now I'm thinking about Karl's betrayal, so obvious in hindsight.

"Hey, maybe he takes in orphans too, I don't know." He laughs. "My advice: he should probably quit movies and channel himself into his charitable work."

"Never mind," I say. "Bad example. Let's say you're Sam in *Brazil* instead, and say you actually do what Sam and Jill can't and you escape from all this."

Anton's eyes light up. "*Brazil*? You know what, that's my favorite movie, man. No one ever talks about that one anymore. You a big movie guy too?"

"Well, maybe not as big as I thought I was. Anyway, is there any chance you don't go for it? I mean, you'd absolutely take the offer. Right?"

"So, in this hypothetical, say Sam and Jill get away," Anton says. "Then what?"

"Then they live happily ever after. Obviously."

"Yeah, see, that's where you lose me," he says with a shrug. "I guess that bit doesn't ring true for me."

"Why not?"

He drums his fingers on the counter as he tries to find the right words. "It doesn't … it's not … basically. First off, why wouldn't the rest of the world be just like the one they left?"

"Well, because they fled the fascists and got away. That's why. All their problems are gone."

"Yeah, man, I don't know," he says. "I mean it sounds nice, and that idea is part of the appeal for sure. But, if you're asking about what I'd *really* do, in real life? Someone offers that deal. Honestly, I'd have to think about it. I've got a lot here to be thankful for." He looks around his shop with an air of reverence and I so badly want to tell him how things ended in those other branches. "Where are you going with this anyway?"

"I don't know," I say. "Thinking about life, I guess. Winter blues or something. I just think it would be nice for you to get away once in a while if you can. So you're not cooped up in this shop all winter. You know, take your daughter on a vacation or something."

"Sounds to me like you need a pick-me-up," Anton says. "Like you told me, you need a little music back in your life, music guy." He says it with a wide smile, then a eureka flick of his finger. "Speaking of which, that metronome."

Just then the door chimes behind me. Probably Jill, back to let me have it again. Or maybe she actually took my words to heart and thought about what she might want to say to her dad.

But then I see the look on Anton's face.

"Got a report of a male suspect." An officer's voice.

I'm relieved to see it's not Petkoff. Instead, it's a young, pale officer. Very young, very pale. His uniform is hanging off of him, so new I can still see the original creases in the fabric. But why is he here?

"Received word there was an assault at the restaurant next door," he says. "Witnesses said the suspect fled in here." He says the words to me, as though I'm the one in charge. "Fits this man's description." But he's not pointing at me.

I don't want the officer to know it's me he's looking for. But suddenly I have the urge to protect Anton, who's already died at the hands of officers more than once.

"There's been a mistake," I say. "This is Anton's store. He wasn't even in that restaurant. I know he wasn't."

"No," the officer says. "No, I'm pretty sure they said it was him." But he doesn't sound sure at all. Now he grips his gun in its holster but he's so young he looks like a kid holding a security blanket.

Anton calmly says "officer, please." The sound of his voice seems to activate the young man and the officer's eyes flit about nervously as he watches Anton holding the metronome.

I kind of feel bad for the kid. He doesn't have that look Petkoff had, brined and curdled after years on the force. Far from being in control, he's clearly in over his head, a routine follow-up apparently more than he can handle. But I don't have *too* much sympathy since he's also palming a lethal weapon, the dam seemingly ready to burst at any moment.

Anton looks resigned, like he has a feeling where this is headed. He tells the officer he could clear up any confusion if he could just show his ID. The officer nods his assent but he doesn't look comfortable at all.

Slowly — very slowly — Anton shifts his hand toward his back pocket. But it's not slow enough. The officer's eyes twitch, his grip tightens. The kid draws his sidearm, its barrel now squarely in line with Anton's chest.

This is it. Whatever's going to happen is going to happen very fast. I have to do something. *Take a side.*

And that's when everything goes blank.

No.

Not blank.

Just black.

An empty void.

What happened?

Where am I?

I'm still awake.
But there's … nothing.
Actually, no. I think I
can still see something.

But it's too far away.
Like a pinprick of light
in the far distance.

Like the eye
of a telescope.

But it's too far away.

And I can't move.

Was it another seizure?

No.

And this is no dream.

This is different.

It's like I'm still awake
but I can't see or move.

I can't control anything.

Someone is shouting.
In the far distance.

More voices.

And silence.

BANG. A thunderous, deafening sound.

But I don't know what it is.
Or where.

With a moment to think,
I know I should have done something.

I can't just let
Anton die again,
for no reason at all.

But I don't know what
I could have done.

Realistically, I'm not going
to be able to stop
an armed officer.

And even if I could, what then?
BANG. BANG.
I need to cover my ears
but I don't have any ears
nor hands to cover them.

There's nothing but
that speck of light.

Everything keeps
happening too fast.

It's all too big, too much.

It's quiet now.

A distant booming.

Growing louder.

I can't tell
if the pinprick of light
is getting closer
or just brighter.

The booming is
even louder.

It's a regular beat,
surrounding me.

And now I'm overcome
with the sensation of rushing forward,
like being hurled,
through a tunnel,
or down a deep hole,
through a windstorm ...

I blink.

My eyes adjust, focus. All I see is woodgrain. Fibrous lines, the remnants of tree rings, covered in decades of scratches and a thin faded lacquer. Mom's metronome. I'm standing next to it as it rests on the counter. At Down-Tune Beats. I'm back.

Whatever that was, it's over now.

I'm not sure how much time passed, but I'm in the same room. I'm guessing I never left. Maybe I've passed onto a different branch yet again? Everything feels heightened somehow. Sharper. Like my body is surging with adrenaline. Peak fight-or-flight. But there's no clear danger in sight. If anything, it's too quiet.

My left hand rests on the metronome's pendulum as though I'd been inspecting it. Anton had said it was fixed, finally. I let go of the pendulum but it just falls to one side. Broken.

There's an odd mark on the metronome's wooden face. Strange. I've looked at the metronome thousands of times and it was never there before. I would remember.

I run my finger over the mark, then inside it. It's a hole.

A bullet hole.

Throbbing pain in my right eye. By reflex, I lift my hand and realize I'm holding something. Something heavy.

A gun. *I'm holding a gun.*

What the hell happened?

With my other hand I touch just above my eye and wince at the pain. A raised bruise is forming.

How long have I been standing here?

The shop appears empty. The haphazard spires of instruments are casting long shadows on the ground in the late afternoon light. Where's Anton? Maybe the officer took him? But then why am I holding a gun?

Slowly, I circle the tower of guitars to confirm there's no one else in the shop. The room had always been soundtracked by a Magnavox back beat but now it's deathly quiet. I don't know the first thing about how to hold a handgun properly, but I'm almost certainly holding it for a reason so I level it in front of my chest with both hands, careful to keep my finger away from the trigger.

Just squeeze they always say in movies. Which I've always suspected is bullshit. Just pull the damn thing.

As I round more spires, my shadow passes over mounds of dismembered instruments and I try to understand what could have happened while I was … whatever that was. What have I done?

The gun is surprisingly heavy. But then I've never really held one. Is it the officer's gun? It doesn't look the same. The top piece, whatever it's called, is slid back. Almost like it's halfway cocked. I look it over, and there's something protruding from the side of the barrel, wedged in the groove where the top slides against the base. Something small and thin.

Jesus. It's a fingernail. Part of one anyway. A smear of blood on one side.

Don't panic. Don't panic, I think, but the mantra isn't helping.

Fingers trembling, I reach out to remove the fingernail, but it's jammed in the groove. I grip the barrel, pull hard on the nail. A sudden sensation of heat makes me recoil and the silent room is filled with an ear-piercing sound.

The fingernail falls to the floor.

The gun barrel is very hot. Which means it's been fired recently. And now I've fired again. *Shit.* I didn't keep my finger off the trigger after all. *Just squeeze* is right.

The large window to the left side of the entrance makes a crackling noise. It's spiderwebbed, bits of glass crumbling away at the center where the bullet I just fired passed through. *Some hero.*

And now the sound of rain outside. Unseasonably warm for January, it's coming down hard out there as bits of glass continue to rain from the windowpane.

Something catches my eye. A shoe. From this angle, I see a shoe on the ground protruding from behind the counter. A shoe attached to a leg. But that's all I can see.

I approach the counter again and slowly peer over the top, past the metronome. My heart is pounding fast, the same rhythmic booming I'd heard in the dark.

When I see him, my first thought is of Mom lying in her coffin. It's Anton, his eyes closed. He's crumpled against the back wall beneath the open microwave. Quiet, still, his purple shirt stained dark—almost black—with blood, his plastic bear overturned on the counter. It's slowly dripping thick gobs of honey onto his pant leg.

He's not breathing.

I want to be able to say he looks peaceful. But he doesn't. There's a pained, stricken look on his face. And I know it's my fault. But I don't know why. Did I shoot him? No. Doesn't make any sense. Why would I do that? Why would any version of me do that?

And then it occurs to me what that darkness could have been.

If my consciousness has been passing through all these other versions of me, then where are they? It never made sense.

When that other version of me awoke in the MWI bathroom yesterday, Karl said I'd blacked out the whole morning. Maybe that's it. Maybe the darkness is what it's like for every version of me I'm passing through. Forcibly overwritten, shoved into the background. Maybe for moments, maybe hours, maybe more, depending on how long it takes before I move on. An unfortunate side effect of messing with the multiverse like this. It didn't hurt, exactly. Though I don't recommend it.

But if I'm the one traveling through other branches, why did I get overwritten? Could it be that I'm not the only version of me taking pills? Then again, I know I'm not. I can't be. Every version of me has the same bottle of pills in every branch. I'm just trying to understand why.

The splitting branches. It's something to do with the ever-splitting branches, I think. If every moment brings more branches, and the parasite exists in all of them ... if I had picked up the parasite even seconds apart in different branches, I suppose there could be any number of very slightly different *me*s out there, each carrying a version of the parasite. Right? All drifting, all taking pills, all passing through and trying to get back to our not-quite-identical branches.

And then, along the way, as we all drift closer to the shared trunk of our original timelines, maybe there's a chance some of us even cross paths. Overriding the same branch, and one another, for a short time. A strange race for the prize, even if we might all be winners in the end, each living on in our own slightly different world. At least I hope so. I don't know, maybe that's a stretch. Things have gotten so turned around I'm probably not making any sense. But then again, if other versions of me *are* passing through, it could explain why I abandoned the metronome in this branch. In theory, a *me* from some other branch could have met with Quantgen earlier, dropped off the metronome here, then continued on to the next branch before I — before he — had the chance to pick it up. And the *me* from this branch would have no memory of ever dropping it off. I can't quite grasp the complexity of it, but it's the only way I can think to explain any of this.

But then I don't know this other me. I don't know any of them. They could be capable of anything. This one just shot and ran and left it to me to clean up his mess. Left Anton here on the floor to die alone.

Jill. Suddenly I remember Jill and I'm overcome with anger to the point that it surprises me. Where was she? Her dad needed her and she was off on some selfish adventure when she could have saved him. I tried to tell her but she wouldn't listen.

It's up to me now. I set the bear of honey upright on the counter and help Anton to lie flat, to make him look comfortable even though I know it won't make a difference. I need to spare him one indignity at least. As I place Anton's hands on his chest I inspect his fingernails. All intact. And so are mine. That just leaves the officer. Somehow I was able to get the young man's gun. And that means others could be on their way.

I need to get out of this shop. I need to get out of this branch.

Fingerprints. I need to hide any fingerprints on the gun. In movies they rub it with a cloth for half a second and call it good. And I always think: *Really?* No. I need to take the gun with me, dispose of it somehow.

Outside, it's now sunny and dry. I press on the entrance door and glass shards rain harder from the shattered window. I pause as I spot a small red smear on the door handle. A fingerprint of blood.

When I open the door, its glass sweeps a brief reflection of the sun and for a moment I'm blinded. When I open my eyes again it's much darker and rain is coming down hard once again. As the door shuts behind me, the remaining window glass gives way and falls to the ground but the sound is drowned out by the rain.

I'm trying to see but the rain's pouring so hard I can only make out a few feet in each direction. There's a thin red trail on the sidewalk but it's quickly being washed away. The officer could be anywhere. So could backup. I hold the gun close and start to make my way along the storefronts toward the bus stop, but all the awnings have been put away for the winter so there's nothing to block the deluge.

Something on the sidewalk ahead. I can't make it out. But it's not moving. I'm almost on top of it before I can clearly see. My grip on the gun goes slack. The young, pale officer lies face down, blood gathered around two welts in his back. I'm guessing they're exit wounds but I don't really know. I crouch beside him and check his right hand. The index finger is bruised and bleeding and half the nail is missing. The young man's head is turned to the side and I can see half his face but there's no sign of life, the pounding rain stippling the surface and flowing down over one open eye. I'm pretty sure I shot him trying to protect Anton. But I don't really know. Maybe I was trying to actually be the hero for once. Not that it makes a difference at this point.

So this is how it happens. For one reason or another, they always come. Calling a nervous young officer to this neighborhood is about as helpful as calling a match to save some kindling. Maybe those other branches were misunderstandings too. I don't know. Maybe Anton never did anything at all. I've been searching for a rational reason but maybe it's just blind luck. Maybe fate has simply loaded the dice for some people. But then, at least this time, the officer was sent to Anton's store because of me. It's my fault. And if other officers find out what happened, they'll come after me too. Maybe even after my family. I was so sure things would be better here.

The rain is picking up now, ice pellets intermixing.

So I run. In the direction of home.

I stuff the gun in my coat pocket next to my bottle of pills. A look over my shoulder confirms police cars converging on Down-Tune Beats in the distance, their red-and-blue beacons refracting through the rain. They're not armored trucks anymore, but that's cold comfort now. So I keep running. Much sooner than I expect, I'm completely exhausted. Lungs burning coal. Joints threatening to tear apart the way a roof shears off in a tornado.

Eventually, I've left the Land of Long Yellow Lights, passing homes whose values rapidly increase with each passing block. From cracked stucco and wild-grown lots to vanity-pillared Cape Cods with manicured neon lawns. I don't know how far I am from home anymore but I have to keep moving. I close my eyes and think of Anton on the floor. Of Jill returning to find him. Of the things she'll never get to say to him now. Why did she have to be so blind she couldn't see what was coming?

When I open my eyes again it's sunny and the wind is less cold. At least I can have that much. Then sweat drips in my eye, I wipe it away and now it's snowing heavily. But I keep running. And running. Toward home.

Through the snow. Then the sun. Then the rain.

Then the sun.

Then the snow.

Then the rain.

Then the rain.

Then the rain.

Then the rain.

Then the rain.

CUT TO BLACK.

VOICEOVER: Has this ever happened to you?

CUT TO a Middle-Age Woman, who climbs a tall ladder that leans against a tree. We see a plump, long-haired Cat with a sour expression perched on one of the tree's upper limbs. Woman strains to reach for Cat, misses and falls onto a large trampoline [cue cartoon spring sound effect] and bounces over a fence into her neighbor's pool [cue cartoon splash sound effect].

CUT TO poolside close-up. Woman's head pops up from the water.

MIDDLE-AGE WOMAN: There's got to be a better way!

V.O.: There is! With the 3-in-1 Super Telescoping Reacher from MyRod.

CUT TO various studio shots of the product.

V.O.: With the 3-in-1 Super Telescoping Reacher, success is always within arm's reach.

CUT TO Woman back on the ladder, hooking Cat by its collar and lowering it to the ground as it continues to glower.

V.O.: Made from the highest-quality aluminum, the Titanium of Metals™, the 3-in-1 Super Telescoping Reacher comes with a sixty-day money-back guarantee.

But wait, there's more ...

Nolan is still laughing at the splash into the pool, though I've always thought the cat's expression is what sells it. It's nice to hear Nolan laugh again. He's sitting in the center of the living room couch, cocooned in a wool throw blanket Meredith bought me for Christmas a year ago.

I'm pacing, unable to stay seated. The path I've worn in the living room carpet vaguely resembles a question mark. My left hand won't stop trembling.

Once the gun had ceased to be in my pocket, I knew I'd passed beyond that branch. But I kept running anyway, gripping the bottle of pills until I could see the house again. By the time I arrived at Nolan's preschool on the bus, he'd been waiting for more than an hour. He didn't speak the whole ride home.

No more of this. No more interfering. This is not my life. These are not my problems.

I just have to get through the next two days. By Sunday evening I can take the green pill and all of this will end. But the doubt is gnawing again. I've gotten everything I wanted when this started yet everything seems so much worse. I know the election alone has saved countless lives. I'm being selfish if I wallow in my personal problems. At least we're still alive.

But then there's Anton. And the Meredith lying in the hospital. A call never answered. She might not be alive either. Then there's the Meredith and Nolan from the branch I left. The ones I'd been with all this time. It's not like I changed the outcome of the election for them. I didn't change anything. Meredith was right. I did want to leave. I haven't saved one life, because it's all still happening. I shut it out and fled.

A sniffling sound interrupts the thought. Tears are streaming down Nolan's cheeks as he watches his cartoon of a cocky little aardvark eating its weight in cheese. I ask what's wrong but he won't say.

If there's one thing I've discovered as a parent, the biggest challenges always come when you're least prepared to handle them. I'm on the verge of breaking, and so of course Nolan must be as well. He looks older than my Nolan, like he's been through more, but he's my Nolan. That same shock of dark hair, the rosy wind-whipped cheeks he gets in the dry winter air.

Whatever the problem is, it's too big. Too much. His world has barely begun and it's already broken, his parents now strangers to one another for reasons that I'm sure make no more sense to him than to me. I check once again, but my phone still says "Ex."

I can't solve it. But I also know I have to do something. There's no one else.

I try to convince Nolan to play with his toy trucks, to draw on his easel, but he's not interested. I offer to turn on anything he wants. Anything at all. Maybe *Frozen*, maybe even those weird Polish tractor videos he loves on YouTube. He moves to the corner of the couch, keeping as far from me as possible, arms tucked beneath him, quietly weeping.

I'm out of options, desperate for a way to cheer him. Even if I can't stay here, even if I pass on at any moment, I still need to do something.

I head toward the corner just off the living room. The metronome is back again. Still broken. I sit on the bench, lift the keylid, run my hand over middle C and feel the rounded impression of a finger formed over many years. It's been so long it takes a minute to get my bearings, but soon it comes back to me. Within a few minutes I'm tapping my foot, slowly rocking forward and back as I progress through a cadence of major chords I first learned when I was little.

It isn't long before I hear a tinkling. It's Nolan, pressing some of the sticky higher keys with a bashful look, tears drying in place. Those hopeful eyes he got from his mother. I nod and he sits close beside me. When he reaches out to play, I don't stop him. He taps a few notes. Then he hits the keys harder. Then he mashes them, then hammers away, and now he's yelling at the top of his lungs, pounding and pounding and pounding, a thundering dissonance that fills the entire house and resonates deep within my chest.

Eventually, Nolan stops, now calmer. Then he turns to me.

"I miss mommy," he says.

Then he asks me to play.

Ever get a feeling of melancholy nostalgia for something while you're still doing it? The knowledge that it's a moment that will soon slip away but you'll keep returning to it, burrowing for warmth. That's what it feels like now.

I play one of the few songs I can still perform from memory, a song I used to sing to help him fall asleep when he was a baby, slowly rocking, in that brief window of time when everything was still uncomplicated.

Once there was a way
To get back homeward
Once there was a way
To get back home.

Later, he's lying in bed paging through books with his plastic lantern as I tidy up around the house. I'm in the living room, on my hands and knees, trying to pick up all the little foot-fucking LEGO blocks Nolan's left embedded in the carpet. It's funny. I've been wanting nothing more than to run away and hide from these other lives, and here I am cleaning the house for a version of myself I don't even understand. But everything is such chaos, it's all I can do to try and create the illusion of order. If only for a moment.

I'm brushing my hand across the carpet fibers, sweeping for plastic mines, when I spot two little reflective eyes under the couch. Watching me. I attempt to make some bird sounds, poorly, yet it's enough that I hear a gentle purr. The brown tabby's tail flicks back and forth, its head cocking, its notched ear twitching.

"What do you think I should do?" I ask it. "What would you do if you were me? I mean, I can't solve any of this."

The cat slowly blinks, and I take it as an invitation to explain myself. So I sit on the floor and start at the beginning. By the time I get to Anton helping me to pull Nolan from the wreckage, the cat is sitting in my lap gently rubbing its face against my hands. The purring is so soothing. I want to stay right here. As a kid, I loved Lady, my family's black Lab, more than anything. Even when she grew old, grew sick. She was always there, a constant reassurance until the day she wasn't. I guess I always pictured myself having pets when I grew up. Meredith used to regularly talk about us getting a dog, but there was never time. Life always got in the way. I was on the road so much for work that I barely had time to tuck in Nolan most nights.

Which reminds me. I lift the cat, cradle it, and it snuggles against me as we head to Nolan's room. I guess I've finally won its approval. Maybe I belong now. We're a family, however imperfect. If only everything were this simple.

Nolan's light is out already, but I feel my way to his bed and, after a few misses in the darkness, kiss him on the forehead. I go to close the door but he stops me.

"Dad?"

"Yes?" I call back into the dark.

"Can you leave it open?"

"Of course, Nolan."

"Hey Dad?"

"Yeah, what's up?"

"I love you," he says.

"I love you too, Nolan."

"And Dad?"

"Yes, son."

"Why do you have the neighbor's cat?"

The tabby lets out a low moan in my arms. "Sorry, what?"

"That's Bib Purrtuna," Nolan says. "Why are you holding Maxton's cat? Did it sneak in again?"

"Yes. Um ... yes. Yep. That's exactly what happened," I say. "Good night, Nolan."

"Good night."

Okay, so I'm an idiot. I don my coat and cross the street to the Nguyen's to return the cat, but no one's home. I'm forced to leave it on their front porch instead. Of course, now it follows me back across the street and I try to shoo it away. I have to keep batting it with my foot and eventually I'm whipping little LEGO blocks at it to keep it from entering as I shut the door.

I can't wait for this to be over. As if by instinct, I reach into the coat pocket where I left my pill bottle, to shake it, to hear its reassuring little rattle.

But it's not there.

After everything I've been through, I'd made certain to leave it there so I couldn't lose it. I drop the coat on the floor and check the master bathroom, but the pills aren't there either so I retrace the steps I had taken with Nolan after we arrived home from school. I definitely had it in my pocket *after* we got off the bus. I know that for sure. So I head outside again without bothering with the coat.

It's four blocks to the bus stop. I'm furiously searching every step of the way. Soon, the cat is in close pursuit. The snow's been shoveled recently so I kick up the drifts along the sidewalk, trying to root it out, but there's nothing in the powdery spray but a few cigarette butts. The tabby nabs one out of the air and chews on it.

I pull out my phone and check its history. Nothing. My work phone is in the opposite pocket, but the only calls I've made all week in this branch have been to dial into meetings at MWI.

A deep chill is settling into my lungs so I rush back inside, the cat running beside me, the cigarette butt clamped between its teeth. I shoo it away again and rush to close the door. A moment later there's an awkward thud.

Stupid cat.

The thought is quickly drowned out by the sound of the television blaring, its volume cranked up. Nolan is sitting on the living room couch, once again cocooned in a blanket to the point I can barely see him. He's watching some crime drama that's clearly not appropriate for him. I can tell because a benevolent-sounding detective says the word "*semen*" at least twice in the seconds before I'm able to shut it off and the still quiet of winter returns.

"What are you doing up?" I ask.

Nolan's voice, muffled deep within the blanket: "I dunno."

Another voice startles me.

"Sounds like someone doesn't want dessert with dinner again tomorrow." Meredith emerges from the hallway wearing a satin nightgown and looks at Nolan with mock disapproval. "Right? We agreed on this, kiddo."

She's back. Alive. It's a different Meredith, of course. But I've never been so relieved to see her. And more than that, I want to know what variable made her stay.

I flip on the light and ask what's going on. Nolan emerges from his cocoon. And I stop. Speechless.

It's his face, but not.

"What happened," I gasp. Nolan doesn't know what I mean.

A feathered scar cuts diagonally across his face, from his little chin over his nose to his forehead. I instinctively touch my face, phantom pain registering as my own. It looks as though the scar has been there for some time.

"Right now, kiddo," Meredith says, and starts to count down from five.

Nolan rolls his eyes and drags his feet dramatically as he heads toward bed. Meredith musses his hair as he passes and looks at me with a warm smile I haven't seen in a while. "You coming?"

"His face," I say. "The scar."

"I know, it's really faded, hasn't it," she says optimistically. "Looks like that cream works after all."

"No no," I stammer. "I mean. How it happened … I …"

"I know." She holds me in a tight embrace, speaks in a gentle, reassuring voice like we've had this conversation a hundred times. "But please remember it helps nothing to keep blaming yourself. I'm not sure why it's been weighing on you so much lately. But the crash was two years ago. Your mom had just died. You weren't yourself. Things were different then. Right?"

I feel like I've been kicked in the throat. I can't speak. Whatever happened, it's my fault. I push her away and head to the garage. Inside there's an orange Lexus SUV. Ostentatious and muscular. The last car I could ever imagine myself buying. *Why?* I stagger back to Meredith, who's watching me with concern.

"Just let me know what you need," she says.

I don't respond. I need to get out of here. I need to find my pills. I can't keep doing this.

I search my coat again. Then the bathroom. The bedroom. The garbage. Everything. Nolan quietly watches me from behind his scar as I check under his bed. In his desk. It's physically painful to look at him.

Meredith follows. "If you could just tell me what it is you're searching for?"

"The pills," I remind her. "Quantgen. My seizures. Remember my seizures? The pills I got to treat them?"

"I remember your nausea. Those headaches. Is that what you mean? But that was a long time ago. When did you get a prescription?"

Eventually I'm looking in completely illogical places, places where I'd already looked. The couch cushions. The pantry. The ugly-ass Lexus. The recycling bin. The LEGO bin.

I'm walking in circles in the living room now, with nowhere else to go. Meredith returns in a different nightgown, urging me to come to bed. Is she the same as she was a minute ago? I'm not sure.

Something else feels off now but I don't know what it is. Nolan's light is off. I rush to his room but he's curled up under his covers, asleep.

Pictures, toys, even furniture have been shifting places all week, but this time feels different. I'm home, yet more than ever it feels like it belongs to someone else.

In the corner, the metronome is gone.

No. Not just the metronome. The piano.

"Where's Mom's piano?"

Meredith doesn't know what I mean. "At your parents' house," she says. "Where else would it be? Knowing your mom, she's probably playing it right now."

The room is spinning and I can't make it stop. Mom used to complain of vertigo when I was a kid, and I never knew what she meant. But I'm willing to bet she never felt like this.

I didn't get the parasite on that trip to the Amazon last year. That much is clear. I've been thinking about the timescale of this parasite all wrong. Been thinking of the divergences as building toward a year ago, but Mom died just over two years ago. If she survived, her cancer was probably detected months earlier.

I try calling my parents' cells several times, but they don't answer. Meredith keeps telling me they're just asleep. When she finally heads to bed I book a flight for the three of us. The earliest I can get is the day after tomorrow, which won't get us to my parents' house until Sunday afternoon.

January 24th. It would have been Mom's 65th birthday. *Is* her 65th birthday. Who knows what else may change by the time we get there? But it will take just as long to drive so it's our only option.

Sitting in the living room, I try to remember the call center number I've dialed twice in the past four days. I may not have the pills but the number should still work. But then, no one memorizes phone numbers anymore. I can't remember a single number I've dialed since probably 2002, yet somehow I still know the number of my best friend from fifth grade whom I haven't seen since he trashed my Huffy bike driving into a fire hydrant and then blamed it on my bike's "Pepsi: Gotta Have It!" novelty license plate. *Yeah right, David Dipshit.*

I rack my brain, dial a dozen different number combinations before finally giving up.

Most of the night I lie wide awake, waves of emotion coming and going with little warning. The election on which the fate of the world hinged somehow feels trivial all of a sudden. Abstract. Little more than a perverse thought experiment.

But it's not abstract. Without my pills, by tomorrow night I'm going to regress again and it will all become very real. I only need one white and the green, but there's no guarantee they'll still be there if I regress. I probably just got lucky last time.

I'm so close now. I only hope the next branch fixes things.

SATURDAY

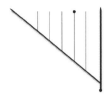

The sound of mutant ants throwing cars stirs me awake. A woman screams but the ants care not for human concerns.

It's 7:45 Saturday morning. One day to go. I'd fallen asleep on the living room couch, wearing sweatpants and an old stained T-shirt, phone in my hand. Nolan is sitting cross-legged on the ground with his back to me, watching some old B-movie as part of an early morning double feature.

My first move is to call my parents. Dad answers. Mom's with her sister for the day but she forgot her cell phone again—her sister, Kim, still refuses to get one—so his guess is as good as mine when she'll be back. I tell him we're coming tomorrow, he says he's overjoyed. He actually sounds emotional about it, which is not like him at all. I'm so excited I head to the bedroom and start to pack before I remember the pills. I search again in all the obvious places, but they're gone. It's as though they'd never existed.

As I enter the kitchen, Meredith is standing by the coffee maker thumbing her phone as she pours a cup. It's not clear where things stand between us, in whatever branch this is. But at least she's here. Her mug filled, she turns toward the breakfast nook, still lost in her phone, and I catch a glimpse of the screen. A man, who looks like he belongs on a magazine cover. Meredith runs her hand over the image and it shifts to another. The same man again. She settles into one of the padded benches in the breakfast nook, puts down her phone and shifts to her laptop. Her familiar look of deep concentration. She hasn't even noticed I'm here. And on her computer screen, the man appears again. She's probing deep into his eyes.

Could it be him? Could he be the missing variable in those other branches? The reason things keep going so horribly wrong. Could she have been seeing him all along without me knowing? Those endless nights I spent doomscrolling. Spent raging. All the hours she spent silently focused on her laptop. She was ten feet away, but where was she? I'm already throttling him in my mind, though it's not working great since he's a two-dimensional portrait.

Maybe this is it. The hinge point. One of those moments where everything is different after, where you finally learn the truth that's been there all along, the part of the sentence you could never see, and there's no turning back. Even if the truth breaks you.

I step forward to confront Meredith. She looks up from her laptop and there's no sign of guilt or shame.

I take a seat opposite her in the nook, trying to decide what to say.

The nook was actually the reason we'd bought this house. Before Nolan was even a passing thought. The house works fine for us but it's nothing special. We were both on the fence about whether to buy it, but as soon as Meredith saw the nook she knew it was the one. Just a simple rounded alcove with built-in benches straddling a wooden table, but there's a comforting warmth to it. Cozy. Safe. Meredith said it looked like a place where we could grow old together. A place to share an early coffee or a late drink. To share our lives. We've shared so many laughs in this nook, I couldn't possibly remember half of them. A few years ago we hung a small flatscreen where the table meets the wall, a TV no one now watches except Nolan. Eventually we stopped eating here altogether. In my old branch, this table is now permanently stacked with mail and half-folded laundry. We haven't sat here for years now. Since before Mom died.

Meredith sips her coffee and makes a face. "Taste this," she says. "Does it taste different to you? I swear they changed something."

Déjà vu. The same comment she made about dinner the other night. The sentences that were identical until they weren't. But this time it doesn't feel like a taunt. Maybe it never was.

She hands me the thrown clay mug and I draw it close, greeted by the scent of toasted almonds. I sip and feel the familiar tightening, senses coming online. But to me it's the same taste as always.

"Maybe it's not the coffee that changed," I suggest. "Maybe it's you."

Meredith looks at me for a few lingering moments, inquisitive eyes searching. Then she bursts with laughter. "Oh my god. You had me there for a second. So serious." Gives me a playful wink as she takes another sip. "Definitely not a good time to be a Nazi."

"What?"

"You know, 'Jojo Rabbit.'"

An inside joke, our private language, but I'm stuck on the outside. I half-remember watching that movie last year, continually scrolling the whole time, struggling to enjoy it as everything hit too close to home.

Now she's distracting me. From the man on her screen. From why things keep breaking. There's a family portrait hanging on the nook wall behind Meredith. She and I are holding Nolan, overjoyed, long before he could even walk. A picture I know well, because it's hanging in my branch too. These branches aren't disconnected what-ifs. A truth in one is a truth in all.

In the picture's glass frame, overlaid upon our young family, I can see the reflection of Meredith's computer screen. The man. She's looking at him again.

This is it. I have to know.

"Who is he?" I ask.

"Who is who?"

"The man on your computer."

Meredith pauses. She looks at me, then at her laptop, and turns the screen toward me. She isn't ashamed at all, and I don't understand.

"Take a peek," she says.

I don't know the man. He's no one to me. A blank slate, an empty vessel ready to be weighted with whatever nightmares my mind can supply. But now, with a closer view, I'm struck by what an incredible image it is. The lighting, the shadows, an ocean fading in the distance. But I don't know where she's going with this. Meredith makes a motion with her thumb like she's dealing cards. I'm not in the mood for charades, but I recognize a motion I've seen her make a thousand times.

I flick the laptop's touchscreen and it advances to the next image. It's the same man again but this time he's facing away from the camera. Out to sea. I flick again, and this time it's a much older man, frail and feeble, the same ocean beyond. Again, and he's looking away. *Flick.* Now an old woman who's lost one eye. *Flick.* An infant barely able to sit up. *Flick. Flick.* There's more, more, more. So many I start flicking rapidly but they keep coming. And then I stop when I see a young girl in braids, relaxed and smiling. The quality isn't as good, the lighting amateur compared to the rest, but the setting is the same. It's Meredith.

And now I finally understand.

They're her youth. Her life. The images she'd taken over the years and eventually built into a massive mosaic. The same life's work she and I once destroyed together, or so she says. She used to tell me she still had the negatives somewhere. She just needed the time to find them. To fix them.

She's been fixing them all along. In every branch, I bet. And I never even noticed. Hours spent toning, tweaking, coping. Finding a way to survive the same as I was these past years. Making a plan, moving forward, all while I lashed out at a thousand virtual Noahs while not getting involved when it came to the real one. Both of us alone together, turning inward instead of toward one another.

"You've been working on this all this time?" I ask. "Why didn't you say anything?"

"I did," Meredith says. "But I'm not sure you were listening." And I know she's right. In every branch, she's right. "Honestly, it's been a great diversion from everything," she says, though with *Him* gone and Mom alive, I'm not sure what *everything* means. "But I want it to be more than a diversion. I don't want to just touch up old photos in my spare time. What I need is to make something new again. Maybe even get into a studio."

And now I know what her meeting had really been about.

"Chaz Bennett," I say. The name startles her.

"What?" she asks.

"He has a studio near your work, doesn't he?"

"How did you know that? I only looked up his name last week."

"Maybe you could display some of your work there," I say. "Though I think I heard he might be having some health issues."

"Yes," she says, confused. "I … heard that too. Wait, how do you know more about this than I do?"

I have to tell her. I can't stand this gap between us, and now it's clear I've been the one pushing her away. It used to be that whenever I was in trouble she could always fix it. I've always hated the movie trope where the hero's wife or girlfriend is unfairly depicted as some nagging obstacle when the real problem is that he won't tell her anything. But I'm just as guilty as they are. And I'm no hero.

"Do you remember those headaches I used to get?" I ask. "The nausea? Maybe even a seizure?"

"I remember you having bad headaches, yes. But not seizures. What is this about? I thought we were talking about Chaz Bennett."

"How long ago?" I ask.

"I don't know, a couple years maybe? Around the time Nolan turned one. You had that bad spell right after his birthday."

"But I was never prescribed anything?" I ask, trying not to appear desperate.

Meredith laughs like I'm teasing her. "Why are you asking *me*? You never said anything about a prescription. Are you having that memory issue again?"

"Memory issue?"

She finishes her coffee. "Now I know you're messing with me."

"I'm sorry, but I'm really not."

Her smile fades and she looks worried. "Three times in the last couple months it was like you briefly had amnesia, didn't know what you were doing. Two weeks ago you didn't show up to work and then afterward couldn't explain why. Last week you told me to remind you not to forget your phone, emphasizing it like it was the most important thing in the world. And later, when I reminded you, you didn't remember telling me. But we talked about all this, and you insisted you were fine. Are you saying you don't remember?"

Other versions of me passing through, leaving nothing but confusion in their wake. Even death. Anton behind the counter. The officer's open eye, a slate gray iris but there's nothing behind it anymore. The rain washing it all away.

I don't know how to explain everything that's happened. But I have to try.

"I can tell you why I don't remember," I say. "But we're both going to need more coffee."

So we sit in the nook, steaming mugs between us, and I tell her. The election. My job. The crash. Quantgen. Her leaving. Her meeting Chaz Bennett. Her hematoma. Life sentences that made no sense. The space between us expanding and contracting. The missing pills.

I leave out some parts, about Anton and Jill, about the other me killing the officer. Things I'd rather not talk about if I don't have to.

She listens patiently. When I'm done, she actually tells me she believes me, that she understands. And for the first time since this began I don't feel alone.

"Okay," she says, still taking it all in. "Can I ask one question?"

"Of course, anything."

She reaches out and gently takes my hand. "What do you think it means that the crash you remember happened because you were upset about the election?"

"What does it mean? I guess I'm not sure I understand the question. It wasn't just the election. I lost my job too, proof that the election was more than just a threat."

"That's okay, never mind," she says, moving on as though I wouldn't understand. "So. Let's figure this out. What do you need? How can I help?"

"I'm not even sure," I say. "I just know I need more pills as soon as possible."

Her face freezes. I can tell she's trying not to react.

"Oh," she says. "Well, let me think about it. This is all still very new."

And now I know why the hero never tells. Because I sound crazy. She doesn't really believe me. Of course not. But she loves me enough to pretend to, trying to hear what it is I actually need. And I suppose right now I sound like some kind of addict, suddenly regretting that I ever told her the stories about those times some friends and I did pills back in college.

"I know you said it's no use," she says, "but maybe we should go to the hospital just in case. Maybe in this branch they can do something for you."

"No. No, they can't help me. Believe me, I've tried."

The space between us is growing again. This was a mistake.

Meredith lets my hand go, even more gentle than before.

She looks around the nook, at the memories it holds, same as I had a few minutes ago. Then she asks if I've picked up the Saturday newspaper yet, mercifully changing the subject. So I go along with it.

Outside, another snowstorm is raging. I try looking away. Blinking. But it's still snowing. So I work through the familiar steps, the elaborate procedure required to do the simplest task in the depths of winter. Coat, scarf, boots, hat, gloves. And I'm longing for the crashing waves of the ocean again, the simple home where my parents await. Where nature is still alive. Where Mom is still alive.

As soon as I step outside I'm blinded by the sun, instantly sweating. It's now at least 60 degrees out here. Not a trace of snow in sight. I trudge to the mailbox, awkwardly clomping in my bulky snow boots, and retrieve the newspaper we'd cancelled years ago in my old branch. Sure, why not. I'm the kind of person who drives an orange SUV now. Who cares about a little unnecessary paper? What's a few carbon emissions between friends? An early-autumn day in January is really pleasant, after all. For now. But by the time Nolan grows up … *Shit.*

The newspaper falls to the ground, grocery flyer entrails spilling out on the lawn. I haven't had any headaches or nausea, so I know I'm still moving forward.

And yet.

My street appears deserted. Strange for an unseasonably warm Saturday morning. The Nguyen kids are almost always in their yard running in circles. Star Wars this. TikTok that. Or something or other. But right now it's totally quiet. I think I know why.

Because there's a yellow tracer mark etched onto our front door. And on those of several neighbors. Across the street, the Nguyens' tracer-marked front door is wide open, as is their single-stall garage door. The gray Civic with a family of Stormtrooper decals in the rear window is still there, but other than that there's no sign anyone is home. I'm relieved when I spot Bib Purrtuna lying in the grass of their front yard. But the cat's not moving.

I gather the dismembered newspaper splayed on the brown grass. As I'm putting everything in its right place I notice a headline on the front page, just below the fold: 'President visits state's expanded internment facility.' But the picture isn't of Him. In fact, it's someone I've never seen before. Never even heard of before. *Shit.* Somehow, I don't know, they must have been able to line up a new nominee here. A young rising star. And somehow the election went differently. Or, rather, the same as I remember it. I'm reminded now of the people in my feeds who always acted like they knew better, before they declared that all is lost, how they would regularly say *He* wasn't the real problem. He was just a symptom.

Back inside, Nolan's wandered into his room but his monster movie continues to blare in the living room. The mutant ants are distraught and absolutely livid. Very relatable. Meredith's still in the breakfast nook, thinking, looking concerned.

"Haven't had any bright ideas yet," she says with a sheepish grin. I haven't moved on yet. I mention the yellow mark on the door, but she waves it off. "Remember, they said it was a mistake. Oh, sorry, you don't remember. Anyway, the patrol's going to clean it off later."

She seems so much happier here. Lighter. How is that possible?

Just then, Nolan enters the kitchen asking for orange juice, and I'm thankful he's here. But then I see his face. It's still bearing the same gruesome scar he'd had last night. It's exactly the same, every inch of gray jagged tissue spread across his sweet little face. And now the scar is all I can think about. How can it still be there? Meredith had blamed the crash on Mom's death. But that's not possible here so it was never about that.I've already told Meredith everything, so there's no harm in asking.

"I need to know how it happened," I say. "How did he end up like this?"

She's clearly worried about me now, but she agrees to remind me of what I should already know. Nolan joins us in the nook, sitting in my lap sipping juice, zoning out to his monster movie on the nook's little wall-mounted TV. And, calmly, patiently, she tells me.

Just over two years ago—shortly after *He* was forced to step down following a bout of flu that triggered a series of debilitating strokes—I became completely obsessed with climate change. It consumed me. I spent most nights on my feeds poring over increasingly dire climate models, worried about the dwindling time that remained to avoid unstoppable runaway effects, distraught that Nolan's time left in a livable world may be dangerously short. One day, Karl and I had a comp day to burn ahead of an overseas work trip, so he came over. We got to talking. And then we got to ranting. Then raging. Then drinking. And soon I'd forgotten I had promised to pick up Nolan at daycare. After the crash, I told Meredith it was the sight of everyone going about their day as if the world wasn't on fire that broke me.

But, she tells me, we feel incredibly lucky every day that both of us only suffered superficial injuries. A steel post within the utility box I hit had pierced the windshield, was driven through my seat and embedded in Nolan's car seat, missing both of us by inches. And beyond that, Meredith says she thinks the crash saved me. I have no idea what she means.

I wipe a tear from my face and look away. Meredith squeezes my hand and rises for more coffee. So that's why she asked about the crash I remember. I hold Nolan tight but he's distracted, watching his movie. On screen, a giant ant engulfed in flames tumbles from a pier as the end titles appear.

VOICEOVER: *Has this ever happened to you?*

It's the 3-in-1 reacher ad again. I desperately need a distraction, so I watch it for the fiftieth time.

[cue cartoon spring sound effect]

[cue cartoon splash sound effect]

This commercial. Nolan loves it, no matter the branch. He laughs so hard it's infectious. But there's something about the ad this time. Strange. I don't know why, but this time I feel like there's something … off about it. The commercial seems wrong. It's basically the same, but something's changed here. On cue, the woman's head pops out of the water. *There's got to be a better way!* And now Nolan is laughing again.

The actress. It's a different actress. They cast someone else here. But what is it about her? Why does she look familiar? With my phone, I'm pulling up the ad on YouTube as Meredith returns with yet another cup of coffee. I ask if she's ever seen the woman in the ad before.

"We've all seen that ad," she says gently. "We just talked about it at dinner last night. You said how they filmed it a few miles from here. Can you remember that?" I'm watching on a loop now, trying to place the woman. Her hair. The woman's wavy black hair is tied back in a ponytail, but when I saw her she wore her hair down. I repeat the clip again. And again.

The doorbell chimes but I tune it out until Meredith gingerly puts her hand in mine and says we need to go.

"Who is she? I know her." I know it's not someone from college or work. In fact, it's someone I met very recently. But I can't place her. She leads me to the front door but I'm still deep in thought.

The half-moon window in the front door reveals a man and woman standing on the stoop outside. It's snowing again. What's going on? Meredith instructs Nolan to go to his room.

[cue cartoon spring sound effect]

The reacher ad is still looping on my phone. I look down and immediately it catches my eye.

The brooch. In the ad's opening shot, the woman climbing the ladder is wearing an emerald brooch pinned to her shirt.

It's the woman from Quantgen.

"She's an actress!" I cry out.

Meredith is now certain I've gone insane. She opens the door to greet two first responders. "Thank you for coming. Sorry about the unusual circumstances."

Oh no.

She's having me committed. Or at least evaluated. She must have called while I was outside. I never should have said anything.

"Wait, I can prove it," I tell Meredith. "She's one of the ones who gave me the pills."

"An actress? Honey, listen to yourself."

The EMTs politely step inside, a man and woman who mainly look bored.

"I know it sounds crazy, Meredith," I say. "I'm sorry for putting you in this position. But somehow I can find her. I have to."

She looks defeated. "I'm sorry, dear. You know I want to believe you. But you hire actors all the time for work. Whatever it is that's driven you to this, she could be part of it."

Of course. Meredith's right. I could hire her. Or try to at least.

I should have let Meredith in from the beginning. Why did I think I could ever do this without her? She completes the sentence. None of it makes sense without her.

For some reason, the first responders aren't doing anything. Now I see there's actually a third person standing outside, a stone-faced man who's been hanging back. Wearing full body armor. In the driveway, the ambulance sits parked beside an armored patrol truck.

Everything's happening too fast, I can't keep up.

"Excuse me, officer," Meredith calls to the hulk outside as he makes asides into a walkie-talkie clipped to his shoulder, "I don't think your help is needed today. But thanks anyway."

The man doesn't move. It's not Petkoff, but he might as well be. The demeanor is unmistakable.

Oh no. The tracer mark on the door.

Meredith looks at me in horror.

"Oh, this mark?" she says to the officer. "They're coming to wash it off. Don't worry. Just a mistake, they said. You can call and verify if you need to."

But he doesn't say anything. Just sniffs, then leans toward his walkie. After a long while he presses the comm button.

"Subject acquired."

Everyone is still for a moment. The only sound is the reacher ad, still looping on the phone in my hand.

VOICEOVER: Has this ever happened to you?

Can't say that it has, no.

The officer proceeds to enter the house and I instinctively look to Nolan's room. The door is shut at least. And then something very strange happens. The officer clenches his fist, steps toward me, and punches himself in the stomach. Though with all that armor I imagine he barely felt it. He calmly grips the walkie.

"Subject has disabled my body cam, over." I can't make out the reply. "Sir!" he screams at me, drawing his gun. "Put down the weapon!"

I'm not holding one.

"Subject appears to be on PCP," he says. "Oof! It seems he has almost superhuman strength!" The officer falls to the ground with a percussive thud, then dramatically writhes on the floor grunting as the rest of us stand motionless.

Meredith and I lock eyes. I know she's blaming herself, but I forced her hand. This is my fault. Of all the branches I've been in, this was the happiest, the most content I've seen her. Both of them, really.

Even with his scar, somehow Nolan looks more at ease here. They remind me of the feeling of those earliest days, right after he was born. Whatever variable was different here, this was one worth holding onto. But now I've ruined it for everyone.

"Backup. Backup!" the officer yells into his walkie as he continues to thrash on the ground, his boots and gear thoroughly scuffing our faux-wood laminate, his gun pointing wildly around the room. "Subject has my sidearm. Over."

I wish I did, but no, I most certainly don't.

"No! Not in the occipital lobe! Jesus Christ! Over." His theatrics become increasingly over the top and eventually his grunts start to take on a sort of lusty quality. One of the EMTs checks her watch. Apparently a typical day for her?

A minute later and the officer's still at it. "The brute has upbraided me and knocked me senseless, over. Now threatening me with a scimitar, over." Meredith and I are tense, fearing what he's likely to do once this ends, but it's just getting tiresome now. "Please! No! Is that a regulation bat? God in heaven, my sciatica! Over." The response from the officer's walkie is garbled but it might be laughter. This is all a power play. He wants us to know he can do whatever he wants to us and get away with it.

The thrashing finally stops and he's back on his feet. "This is your last chance," he says calmly, his gun now aimed at my head. "Put down the weapon. Now."

I drop the only thing on me, my phone, but the ad continues to play.

V.O.: *There's got to be a better way!*

That's when a pair of arms surround me from behind, and I'm drowning again.

The lead officer watches as his partner puts me in a chokehold. In my mind's eye it's Petkoff but I don't actually know. I'm on the ground now. How did that happen? Meredith is screaming, the EMTs she called now restraining her instead of me as a scrum of officers pile on my back. Another officer runs down the hall and kicks at Nolan's door but it holds. I'm terrified for him. I want to help or even just cry out but I'm feeling lightheaded, drifting between agony and serenity. I almost think I can hear whale songs, like the meditation sounds on the phone. No loon though.

V.O.: But wait, there's more.

The officer down the hallway kicks Nolan's door again, breaking the hinges. The room is empty but Nolan's window is open. He's escaped into the snow. Or is it rain?

The lead officer stomps my phone, shattering it. Meredith struggles against the EMTs as they drag her to the patrol truck. The lead officer kneels beside me and calmly produces a syringe. There's chatter on his walkie but the only word I can make out is *"radical."* And then a painful prick in my neck … darkness …

And I sit up.

Alone in the house. Again.

People in caskets never look right. Not that I blame the mortician. Given the things that are done to the body after death, the things the body begins to do with depressing speed as soon as the heart ceases to beat, it's remarkable they're able to make their subjects appear presentable at all. Grandparents, neighbors, an unfortunate coworker. Every funeral I'd attended felt like a necessary formality, but the body who wasn't really the person you knew was largely beside the point. It's that uncanny valley look they always have. That second-rate wax museum effect.

So naturally, when it came time to see Mom, I was terrified. I didn't want to remember her like that. The last thing you see is what you'll remember most. Not like that. But we'd lost her so suddenly. There was no period of illness and decline, not even a moment to take stock, to say our goodbyes and ready ourselves for life without her. She was there, and then she wasn't. So when I entered the sanctuary and saw the yawning casket at the far end, it was like a magnet pulling on me. I asked Meredith to stay back with Nolan. I wasn't sure I wanted to go, but I definitely didn't want this to be his first and only impression of his grandmother. And he was too young to understand any of it.

I approached the lacquered mahogany we'd picked out for her for what seemed an eternity, the distance between us telescoping as I walked. But, eventually, there she was.

Seeing her was not at all what I'd expected. It *was* her. She looked as though she might open her eyes at any moment. Her mouth was slack at the edges — there are some things the living do that can't be faked in death — but otherwise she was perfect. I held Mom's hand, cold yet familiar, the hand I remember holding when mine was small enough to fit inside it. The moment I did, I felt a hundred pounds lighter. The crushing weight would soon return, but for a moment it felt like we were together. I knew it was the closest we would ever be again.

Increasingly, I've begun to regret leaving some of these branches, filled with so much unfinished business, especially the one I had been living in these past years. Maybe I didn't vibrate the same as everyone else, but it felt like my life. My decisions were still my own, even if I didn't always like the outcome. But now it's clear this is what I was meant to do. When this began, it never even occurred to me that I might see Mom again. It seemed like too much to ask, so much more than I deserved. But this is my chance. With everything I've gone through, I'm awake now in a way I wasn't before. Despite everything that's happened, in every branch, I find myself worried the most for Nolan's future, the challenges he'll face because of that scar, a painful reminder of a selfish mistake I don't remember, or at least, remember differently. But then there are still branches to go before the end, chances for things to end up right. Miles to go before I sleep.

But if I can't get the final pills soon, none of it will happen.

uploading

... 1%

... 2%

... 3%

I feel like I'm going to throw up. I haven't smoked in years but I caved and had a cigarette outside with Karl just now. Right before I fired him.

I needed it. And now I feel sick.

It's almost 3:30. In about three hours I'll start to regress if I can't find a way to get more pills. I limp into a lobby bathroom and scrub my shoes. But the stains don't really come clean. So much blood. I don't want to think about what happened today. The attack in our home this morning was enough trauma for a lifetime. And then ...

I keep blinking, hoping I might pass on to a branch where the stains are gone, but I don't. I scrub and scrub but the shoes won't go back to being white. Instead, the stains shift from red-brown to a sort of muddy beige. It'll have to do. I ride the elevator up to the floor where auditions are being held, waiting to see whether there's any chance my plan will work.

Did you know the movies "Carrie" and "Star Wars" were cast from the same set of auditions? Imagine nervously waiting by the phone, not knowing whether you'd landed the role as demented mother Margaret White or, just maybe, Chewbacca. You see, occasionally various directors and producers will link up for joint auditions and consider actors for multiple projects in development all at once. Granted, it's extremely rare when more than one thing spun from a single audition goes on to become a classic, but hungry actors will forever live in hope. And these joint casting calls tend to flush a lot of hidden talent from the underbrush, so if you're having trouble casting your pet project there's value in linking up where you can.

Wait. I'm getting ahead of myself. I should back up.

Earlier this morning, I found myself alone in the house once again. The snow angel of scuff marks in the laminate, gone. The tracer mark on the door, gone. It occurred to me that, somewhere, another me was waking up, pinned to the floor, drugged and probably hauled to a camp for radicals, with no memory of what led to it. So yeah. Not great.

I called Meredith. Five rings, but she answered. I asked if she and Nolan were safe.

"Yes?" she said, confused.

I hung up, overcome with relief but afraid to know any more about where they were this time, who they were this time. Who I was. They're safe, that's all that matters. But if I don't find more pills, I know I'll pass back through that branch again soon.

I called talent agencies in the area until I found the one used to cast the MyRod ad, then used my MWI credentials to get access to their roster. For the first time in my career, I feel fortunate to live in a mid-size metro where the pool of professional actors is only so big. I pulled one file after another, constantly checking the time, but it quickly began to feel like a futile gesture. Then, just as I reached the end of the catalog. Jackpot. She's even wearing the brooch in her headshot.

According to the listing, her name is Lisa LaRoque. I may be shit with names, but I'm certain that wasn't the one she gave at the hospital a week ago. Who knows, maybe it's a stage name. I call the agency back and ask if she's available for a last-minute audition. But she's not. She had a small window of availability today and already booked a 4 o'clock audition downtown at the open casting call for Lev Upton's next project.

Fucking Lev Upton and his coke-addict editing. I think of Anton, smiling, griping about Upton. Anton, lying on the ground. Maybe I could show up outside the audition and confront her? But then, I have no idea who these people are, much less what they're capable of. It needs to be some place where she can't just run away or, God, I don't know, call in a hit or something.

It occurs to me there's one person I could call. But I don't know where things stand here. I'm getting closer to my original branch, that central trunk from which everything spun off, so who knows whether other versions of me have already passed through, messing things up on their way out.

I call Karl, and he picks up right away.

"Dude, I am too hungover today," he says. "Can we talk about this at work Monday?"

At least I haven't burned that bridge here. I tell him I'll let him in on a secret.

"I'm about to quit my job," I say. "I need a new career. Something I can feel good about."

Something that actually makes a difference so I can be more than a complicit hostage in all of this. Even if it's something small, at least it's something.

"So what is it you need?" he asks. I have his full attention.

"You know how you're always telling everyone you know Lev Upton and he owes you one, right? Well, I need you to call in that favor and get me into that audition room. Apparently he's got a couple local commercial directors sitting in to scout talent for other projects, so one more shouldn't matter."

"I mean, sure I knew him," Karl says. "But I can't guarantee he'll remember the favor part."

"So you didn't really work in Hollywood like you've been saying all these years?"

"No I totally did," he says. "Kind of. Lev bought some Molly from me a few times and he told me, he said he owes me one big time.

But, I do seem to recall, at the time he said it he was also, like, *super* into watching this angelfish tank."

That was just before 11 a.m. Then ...

By 2:45 the slate's been wiped clean. I work on Karl again and, again, it works. He meets me in front of the Baker Building downtown, where the auditions are scheduled. Karl says he got through to Lev's people. Lev has agreed to let me sit in as long as I hang back and don't interfere.

Karl lights a cigarette, and I can tell he's only thinking about that promotion. He looks down, points at the blood on my shoes. "Jesus, dude," he says. "What is all that?"

"Oh, look at that," I say, hoping he doesn't notice the tremor in my hand. I don't want to talk about it, don't even want to think about it. "Had a nosebleed earlier," I lie. "A big one. I'll clean it inside before I head up. By the way, Karl, can I bum a smoke? And then we need to have a talk about your future."

… 99%
… 100%
upload complete
PUBLISH
SHARE

Phone down. It's 3:30. I wince with each step, gripping my leg as I push my way past the throng of nervous actors pacing along the long central hallway that spans the Baker Building's 45th floor. Some of them I recognize from past video shoots, though I'm really just looking for Lisa. She's not here yet.

I'm stopped at a set of double doors by an assistant who clearly works for Lev Upton, the obvious facial fillers and overtight goldenrod skin a dead giveaway. He demands silence with one upraised finger as he listens with his ear against the audition doors. After a minute a man's voice says "Okay!" followed by a brisk hand clap, and the assistant takes the cue to open the door and wave me in. I pass a plump young boy and his mother as I enter the room. Both are openly crying as they depart.

It's a small square room, one wall entirely floor-to-ceiling windows with an expansive view of the city skyline. The two local directors I recognize are seated along the back wall. Two men with the same hip young director look they're a decade too old to pull off: zip up hoodies, skinny jeans, horn-rimmed glasses, heads shaved cue-ball bald. They're probably used to being in charge on local projects but seated in the shadow of Lev Upton they're powerless and indistinguishable. Extras without agency. Lev is seated in front, a few feet from the taped X where the talent is supposed to stand.

He's sitting in a cliché cloth-on-wood director's chair bearing his name, a young female assistant standing next to him holding dark red script pages like they're the nuclear launch codes.

There's not much to say about Lev that I couldn't say about every famous person I've met. Compared to the face-melting beauty of the stars in his films he'd be considered pretty homely, not very tall, not very memorable, maybe forty-five give or take, but he still has this weirdly flawless skin and you can sense the gravitational pull he has on everyone, everything warping around him through some combination of enchantment and fear. And you get the sense that he knows it and knows how to wield it. There's some faux humility when he responds to people—I apologize for joining late, to which he gestures at the open chair behind him saying "it happens"—but everyone here knows the score and talks to him as they would talk to their boss' boss' boss. The two local directors sit quietly and nod a lot, occasionally chiming in to say, "Yes, I agree." My hope is that this same universal deference to power will come in handy when it's time to confront a familiar face.

Marketing pro tip: don't try any of this.

First up, an older gentleman enters and steps to the X. Lev banters with the man a bit while idly scrolling his phone the whole time, his jaw flexing rhythmically as he chews a wad of gum. Based on his jitteriness, probably nicotine gum.

I check my phone as well. I'm worried I might pass to another branch before Lisa gets here. Or that I might not pass on and someone will find me here. I look again at the beige blots on my shoes and tuck my feet under my chair. Outside the window the whole city spreads before me, the low January daylight already beginning to dim, streetlights beginning to blink on in the shadows of skyscrapers.

"Okay!" Lev says and claps his hands. I turn to see the old man disappear out the door. Apparently I missed his whole audition.

The next person on the call sheet enters. She's young, with long black hair, a 90s-era black choker, an overall goth-lite thing going on.

Lev greets her, asks if she has brought her own material or would like a side — that is, a short scene from his upcoming film — and I realize I haven't even thought to ask what the film is.

"No, I'm ready," she says, then a moment later erupts in tears, wailing. "Look into my *eyes*! Can't you see there that I'd rather *die* than cause you a moment's *pain*?" Why does this sound so familiar? It's been a while since I ran an audition but I know I heard it recently.

"Until I met you I was so *shy*, so *timid*, uncertain of myself," goth-lite continues, her hands at her sides nervously digging at her cuticles.

Holy shit. She's the woman with the blonde pixie cut. From Quantgen. But she's changed her hair here.

"Always troubled with *longings* and *desires* which you, and you alone, have taught me to *understand*."

I have to say, she's really going for it, and, I have to say, it is not good. But if they gave an award for Most Acting, well, she's at least in the conversation.

"I was so *lonely* that I thought I'd *lose* my *reason*," she continues, devouring everything in sight. "And always I was *searching*, for the one *woman* in the *world* on whom I could pin my *dreams*, my —"

"Okay!" Lev says and claps his hands, sounding upbeat. The assistant outside opens the door and the one beside Lev reaches out and hands the woman a tissue and a small fridge magnet with Lev's face on it. "Loved it, loved it," Lev says, not really looking at her. "So honored you could make it today. We won't forget it. And let's move down the list."

"No, *no*!" Goth Pixie pleads. "I have so much more —"

"Of that I have no doubt," Lev says.

It's over before I even have the chance to say anything. I think I should follow her out and confront her, but I also have a hard time imagining she knows much about, well, anything. She contributed almost nothing when I met her before.

If I'm patient, Lisa will be here soon. It's the only way I can get the final pills. The only way I can see Mom again.

The next four auditions are unmemorable, no one approaching the heights of a Daniel Day Lewis nor the depths of a Tommy Wiseau. I mean, say what you will about Goth Pixie, but at least she makes an impression. Lev seems to agree, constantly checking his phone, chewing his gum to a silent beat. As it gets closer to 4 o'clock, I get increasingly nervous, the tremor in my hand returning. I instinctively grab my phone again to quell my anxiety, pull up my feeds, but there isn't much of a point anymore. The dopamine's run dry.

The next time the door opens, a young man enters. And I hold my breath. The word that immediately comes to mind is dapper. His hair slicked to one side, wearing a dark fitted three-piece and shined Berluti shoes. And I can hear his upper-crust English lilt before he opens his mouth. It's the man from Quantgen. The man in charge.

An assistant reads his name off the call sheet, and I have to suppress a laugh. Jedediah Mundt. Definitely not the name he gave last time.

I tense as his eyes shift from Lev to me, but there's no indication he recognizes me. Compared to last week, when he'd had full control of our meeting—as much as Lev does now—the young man looks smaller. Nervous.

Lev asks if he's going original or wants to start with a side. The man asks for a side and the assistant hands him a few red-tinted pages to read.

"Welcome," Jedediah begins, addressing the assistant who responds by flatly reading the other part.

"Who are you?" the assistant drones. "What is this enchantment? Why have you brought me to this place?"

Jedediah smiles. "Because you, my dear, like everyone else here, are a prisoner of fate. Of forces beyond your control. The die is cast and you have to live with the consequences."

Wait, what is this script?

I start to see an energy building in Jedediah as he progresses, an authority that might come from a personal history with the subject, though I can't be sure.

"However," he says, "unlike everyone else here, you have a special gift. Tell me. If I were to offer you an elixir that allowed you to break free of these … these mortal constraints—to override fate—would you take it?"

The monotone assistant continues. "That very much depends. How do I know what fate has in store for me?"

"Well, you don't of course," Jedediah says. "No one does. But there's no reward without risk. As long as you keep taking the elixir, you can cross through to new worlds. Fate be damned." And the scene ends.

Lev breaks the silence with a slow clap. "That. Was. Brilliant," he says. "Thank you so much, I love it. So Jedediah, I understand from your agent that your main background is in improv?"

"That's right," Jedediah says, shifting his weight back and forth nervously. "I've also done a few of those immersive, experiential gigs. You know, where the mark doesn't know it's all an act. Those can be a lot of fun."

Wait, what? That's it. That's what they were doing. Which would make me the mark. I have to say something.

"Tell us more about those gigs," I interrupt. And now everyone is looking at me. "I only ask because I … I might have some local openings coming up in the experiential field. Would love to know more about your skills."

Lev turns and stares at me, clearly unaccustomed to having someone take over his session. The local directors beside me shift uncomfortably in their seats.

"Better yet," Lev says. "Why don't you give us a demonstration with my man over here." Meaning me, apparently.

The director seated closest to me nods. "Yes, I agree."

"In that case," I say, "I actually would love to continue with the same scene you were running if we could."

Lev's assistant butts in. "Sorry. We're only authorized to release pre-approved excerpts of the 'Elixir' script. Confidentiality issues and all."

"I don't mean the script," I say. "What I mean is, where would *you* go with this scene, Jedediah? Let's see what you've got. Take it from there."

Jedediah squints. "From?"

"From 'fate be damned.' Where you left off. Let's say you're pitching me the elixir. Convince me."

"Right, right," he says, thinking. It's still not clear whether he's worked with Quantgen here. But, if he doesn't know anything, then the odds are none of them know. Which would mean I really am fucked.

Then I see a light go on in Jedediah's eyes. He straightens, his body shifting forward to suggest he's now in charge.

"Don't you want to take control of your life instead of letting it control you?" he asks me.

"Of course. But there's a hole in your plot. If this elixir unlocks brave new worlds, but you have to keep taking it to access them, what if I were to cross through to a world where I no longer have the elixir? If I can't overcome these random twists of fate, I don't see the point in taking you up on the offer. It's in fate's hands, not mine."

Jedediah is now brimming with energy, like he was when I met him last week. "I appreciate your concern. I really do. The choice is yours, of course. But, if I may, you're looking at this all a bit backwards. It's not fate that's in control here."

"It's not? How do you mean?"

"Think about it," he says. "Is what we're doing right now random? Of course not. Right now, you, sitting there, are rife with intention. The choices we all make are anything *but* random. There is always, always a reason. And it's those choices that affect everything that comes after."

"Fine," I say. "But when one random change in the world is the difference between life and death, how can we ever claim to be in control of anything?"

"Because there's more to it than life and death, isn't there?" His demeanor has so transformed that everyone is leaning forward in their seats. Even Lev. "What we do in the face of death matters as much as when and how it comes for us. And it will. Unfortunately, most people never stop to interrogate why we do what we do. And so, as you pass strangers on the street, know that many of them are strangers to themselves, just passing through life feeling fate keeps screwing them over."

"Still," I say. "The cards you're dealt really do matter. If fate gives you a shitty hand, you don't stand much of a chance, no matter who you are. If you're given the option to get dealt a new hand, why not take it?"

"Oh, I strongly advise you to take it," Jedediah says, stepping closer. "Everyone deserves a second chance. But if you think it's fate loading the dice you're bound to be disappointed no matter how many elixirs you drink." He's looking at me intently now, and I know he knows. He must.

"I love it. Love it!" Lev says. "Okay!" He claps his hands to signal his assistants, but he seems interested in Jedediah in a way he hadn't been in the others.

"*What do you know*?" I demand, rising to confront Jedediah. "Where is the elixir? Where are the pills? *Why are you doing this*?"

"What are you talking about?" Jedediah asks, looking meek and nervous again. Lev's assistant steps between me and Jedediah and hands him a leftover *Escape from Hell* promotional mini-poster.

"Thanks and all that," Lev says to me without looking up from his phone. "But I got what I need. If you two want to keep role playing outside or whatever, have at it. Got a schedule to keep."

This is not working the way I'd hoped. I follow Jedediah into the hall where several dozen people are crouched or pacing, all mouthing monologues to themselves.

"*You know, don't you,*" I call after Jedediah as he weaves around the other people. I'm struggling to keep up, my leg throbbing as I limp after him. "You're with them. I know you are. I need your help. What will it take? Please. *Anything.*"

He stops, and after a moment, turns to me.

"Anything covers quite a lot," he says.

"Anything I have to give, it's yours. Now please."

Jedediah walks toward me, stepping over an actor writhing on the floor that I hope is practicing a death scene.

When I look up again I catch a glimpse of Lisa LaRoque as she passes me on the way to the audition room. For a moment, her emerald brooch catches the light. She's wearing the same tailored suit jacket she'd worn when I first saw her, this time paired with jeans and flats.

"What was this about pills now?" Jedediah asks.

"I need them," I say while continuing to watch as Lisa enters the room and the double doors shut behind her. "To get back where I belong, I need them. Will you help me?"

"Hey, not a problem," Jedediah says. "I've got connections. What do you need?"

"Thank god." A thought of Mom, sitting in my childhood home. Waiting. "A white and a green."

"Okay. Uh, can you be a little more specific? You want, like, Cloud Nine? Meow Meow? Purple Wave?"

"What? No," I say. "Not that kind of pill. Quantgen pills."

He seems legitimately confused. "Okay? So ... you want Bliss? Blue Silk? Little Dilberts?"

"No. *No.* Are you with them or aren't you?"

"Is this about your leg?" he asks. "Is that what the pills are for? What happened, anyway?"

"My leg? I think I was in a car accident."

"You think? You don't know?"

"This isn't about that," I say. "I need you to follow through here. Or what was all that back there? Are you going to take this seriously or not?"

"Oh, okay." He thinks for a moment. "No, it's cool, I got this." Now he wrinkles his brow and affects something approximating a Bronx accent. I think. "I have exactly what you need, kid. What say you get in the car and we'll take a little trip together, if you know what I mean. A little light fantastic and whatnot."

Oh no. *Shit.* Jedediah doesn't know anything at all. He's just some gutter-grift actor hungry for a big break. And I wanted so badly to believe him that I fell for it.

I apologize. "This isn't working out, but best of luck to you. I really have to go."

"Wait wait, no no no no," he pleads. "I've got this. If you need more intense, I'm all over it. Believe me, I've done quinceañeras before." I try to get back to the audition room but Jedediah blocks my path. "*Fate!*" He screams, looking wild eyed and desperate. "You think you can master fate! You little piece of— of— of hunk of slime! You don't know fate. It'll shit down your throat and ask for seconds!"

What.

He lunges at me and tries to grab my shirt but he's still holding his mini-poster and paper cuts his upper lip. Now he's on the ground, dabbing at the cut with his finger like he's never registered pain before, giving me whale eye like a frightened dog. Apparently intense isn't his strong suit.

I leave him behind, rush to the doors and enter over the goldenrod assistant's pleas. The room is quiet. Lisa is standing on her mark while Lev and the others stare at her, transfixed.

"Bravo!" Lev shouts and stands, clapping. I've missed it.

I take my seat and watch Lisa standing there as they continue to clap. Considering how few roles are actually written for middle-age black actresses—unless you want to play some flat, insulting stereotype—this is probably a rare opportunity for her. But then she has this air of confidence about her, like it doesn't really matter whether she gets a part or not. Like she's the one judging whether she wants to work for them.

Lisa glances at me, and for a moment I swear there's a sign of recognition. But then I know it's just going to be Jedediah all over again. What am I doing here? I should be at home with Meredith, with Nolan, spending what little time I have left with them before I'm cast back instead of here with yet another person telling me what I want to hear. A better story than the truth. Though now I would swear Lisa is looking at me for a reason. Studying me.

"I'm so glad you came in today," Lev says to her. "While you're here, I wonder if you'd like to read another side?"

"Certainly," she says. The assistant hands her some pages, feeds her a monotone line. "Actually," she says. "If you don't mind, could I run this scene with him?" Lisa points at me. "If that's all right, of course. It's just that it's a male part and it might help to see a scene with a different partner than the last one."

Lev snaps his gum for a bit, then shrugs. "Sure, why not."

"Whatever," the assistant says and tosses me the pages with an eyeroll.

"Yes, I agree," nods the director next to me.

Lisa tilts her head slightly and squints, as if she's trying to see me better. "What is it you want?" she asks. I check my pages but the line's not there.

"What do I want?" I ask. "I'm not sure what you mean."

"Well, you wouldn't be here if you didn't want something."

"Of course I do."

"So?" She leans toward me. "What is it?"

I don't have time to play mind games with another actor. I struggle to my feet, wincing at the pain as I stand, and excuse myself.

Lisa looks at her hands for a moment, purses her lips and lets out a short whistle. After a moment of confusion, I place it.

Da-dee-dum-dum-da.

It's the melody. She knows. She really knows.

I sit down.

"What is it you want?" she asks again.

"One white and one green."

Just for a moment, Lisa's eyes widen with a look of recognition. "So you're close," she says. "And what is it you want?"

"I just told you."

"No. That's what you need in order to get what you want."

And then, without planning to say anything, I say it.

"I want to see my mother again."

She brightens, now more relaxed as she gets an answer. "I see. Thank you."

Lev and his assistant are paging through scripts now, trying to figure out which scene we're doing.

"Now," Lisa says, "I take it you misplaced your medication and need a refill?"

"More or less," I say. "Except I didn't misplace them. It's as though they never existed." The directors seated next to me are practically falling out of their chairs trying to read the script in my hands. "The problem started around the time divergences from two years ago began to take effect."

"Ah," Lisa says. "So you're one of the real ones."

"Real ones? What does that mean?"

"Sounds like we should really continue this in private," she says. She retrieves a black leather clutch that had been lying at her feet, turns and pushes hard on the double doors. There's a thud as the goldenrod assistant outside falls to the ground.

"Wait, hold up," Lev calls after her, chewing his gum nervously. "That's it? You're leaving the audition?"

"You've seen enough to get a sense," Lisa says, smiling with a confidence Jedediah could never hope to match. "You've got my information, so I think we're good here. Thanks everyone."

"Yes, I agree," the director beside me says. "It's been an honor, Ms. LaRoque!"

I follow Lisa into the hallway and catch a final glimpse of Lev sitting in his director's chair — awed, stunned — as the doors close. She effortlessly threads the other actors in the hallway then starts opening random doors along the corridor before finding one she likes.

"This will do," she says, entering what appears to be some executive's personal office with a picture window view of the city. Bookcases line the walls, but when I look closer they're just book spines. Decoys to convey the illusion of depth.

Once the door clicks shut, Lisa sits behind the rosewood desk. She pauses to check something on her phone and for a moment I wonder whether she's just going to ignore me. Then she looks up again, opens her leather clutch and extracts a nearly empty pack of clove cigarettes.

"Now," she says. "Let's talk."

"Can we please just do this? Can you get me the pills or not?"

"This needs to be a two-way relationship," she says as she extracts a black cigarette from its container. "You want me to give you something, you give me something."

"I'm not sure what you want," I say. Are you with them? Are you with Quantgen?"

Lisa shakes her head. "I'm not *with* anyone. But I do know the people you're talking about. And while I might not approve of what they're doing, they still owe me a favor. So I might just be able to get you what you need. If you tell me what you want."

"What do you want to know?" I ask.

"Your mother," she says.

"Yes, my mother. She died two years ago. Pancreatic—"

"The how doesn't really matter."

"It matters to me."

"Yeah, but not to me." She lights her cigarette and gestures at me, flicking ash on the desk. "What I want to know is: why do you want to see her again?"

"Look, I've told you something," I say. "Now it's your turn."

"I remember you, you know," Lisa says, leaning back in the executive's chair. "Not this you but another you. A few months back. See, I've done this gig a few times before. I remember you struck me as more determined than the others. It didn't take any effort at all to convince you."

"I don't know the me from this branch. No idea what he wants, who he is. I was just trying to change the election. Or maybe I wanted my Mom back. Neither of which would even apply here."

"Well, that's your memory. Like I said, different you."

"You said you did 'this gig.' What's the gig?"

"Okay, here's the deal," Lisa says. "I'm nobody. I'm not supposed to know anything about anything. Certainly none of those other actors you may have met would know fuck all. But as it happens ..." She seems unsure of her words for the first time. "I became involved with the recruiter who first brought me in. It wasn't that serious, but serious enough she started talking about her work. Serious enough to learn that they hire actors, like me, for every face-to-face. They pick them from local call sheets using a random number generator. Same with the company name, each time selected from a long list at random. I'm guessing that one threw you for a loop too."

"You could say that, yes."

"It's all just a way for them to make it so someone like you can't later find someone like me."

"I don't understand."

"There's an almost infinite number of branches, every one slightly different," she says. "Every time, random variables change. You can't predict what those changes will be in any one branch, but you pass through enough of them—millions upon billions—and the odds start to work in your favor. If you make a choice with rational intent, in nine realities out of ten you'll probably make that same choice no matter what changes. We're sadly very predictable. But if the choice itself is random, it's easier to sever the ties that lead back to them. You never get to speak to anyone who knows anything. In my case, you happened to luck out. So congratulations."

"And the people answering calls. They're actors too?"

She sighs. "Goddamn outsourcing. It's not like actors here get paid much anyway. But. Every penny. It's how they think."

"Again with 'they.' Who are *they*?"

After a slow drag on her cigarette, Lisa plays with the rings on her fingers for a minute. "What do you want to say to your mother? When you see her?"

"I don't know," I say.

"Sure you do. You've been thinking about it this whole time."

"No, I really don't. I just want to see her again."

"Why?"

"I don't know. Does it matter why? Who wouldn't want to see their dead mother again?"

"Plenty of people," she says.

"I just … I want to feel the warmth in her hand again. Okay? I have this memory of her cold hand, lying in her casket. It was still her hand, but … you could feel she wasn't there. I never got the chance to hold it at her bedside while it was still warm. I need to feel that warmth again. To know it's been undone." That's what I tell Lisa. I don't tell her about all the times I've imagined seeing Mom again. Where we're playing a duet on the piano. Where we're celebrating the birthdays she missed with a sparkler-capped cake. Where she and Meredith are greeting one another on the beach. Where I'm telling her that we're finally free of Him, and she's telling me about that final phone call I didn't answer. But of course none of that would make sense here.

"Thank you," Lisa says softly. "I can understand how hard that must be."

"Please, Lisa. Tell me. Who are these people?"

"Here's where I've got to be careful or I'll get in trouble myself," she says. "What I can say is that they're with a discrete subsidiary of a very major corporation. One I'm quite sure you've heard of."

"Wait," I say. "So you're saying this is all legit? It's really just a company working in quantum pharmacology? Given the elaborate lengths they've gone to, it sounds like some kind of criminal racket."

She laughs. "You say that as though there's a difference. Technically, it's worse than that, since they have contract law on their side. If you stop taking the pills and come back, they get you for $100K or more. And if you go through with it, you're out of their branch forever and you've given them everything they need to rob you blind. Remember, you're not the original you who lived in that branch. When you left that version of you would have come to with a rather significant case of amnesia. However long you've had the parasite, he'll remember none of it. Plus, the hospitals get paid to bring in drug reps. Everybody wins. Except the you who's left behind, of course."

So Meredith was right all along. It is a scam, even if it's real.

"But I told her about Quantgen on the way home from the hospital," I say. "She could expose them."

"Sorry, no," she says. "By the time you walked out the door you'd already left that branch behind."

My head hurts just thinking about all this.

"And why is it that other people shift around when I pass between branches, yet I always stay the same?" I ask.

She sighs. "Dear, some things you're better off just accepting. There are so many branches you can't even perceive. The mind is very good at focusing on what's most consistent and ignoring everything else." The scent of clove is now overwhelming in the small office, the smoke drifting and curling. "Then again, maybe you're just stubborn."

"What did you mean when you said I'm one of the real ones?"

Just then, the lights go out and all I can see is the burning ember of her cigarette. Lisa LaRoque. Deep Throat of the multiverse. I probably shouldn't trust her. But I do. She's the only chance I have left.

It's the motion lights. I stand and wave my arms and they snap on again. Lisa continues as though nothing happened. "So this company, who shall go unnamed, they spent an ungodly amount on this drug. Everything they likely told you about the parasite is true. It's rare, though not as rare as they first thought. They started out treating symptoms, trying to make an anti-seizure drug, and discovered they'd made an anti-multiverse-parasite drug by mistake. At first they discovered how to stop it from drifting farther, to make it want to stay in the same branch forever. Then they realized that if they stunned it they could also send it back, realized not only could they cure the patient, they could literally promise a new and better life so long as the parasite is killed at its weakest, in the branch of the initial infection, before it has a chance to wake up and travel back to them."

"But the subjects don't know whether their new life will be any better."

"Of course not," she says. "But the grass is always greener. Especially these days. Most people jump at the chance. Except, once they got into trials there was a problem."

"I get it," I say, finally putting the pieces together. "The patients crossed into timelines where they'd never taken part in the trial so they couldn't complete the treatment."

Lisa nods. "It's only useful if they can ensure the outcome. To do that, the subject needs to have been infected recently, and the more the company can control the circumstances, account for all the variables, the better."

"But how could they?"

Lisa arches her eyebrows as if the answer should be obvious.

"What. You're saying they're intentionally infecting people? Without their knowledge?"

"Come now," she says. "Companies have always been in the business of solving problems they invented. No one complained about halitosis or restless leg syndrome before the cure was marketed to them. This is just the next thing. They'll do whatever it takes to keep shareholders happy. Supposedly, once enough people are infected, they won't have to go to such extreme lengths anymore and can start marketing it openly. People will be willing to pay pretty much anything."

"Do you really think people will want to do it?"

She snuffs her cigarette on the desk. "He says as he sits here with me now."

"Fair enough."

"Plus," she says, "I hear Hollywood's got some films coming up that might make the concept sound pretty desirable, even downright heroic."

"What, that 'Elixir' movie back there?" I ask, incredulous. "Now this is verging on conspiracy nonsense."

"Oh, I'm sorry," Lisa says with feigned indignity. "Did you think Michael Bay made that Benghazi movie because it was a story that just had to be told?"

"Okay, then if we're going down that road," I say. "Just before I decided to take the pills. There was a shooting at my hospital. Were they behind that, too?"

Lisa shakes her head. "Doubtful. Their goal isn't to create chaos. They simply saw it rising all around and recognized a chance to make a handy profit."

We sit quietly for a minute as she lets me take it all in. It's almost dark outside now, the glow of the city lights forming constellations through the windows.

"You didn't say how they're infecting people."

"Now *that* I don't know for sure," she says. "But I have my theories. If I could tell you the name of the company, I'm sure you would too."

"Again, you called me one of the real ones," I say. "What does that mean?"

"They've been running the controlled trial for less than a year. If what you're saying is true, you must have picked up the parasite naturally. They watch for symptoms that match yours and try to avoid the natural ones. But sometimes I suppose they get it wrong. You're what they would call a 'bad investment.'"

Seems about right. "And what would you call me?"

She looks me up and down. "I don't know you that well, but ... I think you're trying."

"So will you do it? The favor they owe you. Will you help me?"

She smiles. "Oh, my dear. I placed the order the moment we walked in here. They're probably waiting downstairs with your prescription right now." It's all I can do to keep from falling out of my chair. "But you're going to have another problem," she says. "You can't take the green pill until thirty hours after the white, and you'll have passed on to branches where we never met by then." She pulls a pen and paper from her clutch and starts to write something. "Not to worry. The black and white pills are the complex chemistry. The green you can make yourself." She hands me a list of five ingredients with exact volumes. "Of course you'll need to memorize these, but it's mostly off-the-shelf stuff. I trust you can handle it."

"Thank you so much," I say, trying to stay composed. "You can't know how much this means."

"Believe me, I can."

As we wait for the elevator, I ask one last question.

"What's the story with the brooch? There's no way the director of that MyRod commercial would have let you keep it on unless you insisted."

She runs her fingers over the emerald inset for a moment, appears to debate whether to answer. "Let's just say it was from someone very important to me," she says. "And I had to go through a lot to get it back."

We step into the elevator, she thumbs the button and as the doors close the truth finally hits me: she's from another branch. This one is hers, but she probably had to face her own nightmares to get back here. She knows how to make the green pill because she's one of the real ones too. Maybe even one of the original guinea pigs.

"It's all right," I say. "I won't tell anyone. But, as someone still on his way, can you tell me. How does it feel?"

"I will say this," Lisa says. "There are moments when I feel like a fraud, like I entered a cheat code on one of my kid's old video games. Like sooner or later someone's going to catch on and send me back."

"So is it better here than the branch you were in?"

"You wouldn't believe," she says.

"Is that why you're still involved with them? You're trying to convince the people living here to stay rather than take the drug and leave, aren't you. So why are you helping me?"

"Because this is just a way station for you," she says. "You couldn't stop in this branch if you wanted to, and if you've come this far you'll never forgive yourself if you don't see it through to the end. I hope you're able to get what you want. I do."

"I'm glad things are better for you here," I say.

"You know, I was actually a rather famous actress in that branch, believe it or not," Lisa says. "It was a wonderful life in many ways. But compared to the way things are here? That's what I try to tell these people: assuming the grass is always greener takes a certain lack of imagination."

"I hear you," I say, warily eyeing the blood stains on my shoes. "It must have been bad for you to want to leave."

"I mean, I have no way of knowing which branch this version of you is coming from, so I suppose it could be worse."

I think about Him. But I don't even want to talk about Him anymore. Not after today. So I simply say, "Trust me. It's bad."

"Put it this way," she says. "Does the phrase 'social distancing' mean anything to you?"

"I'm not really sure. I don't think so. Is that like Pokémon Go or something?"

"Never mind," she says. "Forget it."

The elevator pings and the doors open on the ground floor. A courier van is parked outside the glass double doors.

I ask Lisa if she ever regrets her decision to come back here. She doesn't hesitate.

"Never."

I know.
I skipped over part of Saturday.
I know I did.

To be honest, I'd rather not tell it. But then, I also know it won't make sense if I don't. And it needs to be told.

It was just after 11 a.m. The tracer mark and the armor-clad officers were gone. Meredith and Nolan were safe. Karl said he could get me into Lev Upton's audition, but I'm skeptical. And Lisa wouldn't arrive there for another five hours.

I'm in my empty home again. But it no longer feels safe, the doors and windows now trivially thin and useless. As if the walls could actually keep the world out anyway. Just more security theater.

Framed family photos are hung on the wall beside our bed. Scenes from a life not lived. In one, Nolan lies in a hospital room, a bandage taped across his face, Meredith and I on either side of him, holding him tight. You can see the pain, the fear. And yet, somehow, we're smiling. Why would I have hung this picture on my wall? Why would anyone want to be reminded of such pain? Every other version of me is a stranger. I don't understand them at all.

One more day, I remind myself. I lie in the bed, close my eyes to rest. I'm starting to drift off when I'm jolted by a burst of pain, like a series of jagged glass shards have embedded themselves up and down my right leg.

I sit up and pull off my sweatpants to see a long gnarly scar running the full length of my leg. There are several straight hairline scars that appear to be from surgical incisions.

Ten feet away, a small bottle of pills rests on the master bathroom vanity with a note taped to them. My pills. I rush to get to them but slump to the ground from the pain. Like a knife blade is being twisted under my kneecap. I pull myself along the floor until I'm directly under the vanity and grasp for the little bottle. It feels heavier than it should, rattles like it's almost full to the top. It's not the Quantgen pills at all. They're white but smaller. Painkillers. The searing in my leg is getting worse so I take two. The note taped to the bottle just says "DON'T FORGET YOUR PHONE" in all caps. It looks like my handwriting. After a few minutes seated on the cool tile floor, I pull myself to my feet. My arms feel stronger here at least.

The photos on the wall have now changed. It's not Nolan lying in the hospital anymore. It's me. In the photo, we all have the same tired smile as before, but Nolan's scar is gone. I make my way out of the bedroom and check in the garage to see the same orange SUV. The crash is still with us. It just took a slightly different turn here. I'm grateful for that, at least.

The piano and metronome are still gone. And I still have that feeling. Like I need to do something. But who knows what dangers lie outside? All I can do now is wait to confront Lisa LaRoque and hope things don't get even worse. Seated again in the living room, I keep blinking at the snow outside, hitting refresh on the universe, but the changes in the weather seem to be slowing. Maybe it's because the pills are wearing off, maybe it's because I'm getting close to my original branch, I don't know.

My phone is resting on the dresser, charging. I have to know how bad things are here, so I pull up my feeds. All the Noahs are still there. All the people who know better are still bleating, the conversations somehow totally unfamiliar yet very much the same. I'm no longer sharing, commenting, lashing out. Just taking it in.

But the details are so odd and alien that I'm forced to search for answers. And as I do I find another change. A big one.

He never won here. Not the first time. Not ever. A margin of less than 4,000 votes in one state, and a prolonged court fight. But He failed. There's no sign of camps. No neighborhoods being swept and marked for removal.

Maybe that was the key. Maybe things are finally good here.

And then everything goes black.

I'm still here.

A speck of light
in the far distance.

We're crossing paths again.

Another me.

Here, in the darkness,
I have time to think.
About *Him.*

About how things
would be different
in a world where He
had never infected us
in the first place.

All the ways
He wasn't able
to poison this world.

To poison Meredith's
brother Noah.

To poison Trent.

To poison millions more.

Maybe that's the answer.
The missing part
of every sentence.

Infections are hard
to cure, after all.

As I now know
all too well.

Branches

And now, all these other *mes*
from other branches.

How many times
have we crossed paths,
will we cross paths?

As we get closer
to the source,
more of us overlap.

All headed to
the same place
but at slightly
different moments.

And what's he going to do?
This other me.

Who messes things up.

Shit that makes him
feel better in the moment
but doesn't help anything.

And then
I have to
be the one
to fix it.

At least it's quiet this time.

Peaceful.

Got to appreciate the wins
when you get them.

And the light rushes forward.
I'm falling harder and faster
than I've ever fallen before …

And I'm back.
Now outside. In bright sunlight.
I'm in the Land of Long Yellow Lights. On the sidewalk.
In front of Down-Tune Beats.
My ugly orange Lexus parked beside me.
And in front of me … she's crying.

Jill. She's crying and I'm standing five feet from where I last saw the dead officer and I don't know what he's done this time. This other me. Is he really a killer? Are any of them? And if not, why would he have brought me here again? I don't even have the metronome anymore. It's more than a thousand miles away in this branch, resting on Mom's piano. Whom I'll never see if I can't get my pills.

Then Jill smiles through her tears. And I see they're not tears of grief.

"Thank you," she says, and hugs me so tight I feel if I try to breathe I'll wheeze like Nolan. "For everything. It's gonna be okay." But I haven't done anything good and now I just feel embarrassed. Jill releases me. She's wearing the same backpack she'd had last time. Dressed like she's about to go for a run.

"I hope everything goes well for Meredith," she says as she walks away.

What? How does she even know who Meredith is?

A block away she turns to wave goodbye, points at my feet. "Your shoe," Jill calls out, then walks another two blocks and boards a city bus.

My lace is undone. Apparently the other me got dressed and came here. But why? I try not to look at the spot on the pavement where the officer died as I tie my new white sneakers with blue trim. At least I have better taste in footwear than cars here.

There's still pain in my leg, but it's slightly less sharp than before, the edge taken off. Maybe the painkillers have kicked in. Which means I'm likely still in the same branch. But I don't understand why I've been brought *here*.

I jump when I hear the familiar door chime. I don't want to be back here again. Don't want to see what's on the other side of that door. But then a customer exits Down-Tune Beats holding a guitar case and I know Anton is alive again.

Of course he would be alive here. Things are better here. *His* stain is finally gone.

Inside, the scaffold of guitars isn't there, but the remaining stacks of instruments are as freeform and haphazard as ever. Prince is playing low on the Magnavox. I don't see Anton so I wander his shop and its chaotic assemblage of instruments, once again taking in this room-sized monument to the way his mind works. The more I look at the chaos, the more it makes sense to me. There's patterns here, a method to it all. I just have to try and see it the way Anton sees it. I've never even thought to ask what instrument he plays.

When he emerges from the back I resist the urge to cry. And now I'm thinking how overwhelming it will be to see Mom again.

"Hey man," Anton says with a warm smile as he jogs across the shop in beat to the music and takes his usual perch behind the counter.

His hair is longer here, a mess of twisted dreads graying at the roots. "What's up?"

I can't think of anything to say. I have no reason to be here.

"Just wanted to stop in and see your shop," I say.

Anton laughs. "Are you messing with me again?"

So I have been here before. "Yeah. Just wanted to say hi. See how you're doing?"

"Fear not," he says with a grin. "Not much has changed in the last three hours."

I'm just going to make a fool of myself if I keep this up.

"I'll get out of your hair and let you get back to work," I tell him. "By the way, I like the dreads. They suit you."

He laughs, hard. But I'm not sure why.

"Come on, man," he says. "Are we really gonna do this again?"

"Do what again?"

"Okay, I guess we are." He shakes his head and continues chuckling to himself. "I'll explain it again. Every day you come in here. You talk to me like it's the first time in ages. Compliment me on my hair like you've never seen it like this."

"What do you mean?" I ask. "Every day?"

"I mean, sometimes you don't show for a few days, then you make up for it by coming hours apart. Right? I mean, you were just in here, man. And every time you stand right there and we always start with the same conversation like you're straight out of *Memento* or something. You bring me instruments that aren't even broken just so you have an excuse to talk, or, like today apparently, you don't bring anything at all."

I've never been more a stranger to myself than at this moment. Who are all these people? Why do they keep coming?

"And the other thing. You always insist on giving me money," Anton says. "And, look, I can't tell you how much I appreciate it, man. How much Jill appreciates it. Pretty soon we'll be set for life you keep this up." He laughs again. "But seriously, what are we doing here?

I mean, you're a great guy and we enjoy hanging out. Jill and I both love seeing little man Nolan. But, and I'm sorry man but I've gotta call it out, you seem like you have some serious kind of problem you're not telling me about."

"I'm not sure," I say. "I suppose I'm trying in some way to make things right."

"And I appreciate that," Anton says. "But I feel like I should be asking if there's anything I can do to help *you* at this point."

There's no explanation I can offer. I don't even know why *I'm* here right now, much less the others. "You owe me nothing, Anton. All I ask is that you remember to appreciate the time you have with Jill."

"You've told me that before," Anton says. "See, this is what I'm talking about. As if we didn't all go to that march together last week. But thanks for the reminder."

I'm struggling to understand what we'd even be marching for here.

"Sorry, I know I can be difficult," I say. "Maybe I just want you to believe in a better branch."

"You said that before too. But I still don't know what it means."

I know he doesn't.

"Hey man," he says. "Come here, bring it in." Anton hugs me. "I hope you get to see your mom again. I know you've been trying. And I know it's been tough, even if you don't like to talk about it. I want you to know, even if you don't get to see her, man, you'll be okay."

I don't know what to say. He's comforting *me*? All those other versions of me, pouring their hearts out to a man I just met three days ago. Who are they? Kind Samaritans? Killers? I'm neither one. I know I'm not.

The door chimes and I tense. But Anton grins.

"Meredith!" He says it like they're close friends.

She enters the shop carrying something under her coat, shielding it against the rain now coming down outside. I expect her to be surprised to see me, but she's not.

"Did you know I was here?" I ask.

"Where else would you be?" she says. "You're always here."

Anton clears his throat like he's impatiently waiting for us to pay attention to him. Such a Nolan move.

"Right," Meredith says. "Here it is, hot off the presses."

She produces a flat rectangular package and hands it to Anton, who sets it on the counter and eagerly opens the brown paper wrapping. Inside is an 8x10 black-and-white print inside a glass picture frame. Anton and Jill, their arms linked, beaming. They're positioned like all those people in Meredith's old photos. Except instead of the ocean there's a sea of people spread out behind them, filling a city street as downtown buildings loom in the margins. Some are wearing backpacks, others hold kids on their shoulders, signs are held high though they appear too small to read clearly. I don't know what it's about but I know Anton and Jill are together here.

Anton hugs Meredith. I'm just taking up space at this point so I offer to hang the picture behind the counter. I'm so focused on getting it level I barely hear the chime until Anton says, "good morning, officer."

In the frame's glass, a reflection of Petkoff enters the shop. He stands in the doorway, looking imperious yet vaguely pathetic, his uniform straining against his bullfrog neck.

Meredith has barely noticed him. She's looking at a pile of recorders on the opposite side of the shop, picks one up and waves it in my direction.

"Think Nolan's ready for hot cross buns?"

I force a smile. "Probably, but I'm not sure I am. Where is Nolan anyway?"

"Still at my parents' house."

Petkoff isn't saying anything. Just standing in the doorway, thumbs in his belt loops, looking at the ground. Like he's waiting for something.

"Don't you think it's time we picked him up?" I suggest as I step out from behind the counter and move toward Meredith.

"It's lunchtime, my dad's got it covered," she says, waving me off while she inspects a small piano.

Anton approaches Petkoff. "Something I can help you find?"

Petkoff begins to wander the shop like Anton's not even there. Eventually he steps to the counter and stares at the new portrait.

"Browsing," Petkoff says.

Anton politely steps past him as he crosses behind the counter and places a mug of water in the microwave. "Well let me know if I can be of any help."

This is all wrong. I don't know why, but it's happening again. We need to get out of here. But I can't leave Anton behind.

"Oh, I *forgot*," I tell Meredith. "Bib Purrtuna got in the house again this morning but I wasn't able to get him out. And I had to leave in a hurry. I bet he's still there." I don't want to lie to her, but it's the only way.

"Oh god," she groans. "Our cat is going to have a fit."

"Yeah. Definitely not a good time to be a Nazi," I say. And she laughs. Our private language.

"You know, I have to run home anyway," she says, checking her watch. "I'll just go now and get him back to the Nguyens."

As she goes to leave, Petkoff makes his way back to the doorway to intercept.

Meredith says goodbye to Anton and Anton thanks her again for the portrait. "Good luck with the exhibition next week," he says.

When Meredith approaches the door, Petkoff looks at her, finally acknowledging there are other people present. He grips the door handle and she stops. I hold my breath.

Petkoff smiles. "You have a good day now, ma'am." He holds the door open for her as she exits.

The chime fades. It's just the three of us now, our bodies forming a triangle on opposite sides of the shop. I'm terrified for Anton. *Ping.* The microwave signals that Anton's water is hot and the sound makes me jump, which makes Petkoff smile.

"Got a report of a male suspect," he says. "Fits your description." This time he's pointing at me. "Owner of that Lexus parked outside."

"Me?" Not that it's any less ridiculous than him coming for Anton. "Why me? What do I have to do with anything?"

Petkoff extends his fingers and counts them one by one. "Aggravated assault. Destruction of private property. Arson. Public urination. Jaywalking. I could go on."

"Assault? When?"

"Took sworn testimony from Trent Gadsden last week." Petkoff smiles. "Old friend of the force. Says a disgruntled employee attacked him at his place of business. Plenty of witnesses can corroborate. He says hi by the way."

What did he do now? The other me. He gave Trent the kiss off here too. Only thinking of himself. Blowing off steam and moving on with no thought for what comes after.

Anton calmly interjects. "Listen, officer. If it helps, I would speak on this man's behalf."

"Anton," I say. "You don't have to —"

"No," he says. "No, I want to. Look, officer, I don't know this Trent, but what you're describing doesn't sound like something the man I know would do. I mean, this guy, he's practically like a saint or something. Six months ago, here I was, facing the prospect of closing down because of a broken window I couldn't afford to repair. When out of nowhere this man shows up and not only does he give me the money to fix it, he personally orders the replacement and has it done the next day. These are folks I couldn't even get to return my calls when I had *cash in hand*, you hear me? And since then, his family and mine, we've grown close. He even helped get my daughter and me back on speaking terms again. So yeah, I know this man, maybe better than he knows himself. And if you're saying he's some kind of hardened criminal, I don't believe it. The man you're describing wouldn't help to replace—"

"You're not going to replace anything," Petkoff cuts him off. He places a hand on his sidearm and makes a show of unbuttoning the sheath. "You think we don't see the kinds of people who come through this place? We're always watching, An-*ton*. The fact that this criminal keeps haunting your doorway is enough to make anything you say meaningless. Hell, you're probably the one put him up to it."

Petkoff draws his gun, playfully tests the weight of it to suggest he's in no rush to do what he came to do. I can't tell if the threat is directed at Anton or me. Probably both.

It's now or never. I have to take a side. But I'm not a killer. And I've seen what happens when I try. What would it accomplish? There's nothing I can do that won't be wiped out by the next person who comes calling. If it were always my fault, I could stay away to keep Anton safe. But it happens whether I'm here or not. Every obstacle had been removed here, *He* never even came to dominate our lives here, and yet this always stays the same. Think. What can I do? I don't even have a weapon. Nothing more than a phone.

Wait. That's it. The note from the bathroom. What Meredith said I'd told her to remind me. Messages from myself.

DON'T FORGET YOUR PHONE.

Maybe I can do this. Yes. I can get us out of here. There's no doubt Petkoff's body cam is off, but he's not the only one armed with a camera.

I pull my phone from my pocket and warn Petkoff to back up. "I'm recording everything," I say. "You can't do this, Petkoff. Not this time. Everyone will know."

And just like that, Petkoff pauses, uncertain.

This is what I can do. This is how I make a difference. I look to Anton for reassurance but his eyes are somewhere else. Like he knows this is it. A look I'm sure he's made countless times before. Not this time. I'm going to save us. This time I can be the hero.

I hold up the phone, just as if I were pulling up my feeds, and press my thumb against the round button.

And nothing happens. It doesn't recognize my thumbprint.

Fuck.

Petkoff sees me flinch, scopes my weakness immediately. "Threaten *me*?" he snaps, approaching rapidly, his gun now in my face, close enough I can see the pulsing vein below his right eye, can smell the sickly sweet tang of 5 Hour Energy on his breath. He snatches the phone from my hand before I have a chance to react. "You really are a radical, huh."

"Now hold up," Anton says, stepping from behind his counter and pressing himself between us. "This shit has got to *stop*."

"*You do not get to speak*," Petkoff barks, spittle flitting. "Because you? Don't matter. You're the whole reason I have to enter a fuckin four-digit code every time I enter my country home. Because you're children who can't be civilized on your own. And someday, sooner than you think, you'll all be gone. We'll finally be free of you." He gestures at me with his bulbous chin. "You too, traitor."

"You're wrong," Anton says. "You been harassing everyone I know forever. I can't drive down the street without you threatening to lock me away for no other reason than I looked at you wrong. My family isn't safe in our own home because of you." The pain he's kept hidden is surfacing now. The band kid who's finally had enough. "You really think we don't see your friends breaking our windows at night? If everyone only knew what we know about you. Sooner or later, things are gonna catch up. Just because shit's been this way doesn't mean it has to. There's more of us now. It's us who'll be free."

Anton's rage is building. He came for me, but now it's like I'm not even here. Maybe this is my chance. Even if I can't get his gun, maybe I can get my phone back.

As if he'd heard my thoughts, Petkoff drops my phone to the ground.

Stomps it. Shatters it.

It's gone.

No. No. No. *Wait.* It's not too late. It can't be. Maybe … Anton's water. Yes. If I can get to the mug steaming in the microwave, I could blind Petkoff with the water, hit him with the mug and get his gun. But it's too far away. I'd never make it. Come on. *Keep trying.* I can fix this. In spite of everything. Do this enough times and I can get it right.

Then Petkoff looks at me, and I know it's too late. Now he raises his gun, the same kind I'd held in my hand yesterday. I can feel the weight of it as he levels it, steadies it. *Just squeeze.* And then time slows to a stop. Vertigo Effect. A million silent cries from a million different branches.

A shooting in real life doesn't look anything like it does in the movies. There aren't dramatic squibs of blood or balletic slow-motion acts of heroism. There's no clean dividing line between living and dead. Just a sudden startle reflex from the noise, same as if cooking pots are being smacked together or a mallet strikes a drum, and now one person isn't on their feet anymore, but you're both in shock so you're not sure which one it is. You're in purgatory together. Alive. Dead. Alive again. We're both gone. Together. One ghost upright, the other on the ground. How many times have we done this? I know it isn't always my fault but once is enough. And it's far more than that.

Petkoff fires his entire clip. But he doesn't shoot me.

By the time the ringing in my ears stops and Prince can be heard crooning on the Magnavox again, he's already on his way out.

"Remember," Petkoff says solemnly, framed in the doorway. "He grabbed my gun. I saved you from him. If that's going to be a problem, someday you may find we have to save someone from you."

Someday is the key word. For now, killing someone like me would be hard for him to explain away here. And I'm sure this is how Trent wants it anyway. Torturing me by torturing others. It's clear now Trent was always just a kid pulling the wings off insects, and Petkoff worse than that. They didn't need *Him* to poison them. *He* just gave them permission to take things further, to reveal who they always were, to treat anyone they don't like with impunity, same as they've always treated someone like Anton. Apparently the choice between branches was never a question of whether they're in control, just a question of who's protected and who's prey.

A final chime and Petkoff's gone.

I kneel next to Anton, lying amid the stacks and spires of his shop. I want to call an ambulance but my phone is gone and there are so many wounds I know it won't be enough. He looks at me. We're both in shock, peering through a thousand miles of ice but melting fast. I can only hope he's the hero in the movie who doesn't even register the pain and keeps going against all reason. I ask where his phone is so I can call for help, but he shakes his head. Even though he's never seen those other branches, somehow he's more prepared for this than I am.

Then Anton says he's sorry, which is enough to break me all on its own. I'm the one. It's my fault. I just wanted to believe he might have one branch that's better than my worst.

"Listen kid," he says, a slight smirk creeping into the corner of his mouth. "We're all in it together."

But we're not. Not in the same way. They've killed him so many times. To punish me. To punish Jill. Or for no reason at all. Someone who shouldn't even be here, in a split second projecting fear, pain, impotence, dominance. Tears are coming now, in a way they haven't in a long time. Yet I try to smile.

"We're all in it together," I say. "*Brazil*. I get the reference."

"You know what," Anton says. "That's my favorite movie."

"I know," I say. "I know it is." His eyes are drifting now but I need him to stay with me. "Hey, you never told me what instrument you play. Mister music guy, right?"

"I'm just a guy, you know," he says. "Seventeen."

"Seventeen what?"

"I play … seventeen instruments, actually." He looks at the portrait on the wall. "I know it'll be hard. Just tell her …" Then he's quiet for a while. He seems to be trying to think of a way to put it into words. But he doesn't complete the sentence.

He said more. I'd like to say his actual last words were profound, but death isn't clean like it is in the movies. After a minute he was still talking but not really making sense and humming the notes to a song I couldn't place. Calm but distant. All I could do was hold his hand while it was still warm.

Hours later, after I say my farewells to Lisa LaRoque and take the final white pill, I arrive home with Anton's blood still on my shoes and find Meredith and Nolan waiting for me. I hold them both for a long time.

"It's time to go," I announced.

But there was no one else in the house.

It was one week ago, an hour after I answered the phone call on the beach that set everything in motion. Our bags were gathered in Dad's small kitchen. Mom was everywhere around, everything as she'd left it, but she wasn't there. It didn't really seem like home, like someone built a convincing facsimile but didn't quite get the feeling right. Dad still lives there, of course. It's the closest thing to her that's left but it had only now become clear to us that he felt the absence so much more than he'd let on. Each room an untended wound. And the piano? It wasn't even there. To me, there was more of her in our home than his.

We'd been there less than a day and already we were leaving. It wasn't fair to Dad. But all I could think about was Him and the certain death sentence that awaited me back home. All that mattered was how long. If I could just hold on long enough, maybe I could see things start to change before I'm gone. There was still a lawsuit making its way through the courts, after all. It was all so blatant, so egregious, but then the courts had been nothing but disappointment. Somehow, if I could live to see His end, the end Mom never got to see. That would be enough. Everything would be different. It would all melt away. And Meredith and Nolan could be happy, even if I'm not there to see it.

scroll

As I stepped outside and crossed the path that runs behind the house down to the beach, Nolan's screaming became unbearable. He didn't want to leave. Meredith and Dad kept trying to bargain with him but he kept running back to the water, thoroughly soaking the clothes he was supposed to wear on the plane, aggressively splashing in the waves, the undertow threatening to pull him in.

refresh

"I can't deal with it," I said in the direction of the house as though it were listening. The small rambler sits a few hundred feet from the shoreline but it's less than 10 feet above sea level, about twice as high as the sand berm at the edge of the beach. Within a few decades it'll be washed away. The ocean will swell, and one day a storm surge will mean the end of it. By the time Nolan has grown kids of his own it'll all be over. And then my parents really will be gone. But then the house is only a shell anyway. Mom's already gone.

The storm had wiped us out. We were all just pretending. And I needed to be anywhere else.

SUNDAY

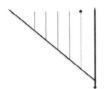

Here we go. Wheels up.

She's really there. And I can't wait.

As the plane leaves the runway, I'm scanning the photos on my phone. Treasured family memories for which I have no context, that feeling I had as a kid peering through old View-Master binoculars where you click the lever to advance the frame and see something new and unfamiliar. Meredith and I holding hands at a baseball game as she appears to laugh at a joke. *Click.* Meredith and Nolan riding a jet ski on some picturesque lake. *Click.* A group of people I don't recognize smiling and pointing as Nolan rides a mini scooter down a garden path that could be anywhere. *Click.* I still see the scar across his face when I look at him, even as it's disappeared from everyone else's memory.

And I'm thinking of the pictures I can't see. Of sitting by Mom's side. Through the chemo. Through the pain of uncertainty, the elation of a future restored. Of everything we'd been deprived simply because things went differently there.

As soon as we reach altitude I try again to call Mom, but her cell battery is dead as usual and goes straight to voicemail, the same outgoing message she's had for a decade. Apparently they've disconnected the landline here. So I call Dad. More voicemail, but it rings first so I know his phone's on. I text to tell him our flight was delayed and within a few minutes he writes back saying not to worry, they'll see us when they see us. We're to let ourselves in once we get there, as he expects they'll be asleep. It's another crushing delay, but I tell him I understand. I just want to get there.

It was bad enough that I couldn't get a flight until Sunday, then had to rebook again this morning in the latest branch. But then after we arrived at the airport a snowstorm delayed our flight by more than four hours. No matter how many times I looked away, it was still there. I'm so close to the end that the changes are now barely noticeable. And I haven't crossed paths with another me all day. Which makes me wonder whether I might be the first one to have made it this far.

As Lisa predicted, the green pill was gone this morning when I awoke, the painkillers for my leg in its place. I immediately grabbed a steno pad and jotted down the ingredients from memory, then read them and re-read them again just in case. Luckily, everything was pretty easy to find. The only thing I had to buy at the store was some clove and a package of hollow pill capsules to put the mixture in. I packed the ingredients and waited to assemble the pill in an airport bathroom. Making it was the easy part. I've never been so grateful for youthful indiscretions as I was when I had to chop up the various components with a credit card and sort them into the right proportions by sight.

I watch my family now, seated across the aisle and a row ahead, Meredith playing a prevent defense in the aisle seat with Nolan in the center. I want so badly to be close to them, but it was the best I could do. Meredith was shocked to learn I'd changed my mind about flying down for Mom's birthday at the last minute, but she also loved the idea of heading somewhere warm after such a brutally cold January. Seeing Meredith on this final day, she reminds me of the Meredith I met in other branches where the crash occurred. Much like the first one I left behind. I don't know whether it's because the crash changed her or me. Or both. But whatever it was, there's less pain here.

Outside the plane, moisture is visibly shedding over the wing in waves as we pass through a cloud. Droplets are beading on the outer lip of the cabin window. Flowing. Gathering. Vibrating.

That's what I'm focused on as I try to distract myself from the man sitting next to me, 34A to my aisle-seat B. Still an hour left to go before we land, and I'm seeking distractions from distractions from distractions. The guy's a classic nervous flyer, scrolling an early-model iPad in his lap with one hand while the other grips his armrest like he's dangling off a cliff. He doesn't seem like the kind of person who wants unsolicited advice—late-career-ish white guy, his demeanor suggesting he sees Tom Selleck when he looks in the mirror, bifocals he seems vaguely embarrassed to be wearing, perusing zoomed-in emails on his tablet with "FW: FW: FW: RE: FW:" in the subject line—so I keep acting like I don't notice he's barely holding it together.

Past him, outside the window, the water is still beading, still vibrating.

There's some moderate turbulence, standard air pocket stuff, and the man instinctively grips my arm then quickly recoils and apologizes. The water on the window is briefly disturbed before returning to normal. Nolan is squealing with glee.

It's fascinating the way so many people are terrified to fly. Sure, you can remind them that they're twice as likely to die on the ride to the airport, but it won't make a difference. What they really fear is handing control of their fate over to someone they can't see. But the thing about planes today, they basically fly themselves. The pilot's little more than a midwife. A thriller set today where the tower needs to talk a passenger down would have all the adrenaline of the in-flight oxygen mask video. *Please enjoy your emergency landing and thank you for choosing to save us today.* Now, if planes only successfully landed when every single passenger agreed on basic obvious facts—only landed when everyone had chosen to inconvenience themselves and do the right thing, day after day across decades for no immediate benefit even when it's hard—otherwise the plane kills everyone on board? Now *that* would be scary. And then, as oxygen masks drop like instant karma, would the passengers even recognize the role they'd played in their own demise? Let's just say I have my doubts.

The man has switched to reading the news now, and the source isn't exactly a surprise. Below the lead story—*"Campus Intolerance"*—there's an article about another militia bombing the state capitol building in Lansing, Michigan. Apparently, it's a rival sect of the militia that's effectively taken over Salem, Oregon and declared it a "Sovereign City." More distressing than the bombing is that it's the third one of its kind this week.

The man seems to be trying and failing to focus on the news, dangerously close to clawing the armrest out of his chair. I lean over and try to help the man take his mind off the immediate. I point out the bombing story and what a shocking tragedy it is.

"Yeah, that's something, isn't it," he grunts. About as non-committal as it gets.

"The bombings don't make you nervous?"

"Not really," he says with a shrug. Then, after thinking about it some more, he starts talking. "Don't get me wrong. Those militia guys are knuckleheads. You're not gonna hear me defend them. Always some bad apples. But you know, what we really should be worried about is that radical *antifa* ..."

He keeps talking but it's clear he's just reciting stenography. Somewhere, at this very moment, other Mad Dads on other planes are saying the same thing, verbatim. A million-man chorus of You Know™ and Actually Technically™.

Even in worlds where *He* is dead and practically forgotten, they're all still there. "... *deadly sanctuary cities* ..." He's a Noah. The most frustrating and probably most numerous kind: the bandwagon believer. "... *tearing down statues and* ..." They mean well, at least they think they do, but they invest zero energy trying to get to the truth of anything, soaking up whatever anxieties, whatever theories appeal to their sensibilities. The prejudices they don't think they have. "*... sharia no-go zones ...*" They fully believe they're being fair and neutral, not seeing the filter they're applying to everything. "*... stand for the flag ...*" Normally this is a Noah I'd have wasted the most time fighting online. He's not a troll or a Nazi, the kind you'd mock and block. "*... you've gotta be a patriot, blue lives matter after all ...*" He sees himself as a thoughtful, rational person. Winnable. Someone open to new ideas. "*... when I was growing up we had equality. No one above anyone else. But this new crew in D.C. thinks they know better ...*" Yet he somehow manages to latch onto every storyline that conveniently casts him as the underdog, the down-on-their-luck hero in need of a stirring third-act comeback. "*... when my dad was fighting in Korea there weren't any safe spaces ...*" But this time, seeing one in person, spouting the same lines in a world where *He* never even took power, the memory of Anton on the floor so fresh, the sharp prick of the syringe in my neck as Meredith is dragged from our home, and here he's talking up some new one about Bill Gates and the metric system. Honestly, at this point I'm just trying not to laugh. But laughing at him, fighting him, fighting every Noah, it was always just a way to make myself feel better for a fleeting moment. Nothing more important or lasting than a kid pulling off a fatality in *Mortal Kombat*. "*... full-on socialism, they say, if you can believe it. Meanwhile, I'm the one who can't afford this cholesterol medication they got me on. You know what I mean?*"

At least he's not freaking out about the flight anymore.

The Noah's finished for the moment, and I'm forcibly suppressing every satisfying rebuttal I have built up inside me. Instead, I blurt out a question.

"Do you have any kids?"

He does.

"What's their take on all this?"

"Well ... they got their own theories," he says. "We don't really talk about it."

"You don't think they agree with you?"

"Honestly? They call me names. I don't know how kids got so disrespectful. Wasn't how I raised them, I can tell you that."

"Yeah," I say. "That must be hard."

"It's fine," he says, his hand gripping the seat rest again. "Agree to disagree, you know. How about you?"

"I guess I was lucky," I say. "My parents and I were pretty well aligned for the most part. At least I think we were. *Are.* But if we weren't, on the important stuff, I would hope they'd talk to me about it."

"Probably right." His grip loosens. "But it's not easy, let me tell you. They can be pretty inflexible."

"Sure. No, I get it. But then maybe you don't need to convince them of anything. Maybe just hear them out, see if they hear you."

"Yeah, I wouldn't hold my breath. But thanks." He's lost in thought a minute, absently drumming his fingers on the iPad, the water outside still gathering.

So many branches. So many changes. Yet he's resisted every single one. I have no doubt he's spouting the same self-serving nonsense in my old branch as he is here. And he's not alone. As it turns out, the butterfly effect isn't what we've all been trained by fiction to expect. There's chaos, sure, but there are also deep patterns, curves, ruts, things that you can barely see much less escape. Jedediah Mundt was in some ways an idiot, but he was right about one thing. Fate isn't fate at all. It's just people, and people are stubborn. The systems they build even more so.

Outside the window, the water is still beading, still vibrating. We're passing through different clouds, in a different time, different place, entirely different water, and yet it looks the same as it did an hour ago, channeled into the same shape. Because the system didn't change. It's still the same plane, after all.

"Speaking of kids," the man says. He removes his bifocals and looks past me, grinning at something in the aisle.

It's Nolan. I see the scar across his face but it's not really there. I don't know if I'll ever be able to unsee it.

"Mommy said I could ask you a question," he says, glancing back at Meredith watching us.

"Of course. What do you need, bud? What's the question?"

"Thank you for letting me see Grandma and Grandpa," he says, eyes sparking, breaths wheezing.

It wasn't really a question, but I get the idea. He can't possibly know how excited I am. I'm certain Nolan has met his grandmother dozens of times by now, but it will be the first time I'm there to see it.

I know Mom underwent prolonged cancer treatment here, but there's also much I don't know, like how long she's been in remission or exactly why things turned out so differently here. Part of me wonders whether I might have even been the one to say something, the one who made her finally see a doctor before it was too late.

"Sure, of course," I tell him. "It's always great to see Grandma and Grandpa."

"And the ocean!" he cries, jumping in place with his hands on my armrest.

Meredith calls him back to his seat. "Okay yes, we get it," she says, trying to calm him. "You've never seen the ocean and you're finally going, I think you've told everyone on the plane now, kiddo." She gives me a sly wink and Nolan crawls over her before she can step out to let him in.

Nolan's been talking about the beach all day, and to me it's déjà vu. Only a little more than a week ago, in my old branch, we took him to the beach for the first time. The same beach we're headed toward now. With the benefit of hindsight, I've packed the plastic pails and shovels we'd forgotten on the first try.

Nolan is now literally bouncing in his seat with excitement and Meredith apologizes to the young man in a Padres hat who's seated in the far window seat. I'd asked him to switch seats and the guy refused, so I figure I'm not going to sweat him dealing with an excited four-year-old for four hours. Nolan bounces hard enough his leg hits his drop-down tray, overturning his ice water, the runoff sluicing down the man's leg. Practically the same thing that happened to me a week ago. *Sorry, Padres. So sad.* He insists it's not a problem, but Meredith keeps trying to smooth things over.

And soon she's making small talk, telling Tony Gwynn, Jr., over there her story of how she and I first met in college. I always tune the story out. But this time, so close to the end and with nowhere to go, I listen.

She's describing how we swung our sledgehammers in sync, destroying her set, breaking things to fix things, wordless yet connected, and it feels a bit like it's breaking me as well. Because the honest truth is that I do remember meeting her that day. But I didn't see *her*. I saw an obstacle in my way. A threat. I was offended. How dare this selfish person who wasn't even in my play derail my career with her vanity art project? I'd wanted to land one of the leads, Hamm or Clov. Instead I got Nagg, a senile old man who lives in a hole. A bit part. A shit part. But all I could see was how important this was for me at that moment, and how close she had come to ruining it. I wasn't even a very good actor. To be one, you first need to know something, to be in touch with something you can tap into. And I didn't. I didn't know what I didn't know. When I met Meredith almost a year later, on the corner by the marquee, I didn't recognize her as the same person. Because I hadn't seen her before. Not really. The truth is that it's not irritation I feel when she tells the story. It's something else.

Nolan is still bouncing, brandishing his plastic sand shovel like a sword, stabbing the air. Meredith rests her hand on his shoulder to calm him. She's so good with him. So patient. The way she said, "okay yes, we get it, you've never seen the ocean," the comment managing to be both warm and reassuring to him and also a little joke for me.

Wait. That can't be right.

Nolan has never seen the ocean. Never seen the ocean? How is that possible? With all that Mom must have gone through, with her treatments, with how tight their money had surely been. I can't imagine them flying to see *us*. Once again there's some variable I've missed. Maybe we only ever visited her in a hospital?

I reach across the aisle and take Meredith's hand. There's a pit in my stomach now as I say how nice it will be to see my parents, to see the old home again and celebrate Mom's birthday.

She agrees. "Honestly, seeing him so excited to finally meet his grandparents in person? I'm just glad you decided to do this."

What? After everything Mom and Dad went through. Her cancer, her recovery. Somehow, we never saw them once? What could have possibly kept us away?

And Meredith reminds me. I didn't think it was a good idea to fly with Nolan so young. Then, with me already flying so much for work, I couldn't justify the emissions of yet another flight. And somehow we'd never found the time to drive it. Meredith wants me to know how glad she is that we're finally going, how much it means to Nolan. To both of them.

And there it is. The variable I've overlooked. The real reason Meredith kept leaving. The missing part of every sentence. The broken limb in every branch.

It's me.

I told everyone it was the election that broke me. But that's not the truth. Apparently, on some level, I think I've been broken a long time, the oxygen mask dangling in front of me but I refused to see it. Things fell apart in so many branches, so many different variables. Not because I'd changed, but because I hadn't. And every time, rather than change the facts on the ground, I told myself a better story.

Yes I cared. Of course I did. I also never really tried. And after all this, after everything I've been through, I'm still not sure how. Another me apparently thought he did. All I could do was follow through on what he started.

Back in Anton's shop, in his final moments. I'd held his hand, did my best to make him comfortable. Made sure he was at least in a position that didn't rob him of his dignity.

And then, after he'd passed, I picked up the phone Petkoff had smashed. The one I'd finally tried to wield believing for a moment I could make a difference. The one that wouldn't unlock. And as I saw the spiderweb of its broken screen catch the light, I realized what had really happened. So I searched all over Down-Tune Beats, looking for a sign from myself. A sign that I was actually capable of doing more than rage and hope someone else could fix it.

There it was.

In the corner. Resting against a broken piano bench.

The phone.

The one the other me had placed there. He had propped it up so it would record everything.

And it had. Petkoff drawing on us. Smashing my work phone. Firing on an unarmed man. Anton's final moments.

The other me. He must have known what was bound to happen, what he'd tried and failed to do in other branches. If he couldn't stop it, he'd at least make sure the world knew what had happened.

I didn't know whether publishing it could make any difference. I still don't. But I did it anyway. I've been futilely sharing anything and everything I could find on my feeds for years. What's one more video going to do? When has a video ever changed anything? But then maybe they know something I don't. Maybe, in a branch somewhere, it changed everything. You never know.

I had to try, at least. If nothing else, so others can bear witness.

Anton deserves that much.

Gunfire. Then more gunfire.

A voice is describing the latest militia bombings in D.C., Portland, Denver and Detroit. In the last few minutes, an armored police truck has breached the White House gate and is now in a standoff with the Secret Service on the west lawn. There are conflicting reports about whether the president has been rushed to a secure location within the residence or if she'd been injured in the most recent blast.

I shut the radio off as I turn our rented Kia hatchback onto the long gravel road that leads to my childhood home. I check my pocket again and confirm the final pill is still there. It's late. Almost 11 p.m. The sky is clear, a waxing gibbous moon illuminating ripples of rolling sand and wild tufts of beach grass as we approach.

Far from being asleep, Nolan is a shaken soda can ready to burst in the back seat. He's been adamant throughout the ninety-minute drive from the airport that we go straight to the beach once we arrive, a slowly building demand that's now on the verge of a full-blown fit.

This is not going to work. In my old branch, he'd melted down for more than forty-five minutes when we arrived. I don't know how, but the kid loves the ocean even though he's never seen it. It's like he just knew. The sight of him racing into the water, of holding our hands along the shore as the tide rushes in. It was like I was living it through him. Or at least I would have if I'd let myself. If I'd been there.

But I wasn't. If I had — if I'd *really* been there with them, on the beach, in that moment — would I be here now? I don't know. I'm not sure I'm even making sense. The point is, I know how Nolan's going to be, and I can't have things go that way. Not now. I don't want to see Mom like that, to have her finally meet her grandson like that. The strain of it. The distraction of it.

I suggest Meredith walk him down the path to the beach for a few minutes while I bring the bags inside. She's not sure it's a good idea, but I assure her I'll be along in a few minutes. It's a warm night and there's a floodlight near the break in the sand berm where the path crosses onto the beach. The shoreline is always well illuminated. Better to get it over with and burn off the energy than fight endlessly until he finally falls asleep.

Meredith wraps herself in a linen shawl and leads Nolan by the hand down the path. And I'm alone once again.

My old house is dark except for a porch light, but it looks alive to me, real in a way it hasn't been for a very long time. I can almost see the faded cedar siding heave and breathe. I wheel our bags into the entryway, searing pain running up my right leg with each step, awkwardly propping open the worn screen door, attempting to avoid making any loud noises.

Inside, the moonlight gives everything a soft glow. It all looks the same as it did a week ago. In that other branch, Dad never took down any of Mom's things when she died, everything preserved the way she'd left it. The smell here is different though. Familiar yet somehow indescribable. Comforting in some elemental way. It's a small house on a narrow tract of land, built long before so much beach property in this area was absorbed by millionaires, speculators and developers. If my parents ever sold it, the house would be razed for sure. But it's home. I peer around the corner into the family room and there's Mom's piano, the keylid open, a classical piece set on the music rest, ready to play. Her metronome stands sentinel on top.

I touch the piano, as if to confirm I'm really here.

As soon as my fingers brush the metronome, its weighted pendulum comes loose from its mooring and begins to swing, weight affixed at 80, the hidden counterweight reacting, equal and opposite, bringing the simple machine to life, ticking an andante beat.

Tick. Tick. Tick. Tick.

It works.

The sound reminds me to check my phone. This is it. Even closer than I'd known. *Tick. Tick. Tick. Tick.* In less than fifteen minutes I'll be locked in, the static fizz of anticipation prickling on my skin as I reach into my pocket for the final, green pill. *Tick. Tick. Tick. Tick.*

But it's not there.

Panic.
Tick.
Terror.
Tick.
No. No. *No.*

The pill. The ingredients. The list. The capsules.
All gone. I've passed beyond them.
Tick. Tick. Tick. Tick.
Back in the kitchen, I reach for the light switch in the dark and flick on a small incandescent bulb over the kitchen sink. I rush to the kitchen table and grab a notepad and pen. I'm trying to remember the ingredients but my mind is locking up. I can't remember anything.
Tick. Tick. Tick. Tick.
Lisa did this, I remind myself. She got through it. I can't even imagine how she made it on her own, with no one to guide her. *Tick. Tick. Tick.* How many times it must have taken her to get the ingredients right, to kill the thing living inside her without killing herself in the process? *Tick. Tick.* Drifting back and forward then back again. I can't. I need this to end. I might not deserve it but I need it.
Deep breaths. Come on. Try to relax. Where is that fucking loon when I actually need it? *Tick. Tick. Tick. Tick.* The nearest house is a mile away, the nearest town with an open grocery store over an hour's drive. But if I can't remember the ingredients it won't matter.
In the living room, Mom's familiar cardigan sweater is draped over a chair.
She's here. Really here. Right now. In this house.
Tick. Tick. Tick. Tick.

Slowly, I feel the block lifting. Clove. I remember that much. And then all at once it comes back. I'm writing furiously, illegibly, but I get it down.

Tick. Tick. Tick. Tick.

Now I just need to find them. There are five ingredients.

Tick. Tick. Tick. Tick. Tick.

I know my old pantry as if I were still in high school. For all I know, a few of the jars on these shelves are probably the same ones now as then. I locate the first three items, gather the jars alongside the kitchen sink.

Tick. Tick. Tick.

For the last two, I riffle through the cabinets in the main floor bathroom. The first, aspirin, is in so many different bottles it's like a parody of an old person's medicine cabinet. All that's left is potassium bromide.

Tick. Tick. Tick. Tick. Tick. Tick. Tick. Tick.

And silence.

The metronome's winder has run down.

Nothing. Nothing. Nothing. *Shit.*

I've come all this way only to lose it all at the last minute, to be cast back with *Him*, back where everything is broken.

Think. In my old branch I'd purchased potassium bromide a few months ago, when I'd been desperate to control my seizures. But other than as an antiepileptic, it's not very commonly used. As far as I know, there's no reason for my parents to deal with seizures.

For some reason, the thought reminds me of a high-pitched tinkling sound. Seizures. An old memory, just out of reach. *Think.* What is it about seizures that triggers that sound?

Then the tinkling connects.

Lady, our old black Labrador. She'd suffered from convulsions in her last year, until the vet finally told us there was nothing more to be done. The tags on her collar would clink together as she seized on the floor. I remember wanting to help her through it but not knowing how, so I watched, helpless. She passed more than a decade ago, but my pack-rat parents never throw anything away. It's possible they might still have some of her old meds.

I head to the nook in the mud room where she used to sleep. Her old bed is still there, tucked in the corner. Above it, there's a small built-in cabinet. In it, there's Lady's faded red collar, a basket of assorted chew toys and for some reason a pile of 4th and 5th place ribbons I got in grade school for God-knows-what. *Gee, thanks.* Of all the things to hang onto.

Behind it all there are some small plastic bottles. The labels are faded so I have to use the light on my phone to read them. Only two contain actual pills, the rest are stale training treats. I palm one called ParaDice and scan the back: "Active ingredient: 500 mg potassium bromide." Jackpot. *Good girl, Lady.*

Back at the sink, I plug the drain, mash and grind the various ingredients into small individual piles in the basin, then draw enough from each to match the volume of the pill I'd made earlier. I don't have any capsules, so the best I can do is tear off a square of toilet paper from the bathroom, roll the mixture into a tight ball and dampen it under the sink. That's it. It's ready.

"I thought I heard you banging around down here."

As soon as I hear the voice, I freeze in place. I might as well be seven years old again. The words are exactly the same.

It's her.

I'm afraid to turn around, certain she'll be gone if I do.

At funerals, there's an unstated rule that the immediate family shouldn't actually see the casket close. They orchestrate the proceedings so those closest to the deceased are spared that final moment where they abruptly crank the body lower in its box and shut the lid forever. The finality of it is too much for most people to bear. But I snuck back into the sanctuary to see Mom. I had to see it.

But here, now, I'm afraid of what I might see.

Slowly, I turn, the pill clenched tight in my fist.

Mom is standing at the foot of the stairs in the ratty house robe she's worn for almost thirty years, leaning on the banister for support. Here. Alive.

My mind searches for all the things I've imagined saying, everything I imagined doing once I saw her again. But now that she's here, I can't think of anything to say. So I just say hi.

Mom smiles. "I'm glad you came."

For some reason, my first instinct is to leave. But I smile back and tell her it's good to see her. She gestures toward the living room and we both sit, she in her chair and me on the couch. Just like when I was a kid.

I still can't think of anything to say.

We sit quietly. A comforting silence. It's only been two years, but she looks much older than she did in her coffin, brittle in a way she's never been. She has the look of someone who knows pain, who's been through things she'd rather not talk about. And for the first time I wonder whether it might have been better that the Mom I knew was spared it.

More than anything, I want to ask her a question. Now that she's really here, I finally know. It's the question that was always there, beneath it all: Does she think I'm a good person? But then, whether the answer was yes or no, I know she'd say yes. I also think she'd believe it. And so it's not necessary to ask. Now I realize it never was. But I also know Mom's not alive for me. It certainly isn't thanks to me. This isn't about me at all. I'm just glad she's here.

I ask how her day was. She talks about a mishap at the grocery store earlier. She'd walked away from her cart and then accidentally took one that belonged to someone else. Totally banal, but she sells it as always. She laughs, and her laugh makes me laugh too.

And suddenly I remember my family, down at the beach.

"I know it's late," I say. "But … do you remember when I was young, how we used to go down to the water at night and watch the waves?"

Of course she does. She tells me to go ahead. Dad's fast asleep, but she'll get changed and meet us by the shore in a few minutes.

I wander down the path I've crossed thousands of times before, feeling weightless, as if the pain in my leg has vanished, the combed beach grass fluttering in a soft breeze, the moon illuminating everything. Meredith is sitting atop the berm with her arms wrapped around her knees, peering out at the water. I think I can hear Nolan laughing somewhere down the beach. She looks at me for a moment, then back at the water.

"You remember how I was telling you I've been feeling like something's missing?" she asks. I don't, but I know. "I'm thinking about starting my photography again. Professionally. Touching up old photos is a nice distraction but it's not enough."

"I think it's a great idea," I say. "Whatever you need, let's do it. I just wish I could have seen the seaside mosaic you made for the play all those years ago, that I could have been there with you from the beginning."

She shines her brightest smile. "But you were there. That's what I'm always telling you."

"No. I wasn't. I was … somewhere else."

The smile fades a bit and she nods. "You're somewhere else a lot." I sit next to her on the berm, cross-legged.

"I know. But I'm here now."

The kiss is like the first kiss we ever had, all those lifetimes ago, walking home after bar close, fingers entwined, the soft embrace of two strangers with their whole lives ahead of them, lives that can wait until tomorrow because this moment is all that matters.

The alarm on my phone chimes. It's time. I've arrived where I belong. Looking at Meredith in the moonglow, she's different somehow. A little younger maybe, more energetic. Maybe it's just the benefit of perspective after the things I've seen. She's as beautiful as she's ever been. There's also something missing, I think, but I don't know what it is. Something in the way she holds herself. More closed off maybe.

My hand is still clenching the homemade pill. But now it's finally time, and I relax. My family is together, here. Alive, here. *He* is gone. We are here. And the night is beautiful. If I could do it over again, I know now I should have done something, anything, to try and make every branch better, whether I was there or not. But this is the branch I have now. Maybe there's even a chance for Anton and Jill to be happy here too. You never know.

I listen to the rhythm of the waves, scan the beach for footprints. The sand appears smooth as glass.

"Where's Nolan?" I ask.

The answer is on Meredith's face before she speaks. I see now it was there from the moment I approached.

"Who?"

Her question drains my blood, hollows me out until there's nothing but a faint outline where I'd been sitting. As much a ghost as Anton in all those endless branches.

Mom approaches along the beaten trail wearing a loose-knit sweater and capri pants she's rolled up to the knee. Meredith rises and wishes her a happy birthday and they exchange pleasantries, recounting how much they enjoyed watching the pageantry of the inauguration and what strange times that it had to be held in an undisclosed location. Meredith tells Mom how her photography has been a welcome distraction from the headaches she's been having, Mom tells how it was her piano that got her through the cancer.

I don't know what to do. But I can't stay here. I step onto the beach, an empty shell drifting closer to the ocean.

Thailand. I can remember the lush foliage, the treks over muddy trails cut through dense jungle, the vegetation already overtaking paths that had been cleared for us days before. Five years ago I went to Khao Sok, Thailand, to oversee a three-day video shoot. Simple job. A client wanted footage of its people conducting field research, a group of not-particularly-photogenic Americans collecting samples of river water with no real explanation. I had never heard of the company. Now I think I know why.

Meredith found out she was pregnant a month later.

So. This is where it ends. This was where it was always going to end. And now I know the truth. That until this moment I've never known what it was to be broken. I've never known anything. After everything that's happened, this is my penance for never seeing what I had, only what I thought was lost. A pain I must bear alone because no one else remembers.

Ahead of me, the immensity of the ocean spreads to the horizon. And I think of Nolan and Meredith. Of Mom and Dad. Of Anton and Jill. Of Him.

Something in the sand catches my eye, in the blank canvas of the beach, in the smooth smoky glass. A crab, no larger than my thumb. It scurries along the shoreline. It's struck, then struck again, by the seawater surging up the shore. Again. Again. But each time it rights itself, regains its footing, and keeps moving toward something out of sight.

And all at once the weight lifts, same as it had when I'd held Mom's hand in the church. Clarity. I'm alive again. Unbroken.

All those other versions of me, the ones who kept showing up at Anton's shop in that branch so close to this one. Kept trying to right the wrongs from other branches, hoping that this time would be different, that maybe this time they could save him. And if not they'd try to make things better, in whatever way they can. I understand them now. They already knew, didn't they. I think they'd already been here, had already made their choice. They had something I didn't. Clarity. Fate isn't fate at all.

I ask Mom to join me at the water's edge. Meredith watches from the old rocking bench. We stand there together, hand in hand in the shining night, like we did when I was little. I'm feeling a hundred pounds lighter, smelling the warm salty air, both of us laughing as the surf washes over our feet, sinking farther with each advance. And yet I'm eager for the days to come. I look one last time at the pill, at a life I could have had, that I very nearly did have, and watch it slowly slip beneath the waves.

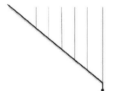

Acknowledgements

I would first like to thank my parents, Jane and Randy, for always encouraging me to read and write. Mom, I miss you every day.

Enduring thanks to my wife, Amanda, who has been supportive of this writing project throughout while surviving eight months (and counting) in a quarantine purgatory, and who also designed this book's cover image. And to my son, Henry, who provided the inspiration for the short story that ultimately became this novel. I love you both and there's no one I'd rather be with in this branch nor any other.

Special thanks to my good friend Scott Boras, who read early drafts of this story and provided valuable feedback and encouragement, and to my copyeditors, Mary Studebaker-Reed and Susan Strecker, whose insights greatly improved the story's final draft.

Branches

About the Author

Adam Peter Johnson lives in Minnesota with his wife, son and golden basset.

Branches is his first published novel.

If you liked this book, please consider leaving a review at bit.ly/reviewbranches

Printed in Great Britain
by Amazon